T0356223

Sunlight Playing over a Mountain

Sunlight Playing over a Mountain

SELINA LI BI

Published in the United States by Soho Teen
an imprint of Soho Press, Inc.
227 W 17th Street
New York, NY 10011
www.sohopress.com

Library of Congress Cataloging-in-Publication Data
Bjorlie, Selina Libi, author.
Title: Sunlight playing over a mountain / Selina Li Bi.
New York, NY : Soho Teen, 2025. | Audience term: Teenagers

ISBN 978-1-64129-648-9
eISBN 978-1-64129-649-6

Subjects: CYAC: Mothers and daughters—Fiction. | Family problem—
Fiction.| Family secret—Fiction. | LCGFT: Novels.
Classification: LCC PZ7.1.B56245 Su 2025 | DDC [Fic]—dc23
LC record available at https://lccn.loc.gov/2024050177

Interior design: Janine Agro, Soho Press, Inc.
Interior art: Xuan Loc Xuan

Printed in the United States of America

10 9 8 7 6 5 4 3 2 1

EU Responsible Person (for authorities only)
eucomply OÜ
Pärnu mnt 139b-14
11317 Tallinn, Estonia
hello@eucompliancepartner.com
www.eucompliancepartner.com

For my family—you are my world

PART I

CHAPTER 1

MY MOTHER AND I came from the moon. My father, a mythical god named Pangu, created the world out of chaos.

This is what I believed as a child.

We were ancient stones misplaced in the world. For years, I dreamed of a new sky filled with clouds so delicate and low, I'd catch them in a jar, like fireflies. When released, Mother and I would join them. Tiny gems hovering above the dark sea.

Though my mother and I came from the moon, we lived in a small Midwestern town called Briarplace. She and I would sit outside on the front steps of the apartment on hot, humid summer nights. Mother with her paper fan, opening it with a flick of the wrist. The paper let off a peculiar odor, a combination of incense and mold. A magnificent phoenix stretched along the folds in luminescent yellow, red, green, black and white feathers. The bird was Feng Huang, a Chinese Phoenix, with the head of a pheasant and the bright tail of a peacock. A symbol of peace and prosperity sent from the heavens. Sent for us.

"Someday we'll be just like this bird and fly away from here," she said. "You and me. Free. Phoenix and Dragon."

To my mother, we were two inseparable entities. A circle of opposing energies. Yin and yang. Darkness and Light.

Phoenix and Dragon. *Sunlight playing over a mountain and a valley.* Something she had read on Taoism.

We were two whimsical creatures with great wing spans, traveling through space and time. We had each other and that's all that mattered.

Everything changed the year I turned fifteen. The stars collided and my life turned upside down and spun, spun, spun, out of control.

Dear Pangu,

As a kid, whenever things got crazy and I started to get stressed out, I'd talk to you—my father.

I was told that you were hairy and fearless. The creator of the universe. I screamed to the heavens. Pangu! Pangu! Where are you? I knew that if I waited long enough and if I kept real quiet, ready to receive, you'd answer me. And the funny thing? I swear you did.

Your breath became the wind, your eyes the sun and moon. Your blood turned into rivers. Your voice the sound of thunder.

Like I said: I was a kid.

At almost fifteen, I know I shouldn't be talking to you, but I still see your image at night, hovering among the stars. You're the only father I've known. Forgive me, but I'm in desperate need of help.

It's my first semester of sophomore year at the new private school, Briarplace Sacred Sacraments, and I already hate it. The one and only person that actually talked to me moved last week. Go figure. I won't even say his name. I'm trying to pretend he doesn't exist because it's easier that way. Just like everything else in my life.

Like the fact that I don't belong at a private school. For one, we can't afford it. Mother had to work double shifts at the restaurant for months. She even sold her favorite pair of jade earrings and a bracelet so I could attend this year. Not that it matters— I'll get kicked out eventually. Moving to the new school hasn't prevented me from cutting classes.

Mother sent me to Sacred Sacraments because she thinks I need help with my faith and I know she's frustrated with the imaginary world I live in. Always drawing. Always in my head. *"Life doesn't exist in your sketchbooks and it's no wonder you suffer from migraines," she says. But the truth is, she's the one filled with stories, she's the one who told me about you, and besides, my art keeps me alive. I live, only to vanish into mysterious worlds. Plus, the saints saw auras, too.*

Mother has no idea, but I believe in God. I pray every night on my knees next to the bed. Last night, I prayed to blend in, like the color beige.

Also, Pangu—my birthday's in a few days. There's something about turning fifteen that makes me nervous. What should I wish for? Do you think I'll feel different? Older and wiser?

Thanks for listening, Pangu.

Yours,

J

CHAPTER 2

A FEW DAYS before my fifteenth birthday, I looked in the small mirror by my bed as soon as I woke up. Nothing had really changed. Freckles and pimples: still there. I dragged myself out of bed, hoping to find Mother in the kitchen, making her homemade rice porridge with gingerroot and scallions. Hoping to hear the kettle, whistling steam for her tea. I loved to drop the dried chrysanthemums into the hot water—watch the petals unfurl. Instead, I heard the echo of the cupboard doors banging against the wall, dishes clanging.

Mother was frantically searching for something, her long hair pulled in a tangled knot on the top of her head. She was in her silk robe and slippers. I was pretty sure her foul mood had to do with her latest boyfriend and the breakup, which I knew was partly my fault. She was going to be so pissed when she found out I had chased him away.

I mean, the dude was lucky. He made enough of an impression to earn one of my catchy nicknames. Yogi. Over the years, her boyfriends had become a simple equation of logic. If I chased them away, then everything would stay the same. Just the two of us.

Another reason I wrote to Pangu: I figure he'd agree with me. It had to be done. He and I were always planning ways to get rid of Mother's endless list of boyfriends.

So—I ignored Mother and pulled out a couple slices of stale bread and made myself a peanut butter and jelly sandwich. That's when I spotted the white paper bag with her pills—tucked in the corner of the counter, next to the rotting banana. The prescription was supposed to help with her episodes, which is what she called them. She also took other herbs she got from a friend to help ease her pain. A pain I didn't know much about. Just that it usually coincided with a breakup. But she swore by the remedy. And she definitely needed something, at that moment.

I grabbed the paper bag from the counter. "Looking for these?"

She whipped around and I tossed the bag to her and she caught it midair. "When did we get this?"

"Yesterday."

How could she have forgotten? Rain had pelted down on us as she and I rode our bikes, pumping our legs and screaming, trying to escape the downpour to get to the drug store on time. Mother insisted that we take bikes to save on gas. "Don't you remember?" I asked her.

"Yes, of course." Her face pinched. "Aren't you going to be late for school?"

I took a bite of the sandwich and swallowed. "I'm going. Don't worry."

Admittedly, she had a right to be concerned. I'd been skipping classes again and one day I was going to pay for it. Especially if the social worker at school got involved—like she did with my friend. I called her the Keeper, because she seemed like the Keeper of my destiny. For a split second, I imagined being dragged down the hall, a door slamming, never seeing my mother again. *You wouldn't let that happen, would you, Pangu?* We didn't usually talk about that kind of stuff, but the threat lingered around me like a ghost.

Changing schools had only made things worse.

LATER THAT MORNING, outside by the bus stop, I thought about the letter to Pangu in my sketchbook, hoping he'd heard my pleas.

I waited for the trees to speak. For the clouds to stir.

A leaf appeared and twirled in the wind. Speckles of sunlight glistened along the sidewalk and it's all I needed for a reply.

CHAPTER 3

I WALKED THE halls of Sacred Sacraments with dread, feeling super uncomfortable in the polo shirt, the stiff collar rubbing against my neck. Strangers stared at me. Everyone was in uniform: tucked-in polo shirts, the girls in checkered skirts or pressed slacks. No jeans or joggers. No distracting hairstyles or baseball caps. No body piercings or funky tattoos. No rap or hip-hop music playing in the hallways. Just nasty whispering. *Go back to where you came from. New China girl.*

The only good thing—I bypassed the miserable back-to-school outfit shopping with Mother at The Flamingo, a secondhand store downtown. There was no arguing this time over what to wear. To meet the dress code at the new school, I had no choice but to order polo shirts and khaki pants online. The pants were a bit long—Mother didn't believe in returning or exchanging things—but they were better than the checkered skirt option. Mother kept smiling and hugging me that day. "Isn't this great? We don't have to spend much on clothes this year." Maybe that's the *real* reason I'm at Sacred Sacraments. I missed my baggy jeans and T-shirt.

School was a drag. All I could think of was Mother and her recent breakup with Yogi and the fact that it was my fault.

Skipping fifth period was the only way to survive the day. So, I did.

THAT EVENING, I lay in bed, wide awake. I wondered if I'd done the right thing, getting rid of Yogi. The door to Mother's room was closed when I came home.

Did I go too far, Pangu? We were just trying to protect our home. Our castle.

I tried to sleep, but my dragon instincts called.

The sweet scent of fire settled on my pillow. My stomach turned and my palms began to sweat. I blamed my restlessness on the wind, the way it teased the silver maple, branches thrashing, nearly snapping just outside my window. I sat upright and puffed up my chest like a sculpted lion guarding the entrance of the Forbidden City.

What if Mother decided to leave, too?

I bolted to Mother's room and was surprised to see her bed still made. Her slippers, the ones embroidered with red lotuses, sat at the foot of the bed.

I found her on the living room floor, surrounded by her large collection of silk flowers, her hands on opposite elbows, cradling herself. Her long black hair hung like silk drapes and her slender legs were spread wide apart in a way that made me shudder. A bottle of pills rested by her side. Next to it was a glass, half-filled with her healing herbs, a smudge of lipstick along the rim.

She was singing a lullaby in Chinese. I didn't understand the words, only her own name repeated over and over. *Suchou, Suchou.* Her melancholy voice, like a violin's long, drawn-out notes, moved through me as I stood over her. The song echoed in my head, a hollow, empty chill.

I thought about calling 911—but this wasn't the first time I'd seen her like this.

She swayed on the floor, hair tousled, still looking beautiful—silk robe lopsided on her shoulders, baring part of her breast, a dark nipple. It was obvious she had been crying. Streaks of mascara ran down her cheeks.

How could she be my mother? I had freckles and wavy, brown hair. "Grow it longer, Jasmine," she said. I never listened. In fact, I had recently cut my hair in the bathroom, watched the locks of wavy curls tumble to the floor.

Mother continued to sing to herself, then she looked up, surprised to see me. "What are you doing? It's late." Her words slurred.

I was checking on her, like I always do. Making sure she was okay. "Yogi left?" I couldn't play totally dumb.

"Yes. He left." Her lids drooped and she stumbled as she stood, grabbed the brush from the table and tossed it to me. "Call him whatever you like. He didn't . . . even . . . leave a note . . . on the lunar calendar. How thoughtless of him."

I started to comb her long hair. The smooth stroke of the pearl-handled brush against her scalp made her feel better. She smelled of Tiger Balm, the menthol-scented ointment she rubbed on my forehead and temples when I had a headache.

"Maybe it's better he left," I said. "You weren't happy anyway. He *was* kinda weird. Just saying."

Mother turned to me and stared as if she hadn't heard a word I'd just said. "Nights like this, it makes me wonder why I even try."

The rain tapped at the window, a rhythmic beat. I didn't want to care, but her eyes were like deep wells, her lids crescent moons. It was no use trying to pretend anymore, no use trying to look past the pain.

"The school called again," she muttered.

"What?" Crap. It was starting all over again, me teetering along the tight rope, my arms spread like wings, trying desperately to keep from falling.

"They said you weren't at fifth period."

"That's phys ed. You know I don't believe in sweating for no reason."

"You can't be skipping school again. It's your first year at the new school and . . ." She bit into her lower lip.

I knew she'd worked hard to get me into Sacred Sacraments, but the thing was—

I didn't *want* to be there. I didn't want to be anywhere. Last year at the public school sucked, too. I skipped a lot and had to meet with the school counselor countless times. I scrunched my toes and looked down.

She took a sip of her herb tincture. "Did you hear me?"

"I'll be better. I promise."

I'd try. We'd both be better with Yogi gone.

"She threatened to call you-know-who," she said.

"CPS?" The evil unspoken words. The Keepers. It wasn't the first time they'd come up. I crossed my arms. "That's not going to happen, right?"

I had heard about foster homes from the only other kid at school that looked like me. He described crying babies. Strange food like meatloaf and potato fritters. Being forced to go to church on Sunday. It almost made me cry, something I rarely allowed myself to do.

This was all her fault. Not mine. Her revolving door of boyfriends needed to stop—it only hurt us, made things more miserable. "It could be just you. You know? No more crazy boyfriends for a while. Okay?"

"*Yogi* wasn't crazy." Mother twisted strands of hair around her index finger and I watched as she drifted into her mythical world. "Ah, the presence of Pangu rattles in my chest. His body opens the heavens wider for us. Dare we enter?"

I transported into the dream, though I was still partially stuck on the idea of being taken from home. But I decided to play along, even though part of me didn't want to, even though I wasn't a child anymore. It was her way of connecting. Thinking of Pangu, I added, "His voice rumbles of thunder. I think he draws near."

Mother pulled me down to sit with her in the corner of the living room, among her garden of silk lilies and orchids. She waved a stalk of bamboo in the air. "No more wasted tears. We belong to the moon. Never forget."

I nodded. And in that moment, I thought she might drown, and a strange mistress of the gods would be sent in her place. I would be abandoned, left beneath the waving palms by the sea. I bit my lip till I tasted blood and let myself dream.

"We belong to the moon," I repeated.

The room grew smaller, the lilies and orchids closed in. Rain still drummed against the window. Droplets of reflections scattering against the black night. I pulled the robe tight over Mother's shoulders, her breast.

I thought of the time I rescued an injured meadowlark after it had blindly smacked against the living room window. I ran outside, found it still, stunned. I scooped it up in my palm, kept it in a box with a towel and a small dish of water. The next morning, I watched it fly out of the box and into the starry sky.

I wanted Mother to flap her wings, move like the Phoenix.

I sat and waited. Waited for the rain to end. Waited for the wind to stop howling.

Time slanted into a pool of water and light. Earth and shadows.

I wanted to know what she was dreaming, with her mind transported to a distant place.

I was born with the ability to sense things. It was hard to explain. Mother called it my gift of knowing and says it lived within me. She spoke of it as if it were a living, breathing creature. The struggle was deciphering it from all the other voices in my head. This knowing often got me in trouble as well.

Right, Pangu? It's exhausting.

I'd much rather have the gift of beauty like my mother. Or the gift of brains, so I can figure out how to keep me and my mother together forever.

She was the Phoenix—exotic, rare and beautiful. And I was the Dragon, the beast meant to save us.

CHAPTER 4

THE NEXT MORNING, I checked the front door to make sure it was locked and grabbed the bottle of pills and glass of herbs from the living room floor and tossed it in the garbage. Mother eventually woke up and retreated to her silk garden.

Over the years, she had gathered her assortment of silk flowers and vases from tiny secondhand shops and peddlers from the Briarplace outdoor market. She planted them everywhere in our apartment—on the kitchen countertop, the living room coffee table, even in the bathroom. The collection grew into a jungle of sprouting silk, including everything from lilies to the birds-of-paradise. "They live forever. They never leave you," she says.

But in the real world, silk petals didn't breathe.

The truth was—she was stressed because of Yogi, and just the week before, after consulting the *I Ching*, she'd quit her job at the local grocery store. A teenage boy had mumbled *chink* under his breath as he was paying for a carton of milk. I couldn't help but think about food and rent. Thank god she had found another job working as a server at a Chinese restaurant on the other end of town.

We lived on the southern edge of Briarplace, in an apartment with dimly lit hallways and wood paneling. The building was tucked between a grove of towering oak and maple trees.

Just behind it stood a ten-foot man-made earthen dike that held back the Blackbird River. Brown murky water rose each spring. Depending on the snow melt and spring rains, it had the potential to flood the entire town and neighboring farms.

During heavy spring rains, water leaked from the ceiling in our kitchen and onto the linoleum floor. Mother caught the incessant, annoying drip in empty tins of Maxwell House canisters she borrowed from an elderly neighbor next door.

Despite our circumstances, Mother always reminded me how lucky we were. I never told her how lost I felt or how I wished I had a family. A place to land. A real father, though I often called on my imaginary one. *Sorry, Pangu.*

In grade school, when my classmates asked me about my father, I told them what I believed—that he was Pangu, a mythical god who created the heavens and earth. I described how he was born from an egg-shaped cloud which contained the universe. They listened in awe until one day, one of the kids started to laugh. I didn't care. It didn't matter what they thought. My father was a heroic god.

"Never forget where you came from," Mother said. But she was the one who told stories that made me feel like I came from everywhere and nowhere. *She* was where I came from. That's all I knew.

My mother, Suchou Cheng, was from the Philippines. She made me study the country, an archipelago of thousands of tropical islands. It's called Asia's "Pearl of the Orient," because of its palm trees and white sandy beaches. On the shores of Cebu, Ferdinand Magellan planted a large wooden cross. This was my mother's home, a mysterious, untouchable world.

Mother said her family was Chinese with a little bit of

Filipino, a little bit of Spanish, and maybe even some Malay. She said with pride, "I'm told I have my mama's spirit and her hands. I wish she had lived long enough for me to hear her voice. Touch her skin. But they say our ancestral spirits live on and guide us."

Come to think of it, I was a mixed breed. A mutt. It made me wonder about my real father's voice, too. Would I recognize it, if he called out to me?

Of course, whenever I asked how we ended up at Briarplace, Mother said, "It's not important." And whenever I asked where I was born, she said with sarcasm, "Briarplace." Then later, she'd whisper, under her breath, "We're so far away from people like us."

Who were we? Where was my real home?

I WAS ALREADY late for school, but I didn't want to disrupt the breakup ritual—so I kept quiet and made Mother a cup of tea.

She took a sip, then disappeared into the bathroom and reappeared with a pair of scissors in one hand and a thin towel in the other. I grabbed a nearly empty carton of milk from the fridge, poured the remainder into a bowl of corn flakes, and followed a trail of white threads into the living room.

"What are you doing?" I asked.

She snipped off the tag from the towel. "Discarding any evidence."

"A towel. Pretty serious. Must be a crime of passion."

"He used this to dry himself in the morning, after his shower." She snapped the towel in the air, dispersing sparkles of colorful dust.

"Lovely."

"I don't want any reminders," she said.

"Why don't you just throw it away? Toss it out the window like they do in the movies."

"Destruction can be healing."

"Go ahead and burn it then."

She cut a crooked line along the edge of the towel and looked satisfied.

"I almost called the ambulance last night." I glanced at the clock. It was almost noon.

"The ambulance?"

"You know, the white van with the siren on top?"

"Nothing's going to happen, silly."

I paused. "Yogi was no good, anyway."

"What makes you say that?"

"He's a freak. You know how he burned candles in every room. It smelled like a temple in here. And he cleared our living room, including your flowers, by the way, just so he could do headstands in his spandex."

She stopped and held the scissors in midair. "What did you do?"

Crap. "Nothing."

"Really?" she said.

"Until I saw him pocket twenty dollars from our Mason jar."

Mother dropped the scissors to the floor. "Bastard." She straightened her back. "And then what happened?"

"I blew out every candle except for one and set his zafu on fire." That was when he drew the line. I had no choice but to chase him away.

"You didn't."

"I did."

"I suppose that's when he left," she said.

"Yep. He yelled *F—you, kid*, gathered his belongings and dashed out the door."

"Ah. You've succeeded once again."

I yanked a sprig of baby's breath from a vase of carnations and tossed it to the floor. "*He's* the one who decided to leave."

Okay—I often had something to do with these sudden disappearances. But her boyfriends were like poison ivy, a toxic weed invading our intimate, serene garden. They offered a dangerous amount of hope. They made my mother happy, but it was always brief. Not true love, I told myself. At least not what I thought love should be. And now, with the possibility of Social Services knocking on our door—I knew I did the right thing with Yogi.

Love only ever caused trouble.

"But I'll never know when the right one comes along," she said, her voice soft and low, "if you keep chasing them away."

Her whole face sagged and I tried not to let it get to me. I hated when she blamed me for things. I was only trying to help.

Mother turned away. "You needed to give him a chance. From now on, stay away, okay?"

"What do you mean? Like leave?" I asked. My stomach tightened, knowing she'd never say that.

"No. If you were a cat, I'd declaw you."

"Right, Ma."

"I'm telling you. You must quit interfering. Tame down those predatory skills. I mean it."

"Okay."

"Promise?"

I brought one hand behind my back and crossed my fingers. "Promise."

CHAPTER 5

I TURNED FIFTEEN on Saturday.

On my fourteenth birthday, Mother surprised me with Halo-halo. A Filipino dessert made with sweet ube, red beans, and coconut ice cream. The year before that she gave me a bracelet made of pig teeth and feathers, an amulet from the Aetas, an indigenous people of the Philippine Islands. Her Filipino nanny, Rosie, had given it to her when she was young, to ward off evil spirits. I kept it under my pillow and waved it in the air at night. It made me feel safe, even brave, knowing I had the power to chase away evil spirits.

That morning, I leaped out of bed and dashed to the bathroom. There were no birthday wishes written on the bathroom mirror. No love poems. No lipstick kisses. Poetry and the written word—Mother's preferred language of love. And in the kitchen, no special omelet with Chinese sausage and scallions.

No mention of my birthday at all.

She totally forgot.

In my room, I escaped into my sketchpad, gripped my charcoal pencil, and drew swirling images of a tornado engulfing everything in sight, as if that would make things better. As if that way, I could escape from the real world. I envisioned the color of light. My anger and disappointment spread across the canvas in vibrant colors.

I imagined Pangu at the beginning of the world. Trapped in an egg with the matter of the universe, a swirl of chaos. *Set me free, Pangu.*

A twinkle of light made its way through the crack in the blind, filling me with hope. Maybe she'd still remember later?

IN THE AFTERNOON, Mother and I watched an old Marlon Brando movie, *On the Waterfront*, at a matinee downtown and took the city bus home.

I kept thinking: *How could she forget my birthday?*

Maybe her forgetfulness was payback for chasing away her boyfriend.

On the ride home, she stared straight ahead like a mannequin, legs crossed. I dug my nails into the seat cushion, holding back the urge to jog her memory.

I pressed my forehead against the bus window, watching the same row of oak trees pass by, latching on to the street signs, an elderly man walking his dog. I longed for something *unfamiliar*, something to surprise and inspire me. Perhaps I was hoping for a sign from the universe, telling me my life was about to change for the better.

The bus stopped and we walked back to the apartment. I grabbed a small rock and threw it across the street, snickered as it grazed a parked car. It was my birthday. I would do as I pleased.

"What's going on?" Mother said. "Have the restless spirits taken hold of you?"

I shrugged. "I don't know what you're talking about. Maybe they've taken hold of you. Some are quite forgetful."

I continued to hint, but she trotted behind, peering up at

the sky. I snapped off a branch from a nearby bush and flung it to the side.

Mother stopped. "Honestly, Jasmine. What are you doing? Your behavior's atrocious."

I bit the inside of my lip. "I think I just need to get out of here. Don't you ever feel like that?"

"Of course, I do."

"We're all going to end up dead anyway," I said, wondering if the thought of death might trigger her memory. Death. Birth. Life. You know what I mean.

"Death is part of the circle of life."

"Well, today's kind of important."

"I don't know what you're talking about."

"I'm fifteen. Hello? Did you forget?"

"What?" Mother stroked my arm. "Of course not."

Nice recovery. But I heard the lie in her voice and could literally see the wheels in her brain turning round and round. A dog barked. I turned my gaze to the cement sidewalk, to the fine cracks and sprouting tendrils of grass.

"When I turned fifteen, I wanted to go to Taiwan. Eat century eggs, spicy hotpot soup. Sip on plum wine."

I didn't want to hear her stories. I wanted to hitchhike to the other end of town and throw a birthday party for myself with balloons and cupcakes. Jon Batiste singing a jazzy version of happy birthday and *What A Wonderful World*, just for me, his fingers dancing along the keys of a grand piano, the stars blinking to each beat.

I planted myself on the edge of the curb, arm extended, thumb raised.

A van, followed by an old pickup truck, zipped by and honked.

Mother gave me a gentle shove and laughed. "What's got into you? What's this all about?"

"I just wanted you to remember. That's all."

Couldn't we celebrate like other kids at school? With birthday cake and candles? Was that too much to ask?

"There will be other birthdays," she said as she pushed away my bangs. "I'll make it up to you. I promise."

But I knew better than to believe her. The words spilled from her lips and nothing more. Like the time she promised we'd take a trip down south to the Florida Keys. Or the time she promised to take me to the salon to get my hair done by a professional. She ended up cutting my bangs in a frenzy before school, leaving a jagged line across my forehead. Another reason for the kids to make fun of me.

"Sometimes, we must drown in the uncertain sea," she whispered.

"Enough, Ma." I rolled my eyes. A *happy birthday* would do just fine.

I tried to remember that we were the lucky ones. Only we saw the stars during the day, the fierce heat from the other side of the world at night.

CHAPTER 6

ON MONDAY, I really dreaded going to school, especially after all the drama from Mother's breakup and her missing my birthday. Just before I left the apartment, I threw a hoodie over my T-shirt to hide my flat chest. Puberty wasn't all it was cracked up to be. I was a thin girl with chubby cheeks. Not to mention the freckles. I still looked like a twelve-year-old. A boyish twelve-year-old. And I hadn't even had my you-know-what-yet. *Mother Nature's gift.*

I stood by my locker, backpack slung over one shoulder. A group of girls buzzed by, like a bunch of bees, dressed in their matching yellow polos and checkered skirts, the fruity scent of hairspray and perfume drifting past. They were giggling and chatting. One of them shot me a side glance, one of those judgy looks that makes my skin break out into an itchy red rash.

I really didn't belong.

It hadn't been that long since summer but I hardly recognized them. They had morphed into women. Curvy women. Hormones gone wild. I wanted to crawl out of my boyish figure and be a woman, too.

C'mon, almighty Pangu. Do your magic. Metamorphosis. Turn this caterpillar into a butterfly.

The hallway shifted, straight lines breaking into waves,

a swirl of chaos. An egg-shaped cloud appeared. Pangu's breath exhaling flames of fire. My arms tingled and stretched, spreading outward like the wings of a butterfly.

I felt a rough shove from behind. A burst of laughter. "Earth to Jasmine." Followed by another burst of laughter. "Frick'n weirdo." I wanted to turn around, but I knew right away who it was—the same dude that had tried to trip me in the hallway the other day.

I sucked in my stomach. Clutching the straps of my backpack, I marched down the hallway, my gaze downward, the speckled linoleum tiles bulging and shifting beneath my feet.

I prayed and prayed for Friday to come.

I PROBABLY SHOULDN'T have cut class. Now I had to meet with the school counselor. Again. I dreaded it the way I dreaded doing homework and taking tests that made me feel stupid.

Miss Carter began the session with a ridiculous breathing exercise. For my *anxiety*. She believed it was the reason I skipped class. She said it stemmed from my unstable home life, from Mother and her boyfriends. She even asked me if I felt safe at home.

Why do my feelings even need a diagnosis? Dumb.

The month before, I had made the mistake of telling her how I couldn't sleep because Yogi was over, an excuse for my tardiness. *Her boyfriends* became a measuring stick of my mental health—

I was fifteen now and I could handle things. I didn't need to meet with her. It reminded me of when I told her how in grade school I sold candy at the playground during recess.

"Hey, dude," I'd say. "Want to try some rice candy?" By the end of recess, I had a fistful of dimes and several quarters. I even sold my Hello Kitty Hair Bows to the popular girls. It never amounted to much, but I remember how it made me feel—like a grown up. And I was proud I had made some contribution in my life.

I didn't dare ask her about Child Protective Services, if she'd really call them. Then it might come true.

Yet, sitting there in the office, I felt a storm coming. My gift of sensing things kicked in. It felt like someone was lurking in the shadows, spying on me. *Pangu?* Paranoia? Perhaps. But I didn't think so. It was called being vigilant, keeping a watchful eye out for possible dangers.

"How's it going, Jasmine? Are you liking it better at Sacred Sacraments?"

I furrowed my brows, as if giving it some serious thought. "Actually, if you want to know the truth, I hate it. I'd rather be back at the public school."

Miss Carter frowned. Her disappointment made me laugh inside. "Oh? Why is that? Is that why you continue to skip classes?"

How much pleasure did she think I received from constant punishment? I paused. "I don't really need this right now."

"Well, Sister Ruth is concerned. It's hard to make up and finish assignments when you're not there." Then she ran her tongue across the top of her teeth, like she had started to enjoy the conversation. "Remind me again. It's just you and your mom, correct?"

"Yep," I said. The *just* part killed me. As if there were a much better way of living? I grew angrier.

"Does she know you've been skipping?"

"Of course she does."

She flashed a smile, teeth. Wrong answer. I felt sick inside. Suddenly, I wanted to throw up.

"And the lunch monitor noticed that you haven't eaten lunch the past few days. She said you asked her for five dollars? I know it's not easy having a single parent."

You don't know anything, I thought. My voice came out staccato. "I wasn't hungry. And I never . . . asked for money. Okay. I asked for money once—to pay a library fine. But that was like—a week ago."

"I see. Do you eat breakfast?"

"Yeah." Duh.

"Who makes you breakfast?"

"I do." A bolt of anger flashed through me. "Why are you asking me these dumb questions? What does this have to do with me skipping?"

I was riding a merry-go-round—spinning, spinning, around and around, with the same stupid questions. And nowhere to go.

AFTER SCHOOL THAT day, Mother surprised me with a used book of haiku.

She felt bad for missing my birthday, even though she'd never admit it.

"What's this for?" I asked.

"Must you ask such silly questions? Read it. Let it speak to you."

I went to my room and held the book in my hands. Receiving any gift from Mother was like winning a prize. I was being seen. I was being loved.

I opened the haiku book and read out loud.

Brushing the leaves, fell
A white camellia blossom
Into the dark well.
                    —Bashō

Mother was right. Poetry was the language of love.

CHAPTER 7

WHEN THE WEEKEND came, Mother danced around the apartment. She dusted and folded a load of laundry with more energy than usual. "Today, we're going to the carnival," she said with a lilt in her voice. "My horoscope says to seek a festive place of amusement for love."

Was that her creative way of saying sorry? Doubtful. I tried not to be salty.

Plus, I detested the carnival.

Every fall, the town held the big festival on the fairgrounds nearby, which included hundreds of acres of land. Exhibition buildings for 4-H Club, home-made crafts, horses and other farm animals. And once a year, it brought crowds of people from all over the state.

Mother urged me down the midway in her long cotton dress.

A disharmony of pops and whistles blared. A whirl of dust in front of us. Hairy chested men, babies in strollers, young kids screaming from the Zipper and the Tilt-A-Whirl. The greasy smell of fried mini-donuts.

Just ahead of us, the roller coaster crawled up the rail at a snail pace, its rusted iron wheels screeching. A dizzy array of kiosks scattered along the midway with popcorn, decorated with hand-dipped caramel apples and brightly colored snow-cones. My hungry stomach gurgled. All the noise made my head pound.

I recalled a time when Mother and I would sit on the front steps of the apartment, sip on sweet grass jelly drinks, and listen to the faint sounds of the carnival from a distance, watching the neon lights flashing in the night sky. As a kid, it was mesmerizing, but now the crowd felt suffocating, the noise debilitating.

Mother yanked me forward as she marched ahead. She bought us a bag of pink cotton candy. I grabbed a handful of the sticky cotton and let it melt on my tongue. A clown wandered by. I wanted to be him at that moment, to wear a rainbow-colored wig, to paint my nose red and curve my lips in a permanent smile. Then no one would guess how I really felt inside, which was miserable.

Mother stopped at the House of Mirrors. After dragging me inside, she stood in front of a full-length image of herself, body becoming wavy and distorted as she flapped her arms like a little girl and giggled. "The power of self-reflection. What do you say?"

"Honestly, I'd rather ride the bumper cars. Throw darts at balloons. Better yet, jump off that bridge which is about a mile from here."

She laughed. "Let's have a little fun for a change."

Yeah. Right. I thought about Child Protective Services again. Thought of my friend. My head throbbed with the sense of danger. A red alert. A storm brewing. More real now than imagined. "Go ahead. Looking at myself might trigger a headache." I narrowed my brows to let her know I was serious. "In fact, I feel one coming on as we speak."

"You're no fun." Mother grabbed my hand and I chased

her through a narrow maze, watched as our stretched alien images were sandwiched between obtuse angles and triangles. She paused in an open area and we stood side by side. A couple of bloated dwarves. Mother stuck out her tongue.

"You look freaky, Ma. Seriously." Her pupils were wide and saucer-like.

"See, you can be anything you want to be. It's all how you perceive things."

I touched the mirror. "I look like a fly."

"No daughter of mine is an insect." She kissed my cheek. "You're a princess. A beautiful princess."

"No. I'm not. Look at me." Thinking of the cool girls at school, I tapped the glass and searched for those desirable curves. Boobs? Butt? Cheekbones? But nope. All I saw was bulging ears and even chubbier cheeks with ginormous freckles. Suddenly, I wanted to scream.

"So, how does it feel to be fifteen?"

"No different than fourteen," I said. I thought about broken promises and missed birthdays. "What did you wish for when you were my age?"

Mother paused. "Hmmm . . . straight teeth. Clear skin. And for my hair to grow down to my toes."

"That's all?"

The tone of her voice shifted to a soft whisper. "And for my papa to love me."

I was shocked. I couldn't imagine my mother being unloved. "How could he not love you?" I asked. "Must have not been like Pangu."

What did I know about fathers? I only knew an imaginary one, a mythological creature who loved me more than the heavens. As a little girl, the words had jumped off my tongue. *Where's my daddy?*

Use your imagination, Mother said. Then, like she always did, she hummed the familiar tune as she lightly touched my chest. *Your father is always right here. A mighty hero. He is the creator of all things in this world. You are precious to him.*

It was like our little secret and it made me feel safe. I didn't care what other people said after that. I had a hero for my father. The great Pangu. But standing in the House of Mirrors, the words seemed empty. Like I'd been robbed of the truth. Maybe I was tired of living in the fantasy world.

In English class, we had read a quote by Kierkegaard, a philosopher and poet: *Life can only be understood backwards, but it must be lived forward.* Maybe that's what was missing in my life. The truth of my past.

The mirror caught my attention. A pulse of light flashed on and off. *Pangu?* A shadow slid along the wall.

Mother sighed. "No, my father's limbs did not create mountains."

I glanced at her. "So *your* father wasn't a giant with a chisel in his hand?"

"No. He was not a giant. Not a god. Not a father who chiseled the world out of rocks. Only a man without emotion. Did you know my mama died the day I was born, giving birth to me? They say she swallowed an evil spirit and bled like a river. Papa was left to care for me. He and my Filipino nanny, Rosie."

"That's sad, Ma. I didn't know that." It felt like someone had flipped on and off a light and I was seeing part of her life flash before me for the first time. The ground beneath me shifted. What else about her didn't I know? "So, maybe it's better just to be a fly."

I waited for her reaction, but a group of young boys crowded in front of the mirror. She found a corner and stared at herself and started picking something out of her tooth.

WE CONTINUED TO walk down the carnival path and ended up in front of a striped tent. A young man leaned over the edge of the booth, his dirty blond hair in a high ponytail, one arm tossing a baseball in the air. He wore a black tank top and jeans.

"Hey ladies, step right up," he said with an impish grin. "I see a winner. I do."

A long dagger tattoo stretched from the top of his left shoulder down the entire length of his arm. I looked away as I caught him scanning the length of my body. It made me feel dirty and naked.

"Name's Sebastian," he said. He had bony hands and long fingernails. "Give it a try? Everyone's a winner."

"No, thank you," Mother said.

He winked and smiled. "How about a Ferris wheel ride later then?"

I pressed my fingers into Mother's back. "Let's go. I'm hungry." I shook my head and glanced at Sebastian.

He looked past me to Mother. Winked again. "Catch you gals, later? Eight o'clock sharp. Meet here."

Mother agreed and Sebastian gave a thumbs up.

"He's kind of creepy, Ma."

"I think he's cute."

"Seriously? You mean in a shipwrecked kinda way? I've seen sexier homeless men downtown."

"He's harmless. And remember your promise to stay away."

Down the midway, I watched the roller coaster dive and turn up ahead. Rock music. Bells and whistles. Children hollering and screaming. My head ready to explode.

CHAPTER 8

WE RODE THE Ferris wheel late that evening, Sebastian and Mother in one cart, and me alone in another, which truly sucked. I gritted my teeth and clung tight to the cool handlebar. I despised her for agreeing to this and making me tag along.

The ride paused when my cart was almost at the peak, causing it to sway slowly back and forth. Below me, the city exploded with bright lights. A warm breeze blew through my hair. But I smelled trouble.

The cart beneath mine started to swing, too. It creaked, very loud, and the sound was followed by Mother's piercing voice. I looked down, out of breath with fear. She had unlatched herself and was standing on the seat, clutching the sidebar with one hand.

"I can touch the stars from here. Pinch the clouds," she said, waving the edge of her dress in the air.

"Sit down," I shouted, wishing I was closer so I could pull her down.

Mother raised one bare leg. "Oh, you're such a killjoy." Her body swayed with the cart.

I shuddered from the familiarity of the situation. Her episodes where she thought she was invincible. *Pangu?* I thought, *Please listen to me. Please help my mother.* I wondered if this mythical god ever got sick of my pleas and my bargains. Did he know my biggest fear was losing her one day? I often had nightmares of her drowning, her slender body floating down the river, her long hair like seaweed.

"Grab her, Sebastian. Please?" My neck strained as I peered down. The cart was now swinging like it had a death wish.

"Damn. Your mom's a crazy chick." Sebastian grasped the fleshy part of her upper arm and she toppled to her seat. I saw him plant a kiss along the nape of her neck and gagged. At least my heartbeat slowed down.

I searched the sky, connecting lines to the stars of the Big Dipper, to Polaris, the North Star. *Hey Pangu, this one reminds me of a stray dog. I believe he's earned a nickname. What about Carnie? Perhaps Carnie goes out with a lightning strike? A fall? Give me a sign, okay?* I waited and the lights tremored and opened to a fierce embrace. *Thanks for listening, Pangu. I won't let this continue. I promise.*

LATER THAT NIGHT, Carnie carried a small glass aquarium into our apartment. He set it down on the coffee table in the middle of the living room. I peered inside. A bright green lizard sat in the far corner.

"Here you go, punk," Carnie said.

"Punk?"

"You're just a kid. This here's a little consolation prize. Hard to travel with the little guy. His name's Tony with a *Y*," Carnie said. "He's got a third parietal eye. Senses light. Just a baby. Chinese Water Dragon." He pulled out a plastic bag of chopped carrots from the pocket of his jeans, opened the net covering and tossed a few orange shreds into the tank. "Keep him company?"

He winked and followed Mother to the bedroom.

I grabbed a bag of rice crackers from the cupboard, went back to the living room, turned on the television, and sat on the floor next to the aquarium. Tony didn't move, his brown marble-like eyes staring at me.

"You're a cool little dude. Third eye, huh?" I swear a tiny pinhole of light on his forehead winked at me. "Bet you detect more than just light. I can sense threats, too. We're kinda the same."

Tony continued to stare, but I immediately felt the connection.

About an hour later, Carnie staggered toward the kitchen, barefoot, shirt off, jeans hanging halfway down his butt. "Got any limes?"

"Nope. Lemons, though. Fridge. Second shelf."

We had a Tupperware full of sliced lemons from the Royal Bamboo restaurant where Mother worked. Some-times, she and I pretended we were high class, dropping wedges in our glasses of ice water, sipping with our pinkie fingers in the air while sitting in a booth. Plus, I had read in a magazine how lemons had the power to fade freckles.

"How 'bout it?" Carnie entered the living room, a wedge of lemon in hand. He bit into it, then took a swig of Tequila he had brought with him before offering it to me.

"No, thanks." Didn't he know he could go to jail for that?

"C'mon. You're no fun."

As if I hadn't heard *that* before. "I could give a rip. Been told that a few times," I said, distracted by his devilish grin. I inched close to the glass aquarium. Tony was still as a stone, blending in with his surroundings. What would it be like to be a chame-leon? Blend in with the world around you? "So, does he ever move?" *He's like me—paranoid—*I thought, mind spinning now about the school counselor, Child Protective Services. "I get it," I whispered. "I don't trust many people, either."

"He's maybe scared. New environment and all." Carnie dropped to the floor, crossed his legs and scooted to my side. I took note of the tattooed dagger along his arm. The blade glimmered, as if it had a life of its own.

"Where'd you get the tattoo?" I asked.

He grinned like I had asked the million-dollar question. "You like it? I had to celebrate my first day out of prison, so I went to a tattoo shop with a buddy of mine. Got inked. Hell. Should've seen his."

Do I dare ask? "What was it?"

"A small, teeny tiny bat on his left cheek." Carnie pointed to his butt. "This left cheek." He laughed. "Chicken shit."

"What were you in prison for?"

"Selling weed. After that I became a carnie. Long hours. Low pay."

"Bet you get to see all kinds of places, though."

"Yep. Travel a lot." Carnie smiled, his body letting off an odor of cigarettes and gasoline. He turned toward Mother's silk garden. "Hell, what's your mother growing? Damn jungle in here. Looks like *Alice in Wonderland*."

"It's her thing. She loves flowers. Someday she's going to have her own shop. Suppose I shouldn't make it hard on her."

"What do you mean?"

"New school and I'm in trouble for skipping." I took a deep breath. "I don't want to end up in a foster home."

"What makes you think you could end up there?" Carnie hesitated, like he was thinking real hard about something. "I was in a foster home."

"You were?"

"Yeah. I ran away from home when I was fourteen. At least there, I had a bed to sleep in. Food. I can't say I loved it."

"Maybe it's a fear of mine. One of my friends at school had to move. Got put in a foster home. He said he regrets saying his parents didn't care if he was in school or not." I shrugged. My neck tensed. I didn't know why I was telling Carnie about this, but it felt good. Like someone else got it. And just talking about it made it less scary, at least in that moment.

"It's cool," he said. "What about you? How's home?"

"I mean, sometimes I wish we didn't have to worry about food and crap."

Carnie smiled. "Everyone has fears. Just don't show it. In fact, I fear I'll get fired one day from the carnival. I just don't show it."

"Really? That's interesting."

And good for me to know when it comes to getting rid of you, I thought.

THE NEXT MORNING, I checked on Tony and found his green body clinging to the glass. Carnie trotted into the kitchen, pulling on his jeans.

"Need your mom's keys. I'm late for work."

"She said that was okay?" I pulled a box of Cheerios from the cupboard.

"Yeah. Find them," he said.

I took a survey of the counter and spotted the small empty bowl she usually kept them in. "Don't know where they are. Sorry," I said.

"Go wake her, then. Don't have time for this shit."

I paused, wary of his sudden change in vibe. "Okay. Geez." I went to Mother's room. She was still asleep. "Ma." She lifted her head and blinked a couple times.

"What is it?"

"Your keys. Where are they?"

"In the kitchen. Why?"

"They're not there," I said. "Asshole's taking your car."

Mother sat up. "Tell him to find another ride."

I went back into the kitchen. Carnie digging through a drawer. "She says take the bus."

Carnie darted to the bedroom and I followed, too slow to stop him as he grabbed Mother by the arm. "I need your keys, Suchou."

"You're hurting her," I said. "Leave her alone."

Mother groaned. "I'm fine, honey. The keys, okay?"

I spotted the keys on the floor, next to a sock and tube of lipstick. I grabbed them and dangled them in front of Carnie.

"Give them to me," he said. "Or I'm going to call CPS."

He smiled. His pupils dilated and turned a misty gray, his tongue darting out like a slithering snake.

Are you kidding me? How dare he threaten us. He'd pay for this. I'd make sure of it.

"I need to get something out of the car first," I said.

"Hurry the heck up, then," he said.

I went to the kitchen and grabbed a screwdriver from the drawer and shoved it in my pocket. Pangu and I had a plan. This wasn't the first time we'd delayed a boyfriend from getting to work. And you can learn how to do almost anything on YouTube. Carnie's fear was our win. Asshole.

Mother's car was parked across the street, at the end of a long row of cars and trucks. I twisted off the air valve of the front passenger tire and with the screwdriver, I let out air, pressing it on the metal pin on the valve. We're not even close to the fairgrounds. Mother might not approve, but she didn't have to know.

In the distance, Carnie drew rapidly closer.

I stood up quickly and pocketed the screwdriver, then tossed him the keys. "She's all yours."

He hopped in the car and sped off, not even slowing down as the tires burned the pavement.

I looked up and high-fived Pangu in my mind, even though a gritty sensation gnawed at my insides. She was going to kill me. But I did the right thing. The Phoenix and Dragon would be soaring through the sky again soon, wings flapping.

As I returned to the apartment, the nosy lady next door peeked her head out, gave me a dirty look, then slammed the door shut without a word.

"The car's been working better now?" I asked Mother. Last week, she had a neighbor inspect the engine for a knocking noise.

"Not sure, but it's on empty, so I imagine he didn't get very far. Never fall in love, okay?"

"Why don't you tell yourself that?"

"Love is complex, Jasmine. That's all. Princes in shining armor, disguised." She grabbed my hand. "Don't be fooled."

I pulled away. "Please tell me *he* isn't your prince?"

"Sebastian? No. He was just someone to make me feel young again. Besides, we've got each other, right? And no one compares to your father, Pangu. He split the heavens and earth. He, who has created this world from chaos."

I nodded, inhaling the sweet scent of her. A ray of sun pressed through the window. *I feel your presence, Pangu.* In that moment, his warmth was like the sun embracing us in a pool of light. I felt the scales of my dragon hide thickening, strengthening, ready to protect our world.

THE FOLLOWING MORNING, Mother needed the car to run an errand. I told her we should look for it, knowing Carnie most likely didn't get too far.

We discovered it about a mile from the apartment, alongside the road. Mother crouched near the front tire. It was flat, the rim of the wheel nearly touching the ground.

"What did you do?"

"Me?"

"Don't play stupid. Look. The tire's ruined. I can't afford this," she said. "Some days, I wonder how we're going to eat."

"I'm sorry," I said. "It needed to be done." The gnawing sensation returned. Aswangs darted toward me, one by one—the counselor, the neighbor lady, shape-shifting into vampire-like creatures with wings.

"What are you talking about? Your pranks are getting costly."

I heard Carnie's piercing voice in my mind. *Give them to me. Or I'm going to call CPS.* My pulse raced.

"I had to get rid of him," I finally said.

Carnie showed up late that evening and picked up Tony. "You don't deserve a consolation prize, punk." He cussed at Mother and at me, then left.

Part of me wanted to run away, too. Before my world split apart. Before I was taken far away.

CHAPTER 9

MOTHER'S BOYFRIENDS CAME and went. Just like her practice of religions, from Christianity to Buddhism.

She prayed to many gods—Jesus on the cross, the Buddha in the west corner of our home, and the Holy Mary, Mother of God. "Never get attached," she says. "Remember the Buddhist saying: *Happiness begins at the end of wanting.*"

There was a small shrine in the narrow hallway next to our bedrooms, a walnut shelf with a vase full of incense and in the center, a cross-legged Buddha, hands resting on his knees. Every morning, she knelt, bowing three times with a burning stick in her hands.

Before Carnie, there was Adi, a self-proclaimed Buddhist who taught her the power of meditation. Before that was Victor, the fighter pilot who promised to fly her around the world, but instead took off with cash from her wallet and never came back. There was Rollie, the poet, who scattered Post-it notes with verses from Rumi all over the apartment—on the fridge, kitchen counter, the bathroom mirror, sometimes in our shoes. *Your task is not to seek for love, but merely to seek and find all barriers within yourself that you have built against it . . . When the soul lies down in that grass the world is too full to talk about . . .*

To them, I was an awkward kid in their way. Sometimes,

when they wanted to be alone with Mother, they bribed me with money, junky jewelry, Milk Duds or Hot Tamales. They often filled a need for her, for us, like free dinners, fixing the car or stuff around the apartment. Or maybe their presence filled an aching need, an emptiness neither one of us wanted to admit existed. A replacement for a father I didn't have.

Mother usually had a sense about men. She could sniff out the "wild boys." And even if she knew they'd love and leave her, she played with them anyway. But, in the end, she was always the wounded one. Her notions of love and princes in shining armor faded in the midst of her dreams.

My shoulders tensed, thinking about the next victim.

CHAPTER 10

A WEEK PASSED without any boyfriends or visitors. I celebrated by skipping class here and there. But then, on Monday afternoon after school, Mother was acting kind of strange. She paced the living room and circled her silk garden. She kept shaking her head and mumbling to herself. She looked pale.

"Say, Jasmine. Why don't you take out the garbage, huh? Is that okay?"

I shot her an odd look. "Why?" She rarely asked me to do household chores, especially after school. I just did the dishes after they piled too high in the sink and took out the garbage when the place started to stink. Which, to be fair, it did right now. Like rotten fish.

But then she said, "We have someone coming over. She might be talking to you. Asking you some questions. Be decent. All right?"

I froze. My mind started to race. A fist punch to my ribs. "Who?"

"I don't know." She bent the leaf on one of her lilies and I knew she wasn't telling the truth.

I stepped close. Her breath smelled sour, of the herbs, and all at once I felt ashamed of our lives. Our smelly apartment.

The dishes piled in the sink. The scattered laundry on the floor.

"Tell me." My body seized, thinking about the possibilities. "Who is it?" I yelled. "What happened?"

"Don't raise your voice. You understand?"

"Then tell me the whole truth, for once."

My biggest fear was about to come true. They were coming to take me away.

"You want the truth? Maybe it's that nosy neighbor next door. It's her fault. Who knows. I told you not to skip school."

"I haven't. I didn't."

And then it occurred to me. Carnie. The conversation. My big stupid mouth. "I warned you that Carnie was trouble."

"It wasn't Sebastian."

"Bullshit. I know it was him." I was partly to blame. Me and my big, big, mouth. I was being punished for trusting the creep.

Mother rubbed my shoulder. "No worries. Pangu will protect us."

I clenched my fists and refused to answer.

I surveyed the entire apartment, panicking. I marched into the kitchen and started washing the dishes, scrubbing the crusted food from the plates. The smell of rotten fish grew stronger, more pungent. Mother went to the bathroom, probably to take her pills.

Before I finished cleaning, I peeked out the window and spotted a red Chevelle parked in front. A woman stepped out and began to make her way up the cement stairs of the apartment building. She looked young, maybe thirties, clutching a leather-looking binder.

There was a knock at our door.

Mother didn't budge. She was now lost in the jungle of silk plants in the corner of the living room.

I wiped my sweaty palms on my thighs and took several deep breaths as I headed to the door.

I peered in the peep hole. She appeared normal looking for the most part. What was I expecting? Someone in a uniform with a badge, like a federal agent or something? Her sandy brown hair was pulled back in a ponytail, dangly turquoise earrings, a floral blouse and jeans.

I blinked and she started to morph, her ears growing larger and larger—teeth turning to fangs, a monster-like creature hiding in the shadows.

I stood, paralyzed. I refused to open the door.

She knocked again.

Mother seemed to snap out of her reverie. "Jasmine, open the door, for god's sake."

My hand trembled as I opened the door. The creature moved toward me. I blinked and blinked. The image dissipated. The red lanyard around her neck, coming into view, a dangling rectangular ID badge in clear focus. I fought the urge to slam the door.

"Hello, I'm Sherry Simpleton, from Clarks County Child Protective Services." She held out a hand, the other clutching on to the leather-bound notebook as she scanned our apartment. The fishy smell from the garbage still lingered, mixed with the faint smell of Mother's drugstore perfume which I had squirted in the air several times in a panic.

It was the Keeper. The Keeper of my destiny.

I brought my hands to my hips and frowned at the monster in disguise.

Mother leaned against the wall. "Why are you here?"

"A report has been filed with our agency. My job is to make sure your daughter is in a safe environment."

Mother laughed. "I guess you can leave, then."

"Please, Ms. Cheng. I just have a few questions for your daughter."

Mother looked almost cross-eyed. "Are you even a mother?"

I winced. Seriously? I couldn't believe she just said that.

"No. I'm not."

"Well then. How do you know anything about raising a child?" Mother batted her lashes. She looked like she was high, on one of her pill trips.

A child? Seriously, Ma? I sank into the couch while the Keeper pulled up a chair from the kitchen. An excuse, I thought, to snoop around. She crossed her legs, set the binder on her lap and pulled out a pen. She flipped open the binder, displaying a bright yellow notepad. A sour scent rose up my nostrils, like apple cider vinegar.

"Could I get your name, sweetheart? And your birth-date?" The Keeper stared at me like I was some sort of pathetic creature that needed rescuing.

"It's Jasmine."

"Jasmine what?" She leaned forward.

"Jasmine Cheng."

"And your birthdate?"

"My birthday was a couple weeks ago. I'm fifteen." I cringed as Mother slid onto the couch next to me. I thought about how she missed my birthday. Does that count as negligence?

"Who lives in the household? You, your mother and ...?"

"It's *us*, me and my mother."

"No other guardian? Father perhaps?"

"I don't have one." *What a stupid answer*, I thought. Who says that? Who doesn't know? The lights above tremored on and off. *Pangu? You trying to say something? I know. This whole thing is dumb. Dumb.*

"Do you like school? You were absent during fifth period for several days last week. You don't want to end up on probation like at the public school. Or worse yet, suspension."

I bit into my pinkie fingernail, felt my calf rubbing against the edge of the couch as I shook my leg up and down. How did she know about last year? She must have talked to Miss Carter. "I only missed a class or two last year. I think I had some sort of stomach virus. Good thing I didn't spread it to anyone."

She started writing in her yellow notebook, then sneezed. She looked up, her gaze shifting to the corner of the living room. A flash of ominous red streaks darted across the wall. "Lots of plants in here."

"They're not real."

"Artificial flowers collect a lot of dust. It's not healthy." She cleared her throat. "Anyway."

"Why are you here?" I asked.

"Well . . ."

This was it. I held my breath. Lights flashed in the periphery of my vision.

"We received a call from someone, notifying us that they were concerned about you and your mother's wellbeing." She paused. "Do you feel safe in your home?"

"I don't know. Do you feel safe in *your* home?" I crossed my arms. "And who called you?"

"The caller said he feared for your safety."

"He?"

"Well. He or she. That's not important. What's important is that you are well taken care of. That's my job." The Keeper rapped her pen against the notebook. "Do you ever feel hungry? Like there's not enough food in the house?"

"What kind of question is that?"

"Do you?" she repeated.

I turned to Mother. It was as if she was frozen in time. She didn't even look like a mother. *Too much make-up on today, inappropriate for a child protection visit*, I thought. Lids half drooping. Plus, I noticed that she had a silk flower petal stuck in her hair. What was she thinking? Couldn't she just be a normal mother for a change?

"Do you feel safe in your home, Jasmine?"

I thought of the incident on the Ferris wheel, the vision of Mother falling, tumbling to the ground. And the time when her boyfriend, the one that looked like a Buddhist monk, had left in a fury. Barefoot, she dashed out of the apartment, frantic. "Adi, come back," she had hollered. It was six o'clock in the morning. She took off down the street and I remember thinking, *She's not coming back*. But she did. I plucked every dandelion in the front of the apartment, believing the brightly disguised weeds had infected our lives.

Mother leaned close to me. "People ought to mind their own business. Besides, you're not even a mother. What do you know about being a parent? Whoever called must be mistaken. You can't believe everything you hear. With all due respect, I'm going to have to ask you to leave. I'm not sure why you're here."

I nudged Mother in the rib. "Stop," I whispered. I flicked

the silk petal from her hair and watched as it dropped to the floor.

The Keeper jotted down a few notes then clasped both hands on her lap. "By law, I have the right to check on this household. The job of our agency is to make sure every child grows up in a safe and loving environment. Jasmine deserves to be in a safe home."

An image of an aswang dove passed, then disappeared.

"You call yourself a child protector? I should be reporting *you*." She let out one of her scary guttural laughs and I knew we were in trouble. "Pangu will not be happy about this. Now, get out of our home, please. I know you can't be here without my permission."

The Keeper jotted down a few more notes and closed the binder. She stood. "I'll leave. I do ask for your cooperation, Ms. Cheng. This is a serious matter. You'll have to prove you offer this child a stable and safe home. You've got a month. Thirty days, to be exact."

"Listen, Ms. whoever you are. I'm trying the best I can. Jasmine is a happy young lady." She pulled me close. "Aren't you?"

The Keeper appeared disinterested, looking around the apartment.

"Please leave. Now," Mother said.

AFTER THE KEEPER left, I held Mother's attention as long as I could. "You're not taking this seriously, Ma. *Pangu will not be happy?* Really? I'm going to end up somewhere else."

"You think I'm a bad mother?"

"Stop. No more men, okay?"

"What does that have to do with anything?"

"You get all screwed up. Especially when they leave. You don't think clear. The house is a mess. We have no food."

Her nostrils flared as she breathed in and out. "We aren't like everyone else. We're the birds-of-paradise. We come from the moon."

I wanted to believe her, but the dragon inside me snickered. Was I being fooled? I groaned. I was sick of living in my daydream world.

She reached down, pulled out a compact from her purse, and powdered her forehead and nose. She started to hum a Beatles tune "Here Comes the Sun."

"Come on, let's dance." She grabbed my hands and interlocked our fingers.

"I don't feel like dancing." This was her way of not dealing with important matters and it made me feel like a little kid. I dug my heels into the floor.

She yanked me forward. "Good god. Come on, Jasmine."

She twirled me around in a circle and we spun into the living room until we both collapsed in a dizzy spell. I fell into her arms, her hair tickling the tip of my nose, fragrant like lilacs. We both laughed, tears streaming down our cheeks.

As the room swirled, a sharp pain rose within me. I clenched my fist, not wanting to let go of this moment, squeezing so hard it made my head hurt.

I swallowed the pebble in my throat. "I'm scared, Ma. I'm really, really scared."

CHAPTER 11

I COULDN'T SLEEP. I tossed and flipped around in the bed. I'd been reading way too much Filipino folklore.

The aswangs circled my room like bats above my head.

Tiktik. Tiktik. Tiktik.

They dove and swooped, starved for human flesh and blood.

Ominous shape-shifters. Humans during the day. Vampires, ghosts, reptiles at nightfall.

I screamed and flicked on the light by my bed.

High-pitched screeches filled the room.

Bloodshot eyes flashed on and off. Purple-skinned, hairy beasts.

Winged creatures swirled and scattered above me, then vanished into the air.

CHAPTER 12

AFTER THE VISIT from the Keeper, all I wanted to do was forget and daydream. Draw purple sandcastles and neon orange clouds. Yellow rivers and sacred mountains. The sky rising. Earth thickening. Pangu and his magical axe. Color had energy and power. The blank canvas once again my escape from reality. My colored pencils and paint palette tools for creating new worlds.

"Jasmine, what are you doing? Hurry up," Mother said. It was close to supper time, and she needed to run an errand at the grocery store. She insisted I come with to help *carry the bags*. What she really meant was: *You spend too much time alone with your thoughts. It's unhealthy.*

Plus, she was trying to assure me that she had settled things with the Keeper. Yeah, right.

I ignored her. In the bathroom, I picked at every pore on my face and examined my freckles, the cinnamon-colored dots I wanted so desperately to erase. I rubbed a lemon wedge across my cheeks and imagined a magic lantern. A genie floating in a cloud of purple smoke. *Your wish shall be granted.*

I crossed my fingers as I moved the peel back and forth like a sponge, until my skin felt raw and burned a bright red. Where did these awful freckles come from anyway? My mind shifted to biology class. Genetics. Was this my biological father's fault?

Mother once laughed at a picture of me, saying I had my father's nose. *Do you mean Pangu? Or my real father?* I asked. She ignored the question. Who was my real father? Would it be the mystery of my life forever? I began to wonder if it was the missing link to solve all my problems. *Life can only be understood backwards . . .*

The light in the bathroom blinked and blinked. *Pangu? That you?* It blinked again, then went out.

Mother rapped at the bathroom door. "What the hell are you doing in there?"

I envisioned furrowed brows, her glare on the other side of the door.

"Just a second."

I flushed the lemon down the toilet and flung the bathroom door open. With one hand at her hip, Mother stood in front of me in a gray wool coat, the one with holes in the pockets she had found at the secondhand store.

"What are you doing?" she asked.

"Going to the bathroom," I said. "Making myself look decent."

"My god. Your cheeks are red. You don't need makeup. You're beautiful, Jasmine. Back home, Papa never allowed me to wear makeup."

My right lid twitched. Easy for her to say. She was the beautiful Phoenix. Something I would never be. "Chill."

I put on a jacket and followed her to C&S, which was more of a convenience store with an odd mix of world cuisine than a full grocery store. The shelves were lined with seasonings and canned goods from all over the globe. It was owned by an elderly couple and just a few blocks from our apartment, next to a music records shop in a small strip mall.

By the time we had walked halfway there, it was night-time. The evening chill sliced through me, my breath forming a cloud midair. It started to rain and I tilted my head back, trying to catch a few raindrops on the tip of my tongue.

"You're so silly," Mother said.

As soon as we entered the grocery store, she whispered, "I'm craving pad thai."

We searched the aisles, and I pulled a box from the shelf. "Right here, Ma."

Excited, she knocked down a couple boxes onto the floor. Macaroni and rotini pasta. I dove for the macaroni box. As I straightened, a stranger in brown cowboy boots blocked my path, the box of rotini in his hand.

The stranger wore a tan suede coat and jeans. Maybe in his mid-forties with slicked back, graying dark hair and chiseled cheeks.

"In a hurry?" His voice was deep. He turned in the direction of Mother and his eyes widened, shining a greenish blue in the fluorescent lights. "Suchou?"

"C-Cal?" Mother said. "What are you ... I mean, I haven't seen you for a long time."

"Yeah, right? Heck. It's been a while. I thought you were on the West Coast somewhere. You came back?"

Mother fidgeted with the bottom hem of her coat. "I've been here for some time. Didn't know you were still around."

Cal laughed. "You know me. I come and go as I please." His gaze turned to me. "And who is this young lady?"

Mother pulled me close. "This is Jasmine. She keeps me

on my toes." She glanced at me. "Cal's a contractor. He builds office buildings. Right? Is that what you're still doing?"

"Sort of."

Cal's attention shifted to me. My stomach churned.

I couldn't stand encounters with men she knew. Most of them gave off a peculiar, nervous energy. My vision narrowed like a tunnel, a kaleidoscope of lights blinking in the periphery. I recognized the signs of a migraine and broke away from my mother to search the shelves for Tylenol.

I longed for an unlit room. As a young girl, Mother had to pick me up from school. The grade school teachers complained that I was zigzagging between desks like some crazed, doped up fairy chasing imaginary stars. A nurse later described these episodes as migraine auras—hallucinations. My brain overreacting. An excruciating headache usually followed. It was about to take hold any minute.

"Jasmine." Mother grabbed my hand like I was a two-year-old, pulling me back. Her hands felt rough, like sandpaper.

These were the hands that comforted me at night, rubbing my shoulders. The hands that scrubbed dishes at the restaurant so we had food in our bellies. The same hands bent the leaves and stems of colorful silk orchids and roses, bringing them to life.

I pulled free from her grasp. A garish streak of light appeared above me, a brilliant rainbow of colors.

Mother furrowed her brows. "Just say hi, please," she muttered.

"What's up, Capt'n?" Cal reached out his hand.

I shoved my hands into the front pockets of my coat. I didn't have time for petty talk and this was definitely petty talk. I thought of the Keeper. If I could scare this man away now, then I wouldn't have to chase him later. But he didn't seem frightened at all.

Cal studied his palm. "No handshakes today, Bruno. I don't know about you two, but I don't like all this wet stuff. Makes me want to move somewhere real warm." He paused. "Like where you're from. The tropics. It's ah . . ." He looked at me, as if to jog his memory. "Don't tell me. Hawaii?"

Mother giggled. "Philippines, Cal."

"I'm joking. You know that." He looked at me. "Your mama and I go way back."

I'm sure you do, I thought as I dug my hands deeper into my pockets.

I noticed the way Cal looked at her, and she at him. I grew ill. A halo of lights hovered above them.

What would the Keeper think of Mother and this man? Another distraction from her precious daughter? I felt the rumble of Pangu's presence in my soul.

"I don't feel so good." I dashed down the aisle all the way to the restroom and vomited into the toilet. I sat on the cold floor, an aura of amber and violet fading in and out. Another gift from the spirits, my mother keeps telling me.

Several minutes later, my headache subsided. Mother found me in the bathroom and took me home.

Along with Cal.

CHAPTER 13

BACK AT THE apartment, Cal and Mother huddled in front of the stove while she boiled pad thai noodles and stir-fried leftover chicken breast. Cal's hand touched the small of her back. When the meal was ready, she brought out the "special" porcelain plates, including the one with a large chip on its outer edge. She had broken it after opening a letter from the electric company that threatened to shut off the electricity to our apartment. She screamed and tossed the letter along with the porcelain plate into the sink. She had tried to repair the chip with glue several times, but finally gave up.

Mother slid the plate in front of me. The memory of the big bold red words—PAST DUE. ELECTRIC SERVICE NOTICE—swirled in my head. "Sit there, okay, Jazz?"

Jazz. It sounded so foreign. She only called me *Jazz* when she was in a good mood. A really good mood. She lit a candle and set it in the middle of the table. She glowed, the happiest I'd seen her in a while. As if the Keeper hadn't just visited us a few days earlier.

"You feeling better, Jasmine?" Cal asked.

"It's a headache. Happens all the time." What I really wanted to say was, *Buzz off and leave me alone.*

"They're awful. Very debilitating. Don't let her fool you," Mother added, as she arranged and rearranged the plates.

"Sounds like you're a tough one," Cal said.

I ignored him and pretended like I had better things to do. Set the table, fill the glasses with water and glare at my mother so she knew how angry I was at her for inviting this man into our home.

He appeared more "put together" than her other men, clean-shaven with his tucked-in, pressed shirt. His movements were precise—almost calculated—and there was a familiar, confident energy about him that made me uncomfortable.

After dinner, Cal stretched his arm like a slippery venomous vine across the back of Mother's chair. The lights above blinked an amber hue.

"I forgot how much you amaze me, Suchou. Growing up in a different country and now raising a daughter. We come from different worlds, but I've always felt connected." He took a bite of the noodles. "This is amazing." His head elongated like a crocodile's and I grimaced at the transformation. An aswang in disguise. A shape-shifting evil creature.

An odd squeal of laughter escaped from her mouth as she twirled her hair. "It's instant noodles, Cal. And . . . I mean . . . we're two misfits. That's all."

"Next time I'll make you two my specialty. A sub."

I snickered. "A sub? Seriously? Not sure we're worthy of such fine cuisine."

"We'll see," replied Cal.

Sandwiches. Gross. The smell of bread reminded me of sitting in the grade school cafeteria and plucking out spots of mold from a slice of bread from my homemade lunch.

Mother giggled. It sounded awkward and cringe-worthy. "Yes, next time. Right, Jazz?"

"If there is a next time," I mumbled. I swirled ribbons of noodles around my fork and watched my mother and this man like they were part of a movie. Cal, waiting for his prey, anticipating the bite.

This one seems different, Pangu. Too confident? Sly? More dangerous? And Mother is acting kinda weird. More nervous for some reason. Just saying.

She seemed to lose herself completely and I felt the slow burn of her desire. How could she be so oblivious and ignorant? She was swimming in the swamp of death.

"Jasmine, quit picking at your food." She stared at me. "Any homework?"

I knew what she meant, but there comes a time when you have to stick up for yourself. Ignore the cues. "Nope. Not to my knowledge." I jabbed a piece of chicken with my fork and scowled back, fighting the urge to bare my teeth and hiss.

Mother cleared her throat. "She's always the top of her class. Straight-A student, my girl."

Yeah, right. Her bragging was fake, like her silk flowers. I'd only gotten one A and it was for gym class, because the teacher took pity on me when I got smacked in the forehead with a basketball and continued to play, arms extended, hobbling like a blindfolded Frankenstein. An "A" for effort, he told me. Suck him.

"Tell him whatever you want, Ma. School just started."

"Well, you need to study. You don't want to end up like your mother," she said.

"What's your favorite subject?" Cal asked. A toothpick teetered between his front teeth.

"Art," I answered. That was easy.

"Mine was phys ed. Dodgeball. I had a mean throw."

"I hate dodgeball."

"Why?"

"I'm always the last one left. The moving target."

"You must be fast."

"I'm good at making myself invisible." I laughed. "I have a gift of making others disappear as well. Predator skills." I looked him straight in the eye.

"Jasmine," muttered Mother.

"Much easier to just skip class." I winked.

"Honestly, Jasmine. That's enough."

"I skipped art once," replied Cal. "Maybe twice. Teacher didn't appreciate my work. Maybe it's because I was self-taught."

"You're an artist? For real?"

"I draw."

"What do you draw?"

"Stick people. Celestial stick people. I'm sure you've seen this before? A prehistoric form. My medium is pencil."

"That's dumb." What an idiot.

"She loves to draw," Mother interrupted. "Ever since she was a little girl, she'd sit for hours with colored pencils, painting the world in shades of blue, purple and gold." She leaned back, her hair cascading over her shoulders. "Show Cal your work. The one with chrysanthemums."

"Nah. I don't think so."

Cal leaned forward. "I'd love to see what you've done."

Perhaps it was the innocent yet sly tone of his voice I decided to challenge. The clean soap-like smell of him. Boredom? I'm not sure, but with some reluctance, I went to my room and pulled out my sketchpad.

He flipped through the pages, his expression deep and intense.

"This one's haunting." He pointed to Mother's favorite, a black and white sketch of chrysanthemums, petals drooping in the rain. "The gray clouds in the background look like they're moving. Flying ghosts."

"She's a Picasso, isn't she?" Mother said. "*Art is a lie that makes us realize the truth.* Famous words from the artist himself."

"Beats my stick people. Hands down."

I grew uneasy and reached for the sketchpad. "Enough."

Cal clung tight to the sketchbook. "Hey, I'm not done."

I took a firm grip and snatched it away.

"Strong. Betcha can't arm wrestle." Cal plopped his elbow on the table and let out a belch. "C'mon, let's see what you got."

I set my elbow on the table, made a fist, ready to fight. *C'mon, Pangu, give me muscle.*

"Strength doesn't come from your arm." He pointed to his belly. "It's from your core."

Our hands interlocked and I felt the scaliness of his skin. With all my might and weight, I pushed. It was like trying to move a boulder. A sparkle of light flashed before me. Purples and greens. I thought about my imaginary father, Pangu, busting through his shell of existence. A towering giant with horns and tusks. A mythical god who separated heaven and earth. Trees and plants sprouted from his hair. His body transforming into the soil of the earth.

I stood and pushed again with all my might. A bead of sweat trickled down my back. Another sparkle of light in my periphery. Cal's arm didn't budge.

Mother raised one brow. "I'm sure you have homework to do, Jazz."

I let go of Cal's claw.

"Make you a knuckle sandwich next time?"

"Can't wait." I frowned as he forced a fist-bump. Our eyes met, longer than I was comfortable with.

Cal turned toward Mother. "Now, tell me about this silk floral shop."

Mother paused. "I'd call the shop Forever Floral. Why should beauty be so fleeting?"

Why should beauty be so fleeting? A phrase I had heard a dozen times. I answered in my head: the euphoric image of Cal and my mother bursting into flames; ashes scattered to the earth; the beauty destroyed.

"Why pay for something that's going to die?" she continued. "Why not buy something that lives forever?"

He leaned close to her, enraptured like all the men she brought home. He seemed interested in her dreams, and oddly, mine as well, which I brushed off as deception at its finest. I could see through his disguise.

Later, alone in my room, I heard Mother and Cal chatting and laughing, the rise and fall of their voices unfolding in the night. Outside, the stars blinked, vigilant against the velvet sky. I didn't dare sleep. I dreaded nights like this. I had watched men enter and exit our lives since preschool. Why was this any different?

I needed a plan to get rid of him.

A hot rush tore through my veins. I felt ashamed, but I wondered what it must feel like to have a man kiss you. What it must feel like to have a man love you. I buried my head beneath the pillow and gathered my thoughts.

How to get rid of Cal. *Any thoughts, Pangu? Poison his*

water? Too much. Plus, we'd go to jail. Spoiled food? The sudden case of the stomach flu?

A few hours later, I heard the apartment door shut. From my window, I watched Cal saunter to his pickup.

A sliver of moon punched through the night sky. I reached beneath the mattress and pulled out my sketch-pad, my favorite cloisonné pen resting at the top of the fold. Mother had bought it for me at one of the street markets downtown. It was hand-painted with blue and purple flowers and outlined in gold. I picked up the pen and ran my fingers along its shaft.

I drew a mountain, added droplets of tainted rain falling into a naked blue sea.

CHAPTER 14

THE NEXT MORNING before school, I walked to the bus stop, bundled in my coat and knit cap, backpack straddling my shoulders, hair pulled into a short ponytail. I carried a lunch bag I bought several years ago for a nickel at a garage sale. Originally, it had yellow bumblebees splattered on it, but I had painted it charcoal black and drawn a mythical dragon that stretched along the entire bag.

Stuffed inside was a peanut butter and jelly sandwich. I knew better than to take Mother's leftover sticky rice, for fear I'd be made fun of again.

I detested the long bus ride to Sacred Sacraments. It was a twenty-minute jaunt across town, the complete opposite end from my old public school. The red brick building rested on top of a high hill, apart from the city, unshadowed by trees. It was as if God had placed it there himself, a school as close to heaven as you could get in Briarplace. A life-size marble statue of Saint Joseph stood near the entrance.

I searched the sky for patches of blue as the bus pulled up to the stop.

The bus driver, Mr. Wally, a retired English teacher, swung the door open, greeting me with his toothless grin, gray whiskers sprouting from his chin. "Mornin' Ms. Jasmine . . .

Ah, but love is blind and lovers cannot see. The pretty follies that themselves commit." He chuckled.

"Morning, Mr. W." I paused. "Too easy. Shakespeare. *The Merchant of Venice.*"

He reached in the front pocket of his flannel checkered shirt and pulled out an inhaler. "You got it, my lovely." He took a puff.

We played the quote game every morning. He even loaned me the complete work of Shakespeare. I read the thick, heavy book beginning to end.

I marched down the aisle of the crowded bus, the air thinning, the noise and chatter escalating as I looked for an open seat. The only one left was toward the back. It was faded with cracked vinyl, stuffing protruding through the seams. A thin, brown-skinned girl gazed out the window, her hair pulled back in a braided ponytail, hands jammed in the front pockets of her camel-colored jacket.

Behind her was an upperclassman who ruled the halls of school. Parker. He had dirty blond, unruly hair and a mole on the left side of his cheek. Before I even sat down, he threw a wad of crumpled paper at me.

"Oh, so sorry. Ching-Chong. Ting-Tong," he chanted.

I took a deep breath and looked down. I thought of Jimmy Wong's song on YouTube. Didn't Parker know that Ching-Chong means I love you? *He's saying I love you,* I repeated to myself. Idiot.

I slid into the open seat, careful not to bump shoulders or legs with the girl. I stared forward, every now and then chewing on my pinkie fingernail. Parker let out a vicious cackle. Part of me wanted to turn around and belt him a good one. Scratch him with my Dragon talons. Exhale a breath of fire.

On the bus, another kid joined in laughter. "So, whatcha got for lunch, Dragon girl? Rotting chow mein? Stinky rice again?"

"Don't listen to them," the girl next to me whispered. "They'll smell your fear."

"Yeah. You're right," I mumbled. I thought of what Carnie had said. *Just don't show it.* But I lived in fear, every time I walked down the aisle of the bus, every time I walked the hallways at school. At home, Mother and I ate with wooden chopsticks from the Royal Bamboo. As a child, I wanted to use a fork like other kids, but Mother insisted I be proud of where I came from, her fingers dainty and graceful as she held the chopsticks in the air. I held my breath, focused on the graffiti on the back of the seat when someone yanked on my ponytail.

The girl next to me turned around, reached over the seat, grabbed Parker's hand and twisted until his palm faced us, causing him to raise his body in the air. I spun around and watched as she bent his arm like a pretzel.

He shouted in pain.

"What the hell?" he squealed.

"Leave her alone."

She let go. He dropped to the seat, rubbing his wrist.

"Psycho! You'll pay for this one." He looked at me, his voice penetrating like daggers of death. "Losers. Both of you."

I felt his finger jab into my back as he and the other boy dropped to their seat.

The girl and I did a low-key fist bump. "I'm Jasmine."

"Rani."

"I don't think I've seen you before," I said.

"Just moved here from California."

We exchanged numbers. The bus stopped and the two boys pushed their way to the front and hopped off.

I waited outside for Rani. The lone statue of Saint Joseph stood by the entrance, highlighted by a ray of sun.

"Where did you learn a move like that?" I asked her.

"My father taught me. It's a martial art move."

"You know they'll come after us, now," I said.

"For sure."

Rani drew her lips tight over her teeth, and I knew from that moment we were going to be friends.

CHAPTER 15

AFTER THE BOYS made fun of me on the bus, I found it difficult to concentrate in first period. Math. What was the point in solving equations? I didn't give a crap about decimals and percentages. Fractions. My friend that moved would be in pre-calc. He was a brain. I guess it didn't matter how smart you were—you could still be snatched up by the system. Taken away from your home.

My head spun and a little voice inside screamed, *Get me outta here.* Rani and I agreed to meet during last period. I knew I shouldn't skip, but it was better than getting in trouble for not finishing my homework. It was a vicious cycle—skipping then getting in trouble for missed assignments. But it was survival. *Right, Pangu?*

I shrank inside, thinking about a foster home, being taken away from the life I knew, taken away from my mother.

I started to doodle. I drew comic caricatures of Parker as a cockroach and sketched a colorless world filled with mountains and endless ocean. As Sister Agnes wobbled up and down the aisle between the desks in her habit and black and white gown, I drew my legendary father, Pangu, hairy and fearless. The fluorescent lights above hummed and flickered.

My lids grew heavy and I couldn't help but rest my head

on the desk. I turned and faced the window. Outside, a flock of geese flew overhead in the shape of a *V*. I could hear them squawking, their wings beating wildly. I fell asleep.

A loud thwack awakened me. I flung my lids open and saw Sister Agnes's black leather worn shoes. I shot upright. My blurred vision cleared to the sight of her big boobs then trailed upward to meet her nasty glare, coming from behind her cat-eye glasses.

Unfortunately, Sister Agnes was my teacher for Math *and* English. I was a much more attentive student in her English class, where she quoted Dickens. *It was the best of times, it was the worst of times . . .*

My head spun and I instantly saw ten of her, flying around the room.

"Miz Jasmine. It's about time you joined us from your pleasant dreams." Her nasal voice echoed in my head. "Perhaps you'd like to share?"

The class erupted with laughter.

After that, I couldn't wait to skip.

I texted Rani, just to make sure.

Me: Still meeting?

Rani: 👍

Before last period, I headed to the park, which was just across from the track and field. I spotted Rani, wrapped in her camel coat. Up above, a sliver of sun broke through the sky.

Rani greeted me with a smile and pulled out a pack of cigarettes from the pocket of her jacket. She handed me one and lit it—as if I had smoked before—then she held her own between her index and third finger, squinting as she took a long, slow drag. The ashes turned a fiery red.

"Is it always this bloody cold here?" she asked.

"*Bloody* colder." I liked the sound of *bloody*, the way it rolled off my tongue. "Try two below zero with a biting wind of twenty below." I noticed her long braid that stretched down past her bottom. Brown sandals on her feet. "So, you might want to get a pair of boots. Before winter."

"That's lame." She looked down, wiggled her toes. "What do you do for fun?" She exhaled and a puff of smoke appeared, pasted in the air.

I thought about it. I drew. I dug for treasures in the dumpster—dirty magazines, *Glamour*. I planned ways to get rid of my mother's boyfriends with my father, Pangu.

I swallowed, then lowered my voice to sound more sophisticated. "Well, I'm quite fond of discovering new things. Treasures you might say. I draw. Paint. What do *you* like to do?"

"Chill. Hangout. Smoke."

"Cool. Me, too." I drew on the cigarette and coughed a couple times. "Why did you move here?"

"My dad's in the air force. Fighter pilot. He just got transferred."

I nodded. The air force base was located on the outskirts of Briarplace. Each year, it brought new families to town from all over the country. They had southern drawls. Used East Coast slang. "You're a Baser."

"An air force brat. Whatever you want to call me. I've been around."

"Me, too," I said, even though it was a lie. I didn't exactly want to argue that drawing transports me to faraway exotic lands and my father separated the heavens and earth. But there was Mother. "Actually, my mother's from the

Philippines. Guess I come from two different worlds. Palm trees to the prairie." I laughed then sucked in my belly. "Bet it sucks. Being the new kid in town."

"Sort of. I'm used to it. I don't give a crap anymore. I mean it's not like I belong anywhere and sometimes that's cool. I can reinvent myself every time."

"Guess I never thought of it that way."

I exhaled a puff of smoke. Maybe we had something in common. I never felt like I belonged anywhere either. My father flew, too, and moved mountains. She didn't seem like the type that would go for that, though. It made me want to touch the real world and I wondered what it'd be like to have a real father. Flesh and blood.

Then, I looked across the street. There was the Keeper, lingering on the track and field, near the bleachers.

I froze. Her shadow loomed, her body almost ghoul-like. She had on a pair of purple sunglasses. Was that the red lanyard dangling from her neck? What a loser. I knew Mother hadn't settled things. My palms turned clammy and cold.

I dropped the cigarette and squished the butt with the heel of my tennis shoe. "Let's go."

"Wait."

"Just move," I said.

I took off down the sidewalk. Rani followed.

"Where are we going?" Rani asked, out of breath.

"Just follow," I said. "I'll explain later."

We left the school grounds. We dashed across a busy street and a car blasted its horn.

"What the hell?" Rani shouted.

I kept walking fast, fast, faster. I pumped my arms and

glanced over my shoulder. I saw the Keeper waiting at the crosswalk for a line of cars to pass.

Rani trotted by my side. "Are you in trouble or something?"

"Later. Okay?"

I could tell she thought the chase was cool, but she had no idea how fast and hard my heart was beating and how scared I really was. If the Keeper caught me skipping, I could be suspended. We dodged into a nearby used bookstore, the door chiming as we entered.

The bookstore smelled of fine milled soap, coffee and moldy paper. Behind the counter, a tall man with a beard picked at his front tooth.

He gave us a nod. "Hey."

"Hey," I replied as I walked at a fast pace down the fiction aisle. I stopped and caught my breath.

Rani stood beside me and crossed her arms. "Well? You going to explain?"

"Long story, but the Keeper . . . I mean . . . the social worker, is after me."

"The Keeper?" She raised her eyebrows in amusement. "Sounds like someone out of a fantasy novel."

A warm flush rushed to my ears. "Yeah. I meant social worker."

"*The Keeper*. I like that. It's haunting. Gripping. I totally get it."

I smiled, feeling a bit relieved. "Cool. Anyway, she wants to catch me doing something wrong, like skipping school or whatever, so she can send me to a foster home. She asked me if I felt safe in my own home. I'm like, seriously?"

"Holy shit. That's insane."

"And yeah, before you ask, I don't have a father."

"What happened?"

"Nothing. He just doesn't exist." *Only in my mind*, I wanted to add, but that was too complicated.

"You're a love child."

"Love child?"

"You know. Not conceived in the conventional way."

If only she knew. My father was a mythical god, created from the egg of chaos and I was a Dragon . . .

"Maybe we should go back to class?" said Rani.

"Too late for that." I peeked around the bookshelf. "Is she still following us?"

I sucked in air, tried to catch my breath. "I don't know."

"You're shitting me, aren't you?"

"She's truly out to get me. I'm sure of it." I took in a deep breath. "You don't believe me?"

"No. I mean, yeah. I believe you. Dang. It's just intense." She paused. "What now?"

I brushed against a table, knocking a couple books to the floor. "We should go. Maybe out that door."

Rani and I tore out the back door. We ran through an alley, passing a dumpster. I felt like a criminal, running from the law, but I had no choice. My mother and I had less than a month now to prove we had a stable home. Time was ticking away.

A storm of lights pulsed in the sky.

I imagined the Keeper, a predator in disguise, encompassing both human and monster form, ready for battle.

CHAPTER 16

BREATHE, I TOLD myself as I searched the apartment for signs of the Keeper—a scrap of yellow notebook paper, the scent of apple cider vinegar. What if the school called? I jumped at shadows moving across the walls. Thankfully, I found nothing.

"Anyone stop by, Ma?" I called out. I glanced out the window, searching for a red Chevelle.

I found Mother in her bedroom. She let out an exasperated sigh as she eyed several outfits on the bed. She had the evening off and that meant a night out—for her and Cal. Canned tuna and lots of television for me.

"Hey. What's up?" I asked, even though I knew. I sat on the floor and crossed my legs as she paced. "Going out with what's his face again?"

No nickname yet. Weird.

"Cal."

"He smells too clean, like soap. Makes me a bit suspicious."

"Everything makes you suspicious and, I might add, a bit paranoid." She twisted and spun around in front of the crooked full-length mirror tacked on the wall, admiring the skimpy satin dress she had on.

"Is that the dress you bought at The Flamingo downtown?"

"I finally have a reason to wear it." She stole another

glance in the mirror and ran her fingers along the plunging neckline. "How was school? You *did* attend all periods?"

"For the most part. Met a new girl. You should see her martial art moves."

"That's wonderful, honey."

"And I caught the Keeper spying on me."

She let her hair fall, a curtain of black silk, then looked at me. "That's scary. You sure that was her? Makes me worry."

"Pretty sure. It was creepy," I said, surprised that she didn't call me paranoid again.

"Were you at school?"

"Yes, sort of." Just skipping class and smoking with a friend, no big deal.

"Just ignore her, then. The winds have changed direction. Things are going to be okay."

"You sound so sure." What made her so confident all of a sudden? It was like she knew something I didn't.

"Nothing's for certain. But there's hope."

"Right. Hope." I agreed, dropping the subject before I got caught in a bigger lie.

She dabbed on a cheap drugstore perfume, rolled it along her neck. The room filled with the scent of sweet lavender. Why would any man leave my mother? She was a goddess. She belonged to the moon.

I waited for the impatient boyfriend honk of a vehicle, but Cal came to the door, which I tried not to act surprised by. He smelled like body wash.

"Which one, right or left?" Cal joked. I noticed that both hands were behind his back.

Mother moved to the side, trying to catch a glimpse of whatever he held in secret. He looked monstrous standing next to her. I blinked and saw a reptilian creature with wings. Claws reaching for her.

"Uh, uh, not so fast, pretty lady. Gotta guess which hand."

Mother tapped his right arm.

He swung his empty hand to the front. "Too bad." He winked. "Here, you try, Jasmine."

I shook my head, watched the creature fading in and out. "Nu-uh."

"You two are so silly," Mother cooed as she disappeared into the kitchen.

Cal stared at me. "Oh, come on." Then, from behind his back, he tossed me a yellow rose.

I caught it mid-air then immediately dropped it to the floor as if it were deadly to the touch. It was made of silk. The petals moved. A grayish vapor spiraled toward the ceiling.

Okay, Pangu. Do you see what I see? What do you think?

I needed to find a weak spot.

Cal appeared somewhat irritated as he picked up the flower. He unfolded a leaf gently, as if I had damaged it somehow. A ray of harsh light pierced through the window onto Cal's boots.

"My mother hates when people wear shoes in the house. It's disrespectful."

"My apology." He kicked off the boots and flung them by the door. They landed next to a pair of red satin slippers and my worn tennis shoes.

"Always take off your shoes before entering," Mother chimed in a melodic tone as she returned from the kitchen with a vase in one hand. "You'll track in evil spirits." She reached for the rose and placed it in the vase, then kissed the top of my head. "Make sure to lock the door behind me."

Cal looked at me and winked. "You need a good guard dog."

The word *dog* caught my attention. I've always wanted a dog, but was too afraid to ask. "Guard dog?"

"Yeah. To chase away burglars *and* bad spirits. Like Max. Best buddy in the world. Big German Shepherd. He was gorgeous. Followed me everywhere like my shadow."

"Where's he now?"

"That was a long time ago. Always thought I'd get another dog. Well, maybe someday." The aswang faded and Cal appeared truly human—for a moment.

Cal pulled on his boots and escorted Mother out the door. The elderly neighbor next door popped her head into the hallway then slammed her door shut.

From the window, I watched Cal and Mother leave and I wondered what it felt like to be in love. They strolled along the sidewalk, hand in hand, the bottom edge of Mother's coat flapping in the wind. Cal still looked human and it irked me. Because I knew the aswang was lurking beneath the surface.

In Mother's room, clothes lay stretched on the bed, scattered on the floor, and on the dresser sat a black lacquer jewelry box with its lid propped open. In the bottom drawer I found a pearl necklace hidden in a silk pouch. Probably a gift from a former boyfriend, the rich pilot who flew around the world, or maybe a precious gift from a relative. I ran the pearls along my palm and placed the string around my neck. I thought about the Keeper, skipping class with Rani, smoking the cigarette. And now, Mother and this awful creature, Cal. The poisonous ivy invading our lives.

I was doomed. I ran my finger along the necklace, touching each pearl.

I stared at my reflection in the mirror and imagined myself with long hair like my mother's, full breasts and slender legs, freckle-free porcelain skin. I wanted to be beautiful, flawless, just like her. One day men would fall at my feet.

"Oh, darling," I whispered. "Why must love fade so fast?"

In the kitchen, I opened a can of tuna. I swung around to get a spoon when I spotted a letter.

I reached for the envelope with the words CHILD PROTECTIVE SERVICES stamped on the front.

I opened it. *We will assess whether you are providing an adequate home. Should we determine it to be an unfit and unhealthy environment, your child will be placed in a safer one. The investigation will be completed in 30 days since your last meeting. By law, we have the right to check at any time.*

Mother lied. There was nothing settled with the Keeper. There was no hope.

Lies. Lies. Lies.

I ripped the letter into bits.

CHAPTER 17

ON EVENINGS WHEN Mother was out, I never slept. Especially not that night. Reptilian creatures crept along the walls and on the ceiling. The letter from CPS flashed in my mind. On and off. On and off. The Keeper's lanyard came into focus, distorting and morphing into a monster. *Tiktik.* *Tiktik.* The sound was faint but grew louder and louder. An aswang creeping closer and closer.

I bolted upright and raced out of the bedroom.

I texted Rani.

Me: I was right.

Rani: What???

Me: The Keeper's out to get me. For real. I found a letter.

Rani: No way. OMG. What did it say?

Shit, I thought. Should I have destroyed the evidence?

I headed to the kitchen. *Pangu, where are you? Help me.*

Standing by the counter, I studied the torn bits of the letter on the floor then scooped the scraps of paper into the garbage.

A sound from the corner of the room startled me. A thud. One of Mother's books had fallen to the floor. I picked it up. It was one of her books on spirituality. A sign from Pangu?

I grabbed it and sat among her silk plants. *Awareness is the greatest agent for change.* Eckhart Tolle. Reading a few pages, I envisioned myself as a young monk in a saffron robe, soaking up the teachings. All I had to do was believe. The words seemed so simple. Listen to silence, observe my own nakedness. But how does one become plain, like dust?

Where did Mother go when her mind drifted from this world?

I wanted to escape, too. It wasn't fair.

MOTHER FINALLY CAME home when the clock by my bed said 1 A.M. I pretended, like I always did, that I was sleeping, blanket pulled over me, head turned to the side, one leg stretched along the edge of the mattress.

She stopped in my room and kissed me on the cheek. She smelled of cigarettes and peppermint. Just from her kiss, I knew she must have had a good night. Sometimes, I'd find her in the kitchen, at the table, staring at the wall, lids puffy and red when she had a *bad* night. "Ah, Pangu, where are you now?" she'd say. I'd listen to her tales, how my father turned green grass into blades of gold.

The clock ticked and ticked. We were running out of time.

CHAPTER 18

AFTER READING THE letter from CPS, I became more vigilant and watched for signs of the Keeper. Rani and I both agreed not to skip class. After school she showed me a few martial art moves. How to use my own energy to ward off enemies.

"The best fighter is never angry," she said. "It's a quote from Lao Tzu."

The next week, Cal became a regular visitor. I kept my distance and watched him with a careful eye.

One evening, around dinner time, Cal stood and stretched. "I think it's time for a knuckle sandwich. C'mon, Jasmine." He moved to the kitchen and I followed since I was starving. My stomach growled. Mother headed down the narrow hallway toward the bedroom, yawning.

On the kitchen table lay a paper sack Cal had brought in earlier. "Pay close attention to Monsieur Chef," he said with an awkward French accent. "We have hoagie buns, onion, salami, ham, provolone, pepper jack, jalapeños." He pulled them out. "Oh, and can't forget the mayo, Madame. Exquisite. Has a little kick to it."

I stood impatiently as Cal sliced the bread and spread the mayo. I watched his hands shapeshift into claws then back again.

"Any boyfriends?" he asked. A gray patch of whiskers dominated his chin and upper lip. Rough looking, like sandpaper. The question caught me off guard.

"No," I said, feeling a surge of irritation prickle my skin. "They're all geeks."

Although, the truth was, I was the geek at school, the outsider, the girl from nowhere and everywhere. I tried to ignore the whispers and stares. I came from the moon and that's all that mattered.

Cal turned. "Really? No one?"

"Nope. And if you ask me one more time, I might have to punch you."

"Got it." Cal cracked his knuckles and set the finished sandwiches on the counter. There was dirt beneath his fingernails. He grabbed a sandwich and took a big bite, ripping the edges of the thick bread with his fangs, leaving pieces of ham and cheese protruding out of the bun. "Take one," he said. "Time to be brave."

I tried not to look interested although all I wanted to do was eat—anything was better than canned tuna and peanut butter sandwiches. I bit into a sandwich, then coughed. Something hot and spicy invaded my senses, burned the tip of my tongue. I swallowed. "Frick. It's really hot. What's in here?"

"No questions. Eat, okay?" He took another bite of the sandwich then made a fist, brought it in the air like a high five. "Knuckle sandwich."

With great reluctance, I brought my fist to meet his. I kept swallowing and resisted the impulse to grab a glass of water. I tore off the corner of the bread to cool the burning on my tongue.

"What are you two doing?" Mother emerged from her

bedroom with a bottle of blood-red nail polish. She leaned against the wall, hair puffing up on one side, and shook the polish with one hand.

Cal jutted out his lower jaw, still chewing.

I bit into the sandwich again, a large bite with meat and cheese, this time welcoming the hot spicy flavor—the chili peppers, jalapeño, onion.

"Try one, Ma," I said, raising my partially eaten sandwich in the air. "If you dare."

"Hey," Cal said, as if offended.

I studied the whites of his eyeballs, the tiny blood vessels invading the sea of amber. My throat burned. Still looking at Cal, I blinked and saw the reptilian creature with wings, drinking from a toxic river. It roared to the sky. A thick drool of mucus hanging from its gums. Its body collapsing within minutes to the ground.

This man didn't fool me. Pangu and I had a plan. I just wasn't sure what it was yet.

When Cal left momentarily for the bathroom, I grabbed a jar of hot Szechuan chili sauce from the fridge. I opened it and drizzled a fair amount onto his sandwich when Mother wasn't looking. She was too busy polishing her fingernails that awful blood-like hue.

When he returned, he took a bite, swallowed, and within seconds, turned a bright red. He coughed and sprinted to the sink, gulping water from the faucet, but that seemed to make matters worse. Sweat beaded along his forehead and he gasped. "What the hell?"

"Too spicy?" I mumbled. "Time to be brave."

"Jasmine," Mother said. She stopped painting her nails. "What did you do?"

I shrugged.

She looked stunned. "Drink some more water, Cal." She glared at me. "Szechuan sauce?"

"He asked for it."

"You promised. Honestly."

Cal wiped his forehead with the back of his hand. "All right. I surrender. You got me." His voice sounded strained and raspy. "Well, ladies. I should go."

"Yeah. You should." The words popped out of my mouth.

"Watch your manners," Mother said. "You're acting like a child."

"Well, if he thinks he can just step in and be a part of our family, then he's got another thing coming," I stammered.

"Enough." She flung one hand in the air. The polish made it look like she was bleeding.

"It's okay, Suchou. We're just having a good time, that's all." Cal winked.

But my mother didn't seem to care. "Jasmine, bed. Now."

"Night." Cal raised his fist in the air.

I held a vision of him longer this time, a snapchat—the curve of his jaw, his thick lips. Fangs protruding. He was going down like all the rest of them.

As I left the kitchen, I heard Mother apologizing in a soft whisper. "Sorry, Cal. I don't know what gets into her sometimes."

I glanced back and caught the two of them in a close embrace, Mother resting her head against Cal's shoulder. I imagined her breathing in the smell of him, the hint of hot pepper sandwich still on his breath. Sparks igniting with each exhale.

Outside, the sky was littered with clouds, a light drizzle

of rain. The musty smell of dampness seeped through the walls. I listened for Cal and the sound of his truck leaving, but nothing stirred except the wind wrestling shadows on the wall, the soft voices of my mother and Cal.

Oh, dear Pangu, what do you think of this man? Don't worry. We'll get rid of him. Soon.

CHAPTER 19

STRONG COFFEE BREWED the next morning, a comforting bitter aroma. Cal sat at the kitchen table, leafing through a magazine. He wore the same plaid shirt, his hair damp and combed.

"Great morning, Jasmine. Slept like a baby. How 'bout you?"

I yawned. "What are you still doing here?" A sudden coolness crept up my spine and I grabbed a wedge of lemon from the fridge.

"Got in late last night, so I decided to camp out." Cal let out a soft belch. "Whew. Must have been that knuckle sandwich."

"Where's my mother?" I rubbed the wedge of lemon back and forth along the side of my cheek.

"She's still resting. She took some herbs to help her sleep." He glanced up. "What's with the lemon?"

"Just trying to get rid of something."

"Freckles aren't so bad. They're kind of unique. Like a birthmark."

"I hate birthmarks, then."

Cal yanked up his shirt, displaying a large, thick, vertical scar running alongside his ribcage. "How's that for a birthmark?"

I flinched at the scar. My mind drifted. A battle of the gods and creatures of the sky. Thunder clouds and flashes of lightning. "What happened?" I stole another peek before he released his shirt, letting it drop like a blind.

"Not really a birthmark. Keep it to yourself, okay?"

I took a seat, thrilled in spite of myself. He had a secret.

"I was about your age. My brother and I were fighting. Wrestling in the house over something stupid. He was much bigger and taller than me at the time. There was a sliding glass door that led out to our porch. I was on his back, had a hold of his neck like a vampire, like I was going to bite him. He got real pissed, flipped me off and shoved me into the glass door. I went flying. Shards of glass everywhere." Cal tugged at his collar. "I didn't know what hit me. Blood all over. Anyway."

"That really happened? No lie?"

"Something like that." He glanced at his cell phone as it blinked.

Mother interrupted from the hallway. "Are you telling her your dreadful stories so early in the morning?"

"I don't know what you're talking about," Cal said.

"You know what I mean," she repeated. "And don't be lying."

"Okay, so it wasn't really my brother."

"Who was it then?" I asked.

"Let's save the rest of the story for another time, okay?"

"But that's where the scar came from? A fight. Right?" Acid burned in my stomach. He *was* an aswang in disguise. A vampire. I knew it.

"No school today?"

"Way to change the subject."

I needed to get rid of this man. I knew he was a liar. I ought to destroy liars.

I heard Mother's slippers shuffle against the floor as I tossed the squished lemon in the sink. She squeezed my shoulder and kissed the top of my head. She smelled of sleep, like sour milk. "You two are up early. Want porridge?"

Mother made the best rice porridge, thick with scallions and slices of gingerroot, but I had other things on my mind. "I'm not hungry."

"What's wrong? Not feeling well?" She felt my forehead with the back of her hand.

"I'm fine," I replied.

Go back to sleep, I wanted to say. *Leave us alone. I'll take care of things.*

Mother sat next to him. He sipped his coffee and ran his hand along her back. I watched his fingers transform into sharp talons. Suddenly, I couldn't breathe. I headed to the door.

"Where you going?" Mother asked.

"Outside."

Cal stood. "Want company? I could use some fresh air myself." He pulled a cigarette from the front pocket of his shirt.

"Not really," I muttered. He didn't listen and kept following me.

"Don't be long. Rice porridge," Mother said.

With Cal behind me, I opened the door, annoyed, and headed down the narrow hallway until I was outside. A burst of cold air whipped past, my breath visible as I sat on the brick steps. A deep chill rippled down my back.

Cal sat next to me, a cigarette clamped in his teeth. His nostrils widened. "Best time of day. Don't you think?"

In the natural light, his eyes changed a greenish hue, with flecks of gold. A trace of coffee on his breath.

"Why are you hanging with us? What do you want?"

"I like you and your mom. Why?"

I thought of the Keeper. The investigation. How everything felt like it was lurking, how Mother's boyfriends only brought trouble and heartache. "How do you even know my mother?"

"We go way back. She was the most beautiful woman I had ever seen. And gentle, too. A seeker with a restless soul."

"So you and her were a thing."

Cal laughed. "I guess you could say that."

Before I was around to get rid of you. "Then what happened?"

Cal pulled out a lighter and lit his cigarette. "Haven't you ever done something you're not proud of?"

I lifted a shoulder and tried to think of all the things I had done, like skipping school, chasing away Mother's boyfriends and making her angry. "I don't know. Maybe. You?"

"Oh, man. I've hurt people I care about. Not intentional. Maybe they deserved it." Cal took a puff of the cigarette. "Guess you're just a perfect kiddo."

"I never said that. And don't call me a kid."

"I said *kiddo*."

"That's worse."

"What would you rather me call you?"

I shook my head. "This is stupid. I really don't care what you call me." It didn't really matter. Soon he'd be gone like all the rest.

"All righty. I get it. No more kiddo. Just Jasmine."

Fiery red and gold leaves blossomed on the trees. A couple of geese flew overhead. A sign from Pangu, that nothing ever stayed the same. I blew into my hands, rubbed them together. "You ought to stay away from us."

"Why?" Cal threw his heavy suede jacket over my shoulders.

"You don't belong here."

"Why not?"

"My mother and I don't need anyone. Plus, she has issues."

"Seriously?" He laughed.

"For starters, she's been around, if you know what I mean." Cal nodded. "What else?"

I crunched forward, my bottom losing sensation from the cold. My upper body warmed with the help of Cal's jacket. "She's from the moon. An alien. She'll eat you alive. No kidding. I've seen it too many times. It's not pretty."

"I see. Guess I should be worried about her appetite from now on. Watch my back."

I straightened. "Sorry."

"Damn. I'm in trouble, aren't I?"

"You seem like a nice guy," I said, but not really meaning it. He was just like all the rest of them. "Just thought I'd warn you. Hate to see you all messed up." *Your monster body destroyed.* I smiled inside at the thought.

He gave me a nudge. "Hey, thanks, man. Appreciate it. I owe you one."

"Anytime."

Cal made a fist. "I'm hungry. Want some breakfast?"

I hiked up the stairs toward the apartment, aware of the creature behind me, hoping he'd gotten the message. A gust of wind shook the branches of the oak tree, rustling the leaves.

I searched the sky for Pangu.

CHAPTER 20

FOR THE NEXT week, every day after school, I looked for
signs of Cal—his pickup truck, his boots, a phone message.
But there was no word or hint from him at all.

I pressed my ear to the wall late at night, anticipating bits
of conversation, but I only heard the bed squeak each time
Mother moved.

I tried not to make things worse, so I went to school, did
my homework, cleaned my room, leaving her alone as much
as I could.

Time ticked away. It had been sixteen days since the letter from the CPS.

Mother kept silent. It was as though I didn't exist. She
circled the apartment, paced the kitchen floor, rummaged
through the mail. I caught her glancing at her phone then
slamming it down on the counter.

Was this all my fault? Mother seemed so upset. Did I do
the right thing this time?

Was he gone for good? Would the Keeper leave us alone
now? Did it matter?

Normally, during this autumn season, Mother and I
would be hanging out by the river, fishing by the water's
edge before it froze for the winter. The seasons at Briarplace
could be extreme and sometimes harsh. The wind carried a

hint of what was to come, a cool dampness in the air, the soil of the riverbank now hidden beneath a bed of worn leaves. Before long, I'd be cooped inside for days.

But lately she was too occupied with Cal's disappearance, constantly on the phone and in her own world.

Rani was quickly becoming my BFF. Being a Baser, moving from place to place, she had never been fishing before. So, one day after school, armed with a couple old fishing poles, a net and tackle box, we headed to the dike toward the river.

She followed close behind, her hair in a long braided ponytail, arms steady by her side. The ground was soft and muddy. Dead grass and twigs bordered the dirty brown river and the air smelled musty. A beam of light cut through a grove of trees. We stood side by side, watching the hazy images in the water with the sun warming our backs as we flicked the rods forward and waited.

"This sucks," Rani said after fifteen minutes. "Are there really fish in there?"

"Of course. Trust me. Patience is a virtue," I replied. Damn. I sounded just like Mother.

"Really? This is what you do for kicks?" Rani asked.

A cheery trill echoed from a nearby tree and something poked its head above the water.

"My mother says it's about being one with nature. Aware of what's surrounding you."

Rani lifted her shoulders, unimpressed. "So what's the status of your mom's new dude? Chase him away yet?"

I shrugged. "Maybe. Haven't seen him for a while. Hope he's gone for good. He and I made sandwiches. The hot chili sauce about killed him. I thought he might get pissed, but he asked for it."

Rani laughed.

My forehead tightened. "What?"

"Nothing."

"Why are you laughing?"

Rani pressed her lips together like she was holding back another laugh. "Hot chili sauce? Really? It's going to take a whole hell of a lot more than hot sauce to chase that dude away, from what you've told me."

I squeezed the rod.

"And I was reading online about CPS. They're sneaky. They pretend like they're checking on the family. But then they snatch children away from their homes and put them in jail or some stranger's place."

I lifted the rod and reeled in the slack line. "My friend's in a foster home. He hates it."

Rani whistled through her teeth. "You don't want to be red-flagged."

"Right." *Red-flagged?* I could tell she had done her research. I was impressed and somewhat moved by the gesture. "Too late. The letter."

"Speaking of families. Don't get pissed, but do you ever wonder about your dad? Like where he's at? Shit like that?"

"Yeah. I do." I didn't dare tell her about Pangu. It all sounded so lame, now.

Rani lifted the rod. "My pops took me flying once. We were leaving Seattle and there it was in all the glory, Mount Rainier poking its head through the clouds. Pretty cool."

I thought about the Ferris wheel—Mother and her leg in the air—and shivered. "Heights freak me out."

"Heights freak me out, too," said Rani. "I was just

disappointed we couldn't get closer. I wanted to touch the tip of the mountain."

We went silent. A field mouse burrowed its way beneath a bed of leaves.

Mountains and fathers. The mystery of my own father. Who was he? What was he like? Do I look like him? Act like him? Does he know who I am? Is he still alive? Perhaps he was looking for me, too?

"Anyway," Rani added, "hopefully you got rid of Cal."

I nodded. "No kidding."

She winked. "Good thing I taught you those moves. You never know."

The lazy river barely moved. Rani lifted the rod out of the water and frowned at the string of weeds and mud dangling from the hook.

"I don't even know what I'm waiting for," she said. "Besides a fish. Or maybe some sort of sea creature's going to leap above this brown crappy water. Like the Loch Ness monster."

I smiled. If she only knew what creatures I'd seen dwelling in my midst. I suddenly longed for Pangu. I wanted to feel his presence, like I did when I was younger. But something inside me had shifted, as if I was awakened from a dream.

Rani nudged me. "Frick. I feel something biting. Now, what?"

"Watch the red and white bobber and when you feel a slight tug you need to set your hook."

"What the hell does that mean?" Rani said.

"Give your rod a quick jerk and pull back and up."

She jumped in the air. "Look, that thingy just moved."

"The bobber?"

"Yeah. Whatever you call it."

"Hurry. Lift the rod. Slowly. And reel it in," I said.

Rani reeled, her teeth biting into the side of her bottom lip as the line grew taut. "It's going to get away. Help me."

"Don't let loose." I reached around her, clasped my hands over hers and pulled up on the rod.

She nudged me with her elbow. "I got this." A gray fish sprang out of the water, thrashing its body side to side. "What the hell? We did it. Frick, yeah."

"He's a fighter." I caught the fish with a net, his body squirming in my grasp, then gently backed out the hook from its mouth.

Rani leaned over. "Shit, it's ugly. Look at those whiskers!"

I laughed. "It's a catfish."

"Gross," she said. "Now what? You fry it for dinner? Wait. What are you doing?"

I dropped the net back into the water. Mother and I used to eat the fish we caught, but then some kids at school found out and said, "You eating the river fish? Those aren't koi like at the Royal Bamboo, ya know. You're gonna die or turn into a deformed zombie."

I turned to Rani. "I'm letting it go. I don't think you want to eat anything from this river."

"Why not?"

"Trust me. You just don't." The water sparkled in the sunlight, ripples of waves carrying our figures, side by side. "We just catch and release."

A swarm of gnats hovered above us.

"That stinks." Rani was not amused.

Catch and release. A moment of victory. Just like Mother's boyfriends. Just like Cal.

CHAPTER 21

ON SUNDAY, DAY twenty-two, Mother wanted to attend Mass at St. Mary's Cathedral. It was walking distance from our apartment. A majestic old church with red brick, stained glass windows, and two gray steeples that reminded me of a castle.

I put on my Sunday best and wore my red sweater, just for her. Red for good luck, good fortune. We were the Phoenix and Dragon. Invincible. Even though the wool blend made me itch like crazy, resulting in a pimply red rash on my neck, forearms, and back.

Thirty minutes before Mass, I went to Mother's room, surprised she was still sleeping, her head turned to the side, arm draped across her forehead. I flung open the blinds. The jade Buddha on the edge of the dresser lit up with the sun.

I nudged her side. "Hey, Ma. You need to get ready." I shook her a couple times.

She rubbed her forehead and opened one eye. "What day is it?"

"Today's Sunday. Remember, you wanted to go to church?"

"Oh my god. What time is it?"

I held my breath, made a fist. Was she going into her

funk again? Back to her old ways of being? "Just get ready. I set your clothes on the dresser." I started to leave the room.

"Maybe we shouldn't go," she said.

"Why? You told me to make sure to wake you up. Geez."

"I did?" she said. "I haven't been feeling well."

I wanted to rip off the itchy sweater. Forget the whole idea of going. But something told me I needed to be strong for both of us. I needed to feel God's presence. Love and men always made her sick. Especially when they disappeared. She needed hope. "You'll feel better, Ma. Like you always say, one must believe."

"You're right," she said. "Let's go."

WHILE SHE WAS in the bathroom, I rummaged through her jewelry box, looking for something to wear—earrings, a bracelet? I reached for the familiar pearl necklace in the pouch. I put it on and imagined past ancestors wearing it, dainty women dressed in silk, women of royalty.

I could hear Mother's voice. "Bai fu mei. White and wealthy. Round pearls to whiten your complexion. During the Han dynasty, women of the court had fair skin. White skin was thought to cover your flaws." She pointed her finger in the air, her wrist limp. "When I was your age, my amah made me drink white peony root soup to lighten my skin."

Her vanity was covered with skin creams and cheap perfumes. I smelled the bottles of perfume as if the scent contained magic. Floral, musk, citrus. I sprayed cologne in the air and walked through the heavy mist. I opened a jar of rice cream and smeared it on my face, brushed my cheeks with powder and slapped on some lipstick. "Bai fu mei. I am beautiful," I said to myself. I looked in the mirror and imagined an Empress. A crown of jewels on my head. Beauty and power.

I thought of Cal with a sense of achievement mixed with a tug of disappointment for Mother. I defaulted to Pangu and his everlasting love. All I had to do was use my imagination, just like Mother said, and he appeared in all his glory, muscular and strong, long hair, full beard, limbs reaching for the heavens.

OUTSIDE, THE AIR felt misty and cool after last night's rain. In the distance, the steeples of St. Mary's towered above the buildings downtown, piercing the cloudy sky. I avoided the puddles on the sidewalk, stretching my legs and leaping over the mirrored lakes. Mother followed, her hair flapping in the wind.

My phone pinged. It was a text from Rani: I need to talk to you.

Me: Meet me after church.

WE ENTERED THE dimly lit cathedral and the smell of burning incense rose up my nostrils. I dipped my index finger in the bowl of sacred water and touched my forehead. "In the name of the Father, the Son and Holy Spirit." A wave of warmth filled my body at the sight of the vaulted ceiling reaching to the heavens. Stained glass depicting the saints surrounded us with violet light. A rainbow of color pressed against the windows.

"Study them," Mother whispered and pointed. "They tell a story. The sacraments. Blessed Saints."

I sank to my knees into the soft brown cushion, interlaced

my hands in prayer. An elderly woman sat in the pew in front of us, her floral perfume thick and heavy. Mother pulled out a beaded rosary from her purse—a gift, she said, from Rosie, her nanny—that had been blessed by the Pope.

Mother twisted the rosary between her fingers. When she wasn't looking, I reached in my pocket for a stick of gum. I rubbed the pearl necklace between my fingers, as if it had the power to grant a wish.

Mother handed me a hymnal, her attention at my neck. "Where did you find that?"

I hesitated. "The bottom of your jewelry box."

"Take it off."

"But you never wear it," I whispered.

"Off. Now." She reached for the pearls, ready to yank them away.

"But . . ."

The elderly woman in front of us swung around. "Shhh."

"Put it back when you get home," Mother said.

"Okay. What's the big deal?"

When I was younger, her closet was my playground. I'd try on her pretty dresses, even though they draped to the floor, slipped into high-heeled shoes, wore the clip-on coral earrings, the jade bracelets. I had never seen her so upset over a piece of jewelry.

The sound of the organ vibrated through the air, cutting off her answer. The voices of the choir soared, loud and resonating. We rose to our feet as Father Victor entered. He was short and bald with a powerful voice. The choir sang and I followed each note. I prayed to God. *Forgive me for chasing away my mother's boyfriends. It's for the best, right?* I prayed to Pangu. *Don't ever leave me.*

Mother lifted her veil, her lips moving with each note. She appeared calm, but I sensed a deep sadness. Her stare was blank. A clear sign of the beginning of one of her funky moods. It was all Cal's fault and partly mine for scaring him away. But I had no choice.

Why couldn't she find peace in this situation? It was all for the best. The Phoenix and Dragon, together.

AS FATHER VICTOR delivered the sermon, I studied St. Francis of Assisi standing in a pasture, surrounded by a flock of birds. I approached the altar for communion and envisioned him floating toward me, his presence as comforting and loving as I imagined a father's would be.

"The body of Christ." Father Victor's voice startled me.

"Jasmine." I felt Mother's fingers on my back, pushing me forward.

I cupped my palms, ready to receive communion. "Amen," I whispered. I placed the thin wafer on my tongue and let it dissolve as I turned and headed to our pew.

Looking up, I was surprised to see Rani at the back of the church, leaning against the wall with an unlit cigarette between her fingers. She wore a pair of faded, torn jeans and bright tangerine top.

"What are you doing here?" I asked as I drew closer. I remembered her text. "I said after church."

A rectangular-shaped light stretched onto the floor.

Rani twisted the long braid of her ponytail. "I know, but I couldn't wait. I went to your apartment, but no one was home. I have to tell you something."

"What happened?"

"This woman came to our house yesterday. She asked to

talk to me and asked a bunch of questions about you." I noticed that Rani's hand shook, the unlit cigarette ready to drop to the floor.

"The Keeper?"

"Yeah. I told you they were sneaky."

A hot surge raced to my temples. "So what did she ask you?"

"Like how much time we spend together? What do we do after school? Blah. Blah. Blah. My mother made me talk to her. I think you're in trouble."

"You didn't tell her anything, did you?"

Rani flipped her long braid to the side. "What do *you* think? You think I'd rat on you?"

"No. But shit. I'm screwed."

Rani pulled her top lip tight over her front teeth. "I don't know what to tell you. I heard that they don't have to keep things confidential either. Who knows who else is after you."

The cigarette dropped to the floor and I imagined it erupting into a towering orange red inferno.

CHAPTER 22

I HAD NIGHT terrors about the Keeper that evening, her body shape shifting into an aswang, her top half separating as she flew into the air, sharp claws, wings fanning open. Me squirming, struggling to free myself from her grip.

I screamed and jumped out of bed. Sweat dripped down my temples. I ran outside and peered up at the night sky. *Pangu. Help me. Help me.* I waited until one lone star pulsed then faded. I fell asleep on the concrete steps of the apartment and woke to the sun peeking through the horizon. The birds chirping.

School was really going to suck.

At the corner of the block, the yellow bus screeched to a halt, the door swinging open.

Mr. Wally smiled, a tuft of gray hair sprouting from the back of his head. "Morn'n, Ms. Jasmine." He whispered, "Fear is the only darkness."

I took a deep breath in, clearing my head of the night terrors. Then I recalled the YouTube clip from an old Kung Fu series I had shared with Mr. W last week. "Morning, Master Po."

He nodded. "You doing okay, young grasshopper?"

"Yep," I lied.

His nose wrinkled with a look of concern. "You have a good day now. All righty?"

I scanned the row of seats, looking for Rani, but she wasn't there. I started to panic. My head throbbed. At least the boys in the back of the bus appeared to be preoccupied with their phones. They were laughing and eating gummy bears.

AT SCHOOL, AS I took a drink from the water fountain, someone shoved me from behind. I groaned and took a step back, the front of my shirt drenched. I whipped around. It was Parker. Go figure. He sneered and kept walking past.

In English class, I gazed out the window as a flock of geese flew in the sky. I thought of the haiku by Matsuo Bashō, one of Mother's favorites: *Clouds now and again give a soul some respite from moon-gazing—behold.*

I couldn't wait for school to end, but when I returned to the apartment, Mother was in the kitchen banging dishes, slamming cupboards. She didn't speak or look at me, as if it was my fault Cal still hadn't called. Maybe it was. I attempted to make rice porridge, sliced a shriveled gingerroot from the fridge. I forgot to add enough water and burned the bottom of the pot.

I watched her take her pills and finally asked, "Something wrong?"

She swirled her glass and lit a cigarette. "Oh, my dear Pangu. Where are you when I need you? For eighteen thousand years you sleep. Your sweat turns to rain, the dew upon this earth."

"He's the creator of all," I added, offering her a bowl of rice porridge. "Self-contained in a black egg."

I envisioned angry gods in the sky. The Phoenix rising while she sat at the kitchen table, fixated on the wall. She took a puff of a cigarette, a sign of her unhappiness. The last time I caught her smoking was in fifth grade. I had fractured my arm in gym class. After returning from the hospital, she paged through her checkbook, surrounded by blue smoke. *Gotta be more careful,* she'd said. *That arm's going to cost us.*

Her hand quivered as she took a drag from the cigarette. She exhaled a puff of smoke. "I want to believe that it wasn't you this time. But I wonder, did you say something to him?"

"No. Why?"

"You can be fierce. A true Dragon."

"It wasn't me."

"I hope not. You know what they say: *In order to achieve victory, you must live inside the skin of your opponent.* Perhaps I'll leave this earth on a blue moon. It's a family curse. The fate of a broken heart."

"Stop." Why did she have to talk about death? Didn't we already have enough problems?

She shoved me and laughed. "It's all a dream, anyway. Myths and fairytales. Bones to rocks. Flesh to earth. Limbs, pillars of the world. My hero has broken darkness." She squeezed my hand. Her palm and fingers felt cold. "I'm sorry, Jasmine. I really thought things could be different this time."

Now she was admitting that we lived in a fairytale, which could turn into a nightmare *real soon* if I didn't do something. "Look what it's doing to you. He left, just like all the others."

"Such wasted tears again."

"You have to pull it together, Ma. We have to show the Keeper that things are stable. Don't you care? I saw the letter. We don't have much time."

"What if Cal was the answer? And now you've chased him away." Mother's voice quivered and I thought she might cry. "Please. Stay out of it."

"And what if Cal's not the answer? The Keeper even went to Rani's house and asked her a bunch of questions. They trick you so they can take your kids away from you. Don't you care?"

"I do. If you only knew." She paused. "You'll never understand. You're just a kid. I've got this. Maybe it's time to just run away. Go west."

I wanted to understand, but all I saw was a thin veil shrouding her face.

AROUND EIGHT THAT evening, as Mother and I cleaned up, we heard a knock at the door. The door must not have been locked and it swung open. If I hadn't recognized the eyes, I might have mistaken the intruder for a homeless man, the scruffy stubble on his chin, his hair a disarray.

Cal stood, hands in front of his stomach like a pregnant woman. He flashed a casual smile as if I had just seen him yesterday. The aswang had returned. I was mortified.

"Hey, Jasmine. How you doing? Got a surprise for you," he said.

"Who's at the door?" Mother hollered from the kitchen.

"It's Cal." *Told you, Pangu. This one's scary.*

Pots and pans rattled. "Don't let him in," she said. "Tell him to go back where he came from, like all the rest of them."

I tried to close the door, but he blocked it with his elbow and stepped forward.

"What kind of greeting is that?" He leaned against the frame of the door. "I have something. A gift."

"We don't need anything."

"It's for you."

"I think you should leave," I said.

A brown paper sack dropped to the floor.

"Ma," I hollered.

Something squirmed in the flap of his suede jacket. Yelped.

He knelt and opened the flap of his coat. A small black-and-white puppy darted forward. It circled the floor a couple times, then squatted on Mother's favorite silk rug by the door.

Mother entered the living room and stood. "Long business trip?" She brought her hands to her hips. "You look like hell. And what's that puppy doing in here?"

"Let me explain," Cal said.

"No. Get out."

"C'mon, Suchou. Please. It's been crazy these past weeks."

"Who do you think I am? I really thought you changed."

The puppy scampered toward me and I scooped it in my arms while they talked. Mother called Cal out for promising that things would be different this time—as if they had a serious past, as if his leaving wasn't the first time. I didn't know what to think or feel. I held the puppy tighter. I'd never felt anything so soft, so alive. Its smooth belly felt doughy and warm. Another aswang in disguise? How clever. I tried not to get too excited. *Stay cool. Stay calm.*

"He doesn't have a name yet," Cal called to me. "I nearly

ran over him with my truck yesterday. Right in the middle of the road. No collar. Nothing. Guess he needs a home."

The puppy pawed at my neck and licked my cheek. My whole body clenched. I didn't trust him. It was a scheme; it had to be.

"Are you insane?" said Mother. "I can't afford to feed it."

"He comes with food." Cal pulled out a small sack of puppy food and a leash from the brown paper bag that had dropped on the floor.

Mother tightened the belt of her robe and crossed her arms. "Leave. Now."

Cal reached for Mother and she shoved him back.

"No, Cal." She knelt to the floor. "What are you trying to do? It's not fair. Coming and going as you please. I can't do this anymore."

I squeezed the puppy tight, out of fear.

Cal placed his hand on her shoulder, kissed her on the cheek. "It'll be fine."

She backed away. "I don't know why you're back. How dare you." She buried her head in her palms, sobbing uncontrollably. "I need someone I can count on."

"Enough. Okay, Suchou? I'm here now."

With those words, he drew her close.

AS I LAY on the bed that night, the puppy curled in the crook of my arm. The wind whistled through the windowpane in tiny phantom-like shrieks and leaves quivered, casting shadows of spastic dancers on the wall. I stared at the ceiling, counted the chips in the paint.

Cal and Mother started to fight. I put in my ear buds and listened to music—classic rock, the blues, indie bands. I ran my fingers through the puppy's curly, soft, fur. It wagged its tail and licked my chin.

"I'm going to keep you, Basho," I whispered, thinking about the Japanese poet from the haiku book Mother had given me. "That's a good name. Don't you think?"

Basho tilted his head to the side and barked.

I pulled him close and whispered in his ear. "I never want to fall in love. Not like them. Ever."

CHAPTER 23

WE DROVE FOR miles—at least an hour or so—out of town to go hunting, just me and Cal. By that point, I realized he had weaseled his way back into our lives. Mother had the day off and offered to take care of Basho. Cal said he wanted some bonding time with me. It made me super nervous and suspicious, but it beat the heck out of going to school. Plus, Mother didn't seem to care and even called me in sick. My first excused absence.

I thought about the Keeper, especially after what Rani had told me—that the Keeper had talked to her. But maybe Rani had smoothed things out. Things were eerily quiet. No word from anyone. I crossed my fingers, hoping the Keeper was going to leave me and my mother alone for good.

I had never been hunting before or been that far away from Briarplace. I leaned against the truck's door and gazed out the window—fields of brown, snow-covered pine trees in the middle of nowhere. A dense blanket of fog floated above a winding river. The truck had a musty smell. I focused my attention on the knit cap and a pair of thick beige gloves on the floor in front of me, the potato chip wrappers and silver thermos. The hunting rifle was in a case in the back seat.

• • •

THE RADIO BUZZED, giving off an annoying static sound. Cal didn't seem to mind. He whistled and hummed as if to his favorite tune, broad shoulders hunched, arms resting on the steering wheel in a relaxed manner. He wore a baseball cap marked with "C Construction" in black stitching. His upper lip flaunted a patch of razor stubble and there was a tiny horizontal cut on his chin.

He chewed on his index fingernail, and for the first time, I wondered if he was just as nervous as me.

I moved my finger in sweeping lines against the cold glass, thinking about Rani. I texted her.

Me: Skipping school today. Going hunting with Cal. Yep, hunting.

Rani: WTF? He's back?

Me: Yep. Brought me a puppy.

Rani: OMG. A puppy? For real? No way.

Me: For real

I finally interrupted the awkward silence. "Mind if I change the channel?" I asked.

"Go for it. Not much reception out here. Used to drive for miles with my father on these roads. He never spoke one damn word the whole time."

"You sound mad."

"Not really. Cripes. It was better that way. I left home when I was about seventeen. I remember the day like yesterday. My mom, though, I never could make her understand or stop crying."

"Why? She didn't want you to go?" I scrolled through the channels.

"Something like that. But I couldn't stand the sound of her crying all the time. He wasn't so good to her. But I wasn't afraid of him." Cal took a sip from a can of soda, holding the steering wheel steady with his thighs.

Our bodies bounced up and down as we drove over clumps of dirt and rock. We passed an old farm-house and a dried-up corn field. Acres of flat, barren land stretched toward the horizon.

"It's a perfect day. Snow cover last night helps. Easier to track deer."

I shivered and my shoulders stiffened with anticipation. My breath hung visibly in the air. I stared at his hands, waiting for them to turn to claws. *But the aswangs are afraid of daylight. Right, Pangu?*

We parked on the side of the road, near an open hayfield. Cal threw me a bright orange jacket from the back of the truck. It was cold and stiff and smelled musty like the truck. I pulled it over my shoulders and the bottom edge grazed my knees, making me feel silly and small.

Cal pulled out a tin of chewing tobacco from the back pocket of his jeans, took a pinch, then placed it between his bottom lip and gum. He held the tin in front of me and I stole a pinch as if I had done it a hundred times.

The tobacco tasted gross and salty. It smelled earthy. When he wasn't looking, I spat it onto the ground. A drop of saliva dribbled down my chin. I scanned the prairie, taking in the woods, the cool air filling my lungs. I felt lightheaded.

Cal grabbed the rifle from the pickup. I'd never been around a real gun before. He pulled out something from the case that looked like a block of bullets, then loaded the rifle. "Stick close, okay?" He tossed me a pair of gloves. The wad of chew bulged and protruded from his bottom lip.

We hiked for three quarters of a mile on frost-covered

grass, bits of dried leaves, and twigs crunching beneath our boots. To the left of us was a grove of trees. Up ahead, in the distance, was a field of dried sunflowers, their heads hanging limp and harsh against the sky. A ghost of my breath hovered in the air.

Cal stopped. He held out his thick-gloved hand. "Shhh."

Maybe he could hear the noisy chatter of my mind.

I took a step back and froze.

About a hundred yards in front of us, a herd of deer appeared—a couple of them faced our direction, their ears perked forward. The others moved at a slow pace in the grass, long thin legs, slender necks curved downward as they grazed.

One doe in particular had a long white stripe along its neck. I watched each poised movement. I had never seen such a lovely creature. Mother would have been captivated. She would have danced in the open prairie.

I started to think about life and death. Survival. Fathers. Wanting something I could maybe never have. My mind started spinning. I thought of Pangu. Gods and fairytales.

Pause. Breathe.

Cal and I stopped in our tracks. "Don't move," he whispered. "And don't make a sound." He positioned himself and braced his body against a tree. He drew the rifle to his shoulder and took aim. "Cover your ears."

I stood still, covered my ears, and waited for him to take the shot.

The sound of the gunshot rang through the air and echoed. My body jerked. I felt the blast in my body. I stood, stunned. My knees felt weak.

The deer jumped and darted ahead before falling to the ground. The rest of the herd scattered in different directions, white tails flickering.

I followed Cal like a robot, clumsy and slow, trying to catch my breath. My toes went numb despite the two pairs of socks I had on.

We reached the deer. Splayed on its side, it looked helpless, slim long legs now still, neck craned unnaturally. Eyes opened wide, tongue hanging out.

Cal leaned down and examined the gunshot. It was about two inches wide, a smear of red blood on the hide.

I watched in disbelief.

It was the doe with the white stripe along its neck.

"She's beautiful." I swallowed back tears, wondering why anyone would want to kill something as graceful as this creature.

"Yep, she's a beauty," Cal said as he tagged the deer. "Hang on. This part gets messy."

I stole intermittent peeks while Cal removed the deer's organs.

Afterwards, we dragged the deer back to the truck. Warm tears ran down my cold cheeks.

ONCE INSIDE THE pickup, a storm of emotions erupted in me. This was bonding? What it meant to have a father?

My father, Pangu, split the earth and sky. His image grew hazy in my mind.

Cal sighed. "You know what? We're alike, you and me."

"How?"

"You see things other people don't see." He tapped the steering wheel. "And you protect those you love. It can be a curse." He removed his cap, wisps of gray and black hair flat against his forehead.

I softened for a moment. Maybe there was hope.

But then he said, "Can you keep a secret?"

A nervous shiver shot through me. "Depends." My knee jittered up and down.

"I want to show you something." He reached over to the glove compartment of the truck and pulled out a small red velvet box. "Don't tell her, okay?"

My vision blurred and I thought I might faint.

He set the box on my lap. "Go ahead. Open it."

I studied the box as if it were a coffin. Skeletal remains inside. Ghosts psyched to emerge.

"Go on. It's not going to bite." He laughed.

I touched the velvet with my fingertips, little electric shocks pulsing through me as I opened the lid.

A diamond ring sparkled in the dimness of the truck.

"What do you think? The other ring had a bigger stone, but I like this one better. It has three diamonds, if you look real close."

I pinched my thigh. This wasn't happening. A ring? Mother knew nothing about commitment. She was the Phoenix. A bird with massive wings, soaring across the prairie.

His nose scrunched. "What? Not good enough?"

I snapped the lid shut. "Seems a little soon, don't you think?" I tossed the box back to him. He caught it and stuffed it into the pocket of his jacket.

What made him different from all the others?

My body sank into the cushion of the seat. "She doesn't do well with surprises. Makes her super crabby."

"I know. Seems awfully fast. But I've known your mother

for years." He smiled and I could tell it didn't matter what I had said. "Okay, no more talk about this. And remember. It's a secret."

"My mother and I don't need anyone."

"That's what you think. Time to crack open that stone-cold heart of yours."

"Never," I whispered as I glanced out the window.

Cal started the truck and I watched the world pass by. Trees and fields of brown and gray became smaller and smaller in the distance. The wind wailed through the crack in the window.

I was the hunter, too.

I thought of the Keeper. I was determined to protect the life that was mine and now this man was getting in the way.

Or was he the answer? This monster in disguise?

CHAPTER 24

CAL PROPOSED TO Mother after dinner on the day we went hunting. His hand shook as he opened the box and placed the ring on her finger.

"We'll get married at city hall, save a few bucks. A cozy ceremony, just the three of us," he said.

Mother looked stunned. She covered her face and wept.

I distracted myself by sitting on the floor with Basho on my lap. I scratched him behind his ears and hummed a song in my head, just like Mother used to sing to me.

My body turned numb as I bit into my cheek.

I took Basho outside, watched the sun set, streaks of lavender and pink in the horizon.

Pangu, what's happening?

Our lives were about to change.

CHAPTER 25

DAY THIRTY ARRIVED after Cal proposed. I paced the apartment. Made sure the door was locked and peeked out the windows for the Keeper. I waited for a call. Checked the mail for another letter. Heard phantom knocks on the door.

But there was nothing. Not a word or sound from the Keeper.

A couple days later, I found a letter from CPS on the table—*The investigation has been officially closed.* I felt like a gigantic boulder had been lifted off my body. But my sense told me to stay vigilant. Be cautious.

I still resisted the thought of having a stepfather. Just saying the word made me nauseous. Stepfather. Stepfather. Stepfather.

Even my body was reacting and changing to my new life.

A few mornings after the engagement, I woke up with cramping just below my belly button. My boobs felt full and tender. I pulled down my pajama pants and underwear and noticed a damp, pink stain on the crotch. Blood. I stood for a moment, unable to move. The bedroom walls trembored. I grew lightheaded. I hiked up my underwear and PJs.

It finally happened. My period. I had no idea what to do.

I found Mother in the living room, behind a bouquet of lilies. She appeared in deep thought, fingering the petals.

"I think I've got—my you know what," I whispered.

Her hands dropped to her side. "Finally. My gosh." She strode past me to the bathroom and I followed.

She dug in the cabinet and found a box of tampons. "Rosie made me sit on a banana leaf and jump over blooming orchids so I would smell good."

I snorted. "Unbelievable."

"This is a rite of passage. Womanhood." She pulled a tampon from the box, waved it in the air. "I should grab one of my orchids."

"I'll pass. Seriously."

"Ah, to be young again. Two women in the house. We're truly synchronized now. They say women who live together menstruate together."

"Quit it." I snatched the tampon from her fingers. "I can do this myself."

"You've ripened. A blossom." She planted a kiss on my forehead.

"This isn't fun, Ma." I groaned.

I reached for my phone and texted Rani.

Me: Got my period today. According to my mother—I've finally blossomed.

CHAPTER 26

SPRING FINALLY ARRIVED with the manic song of blackbirds awakening me in the morning. Cal mimicked the life of a stray cat, coming and going as he pleased, leading me to question the whole wedding idea, the notion of trust. But that's what held my mother and Cal together—the engagement, their future plans.

There were moments when I felt like we were a real family. Like breakfast, the three of us at the table, the smell of fresh coffee. Me and mother slurping our rice porridge. Cal eating his fried eggs and burnt toast. Basho curled by my legs, watching for Cal's fallen breadcrumbs.

I thought of Rani's home. What would living there be like? Pictures of her relatives hung on the wall in their living room. Sometimes, we watched cartoons with her little brother, TJ. I liked the way Rani's mother offered me spiced milk tea and biscuits, and how she asked about my drawings. Plus, Rani had a real dad. A pilot who flew all over the world. Maybe that would be me one day?

I wondered what Rani thought of our apartment? She came over a lot, especially now that I had Basho. We worked on homework, our bodies sprawled on the living room floor with Basho curled between us, my phone blaring with music—everything from indie to oldies. Yet, something gnawed at me, an unsettling feeling. Maybe it wasn't the fear of having something, but of losing it.

MOTHER FINALLY PICKED a lucky date for the wedding according to the lunar calendar, following the components of the celestial stem, the earth, metal, the terrestrial branch of the zodiac.

"Madame Charito would be proud," she said.

"Who is that?" I replied, intrigued by the snippets of her life she randomly shared with me. I swallowed these little morsels of truth, filling my soul.

"She's a fortune teller. She reads palms and predicts the future. When I was young, Papa always consulted with her first for business decisions, his health, and planning celebrations. He always met with her first regarding the proper day and time." She kept talking. "I remember when Papa brought me to see her when I was ill. She had a deck of cards and long, pointed fingernails. She felt my pulse and asked Papa when I was born. Her voice was fragile, like the sound of a tiny bird. 'You bring heartache to your papa,' she said as she pointed to the veins in my hand. 'Your life like this. Unpredictable. It goes this way then that way. No pattern.'"

Madame Charito was right. Our lives seemed unpredictable.

With the wedding only a week away, Mother buzzed about the apartment, hummed and sang to herself. She spent hours on her phone, looking at images of brides, models dressed in beaded gowns with long flowing trains.

I imagined her in a bridal gown with a floral lace train, holding a bouquet of roses, smiling. But then the thought vanished and I felt suffocated—the lace wrapping itself around my neck like a serpent.

Mother twisted her hair and pulled it back with a rubber band. "I can't believe this is happening, Jazz."

"All that lace might strangle you," I said.

She didn't respond. "I'm thinking flowers. Orchids or maybe gardenias, lots of them. I wish they had sampaguitas here." She turned. "Do you know 'The Legend of Sampaguita'?"

I shook my head.

"During the time of war, there were two lovers that had to part. They made a vow to each other—'sumpa kita,' which means 'I promise' in Tagalog. The man was killed during battle and the woman died of a broken heart. At the grave site where they were buried, a vine of white flowers bloomed." Mother smacked her lips. "Sampaguitas are a symbol of love and loyalty."

I imagined a trail of white petals floating down the Black River. "Sumpa kita," I whispered.

I thought of all her silk flowers. *They live forever. Never leave you.* Then the thought of false promises hit me and without any warning, the words flooded out. "Don't you think you're rushing things a bit?"

Mother looked at me as if I had stabbed her. "Way to ruin a perfect moment. That's all you can say? That I'm in a hurry? This isn't just about me. It's about us. Our future. I told you that things will be different. You don't have to worry anymore. Okay?"

"Promise?" I wanted to let go of the past. I wanted desperately to believe her.

"I promise." She kissed the top of my head. "Now help me find a dress to wear."

• • •

WE FIRST STOPPED at a thrift shop and found a special collar for Basho, for the wedding day—one with little rhinestones on it.

Then we headed to a bridal shop. The mannequin in the front window was dressed in a white satin gown, a sprig of baby's breath nestled in her hair.

Mother tapped at the glass. "Look, Jazz. Part of me wants the traditional white wedding gown, but another part of me wants to be wrapped in red silk."

"For your wedding dress?"

"It's tradition. Red brings good luck." She gazed at the mannequin as if all her dreams were about to come true.

"I guess it doesn't matter. You're getting married at city hall."

"Yes, but I'm going to look and act like a bride."

I gazed up at the sky and tuned out her voice. Why couldn't I just be happy for her? For them? But my brain shifted to a deep sense of dread, my stomach churning.

I felt a sharp tug as she whisked my body away into the bridal shop.

The wood floor creaked beneath our feet as we entered a room filled with an array of haphazardly placed racks of bridal gowns. Along the wall, shelves brimmed with fancy white high-heeled shoes and accessories—gloves, floral hair barrettes, pearl earrings and bracelets.

Mother pulled a few gowns from the rack and disappeared behind a green curtain in the back. I browsed the long line of gowns, grabbed a fancy barrette with miniature bell-shaped flowers and stuck it in my hair. I reached for a gown, one lined with crystal beads and shiny pearls. I took it off the hanger, unzipped it halfway and stepped in.

It barely slid over my hips. I heard a slight rip and a small pearl dropped to the floor and rolled beneath the rack.

A tall woman in a gingham style dress and Birkenstock sandals appeared beside me. She slid her glasses down her nose and peered at the dress from above the red plastic frames.

"Is there something I can help you with?" Her voice sounded low and gruff. "Looks a little small. Those are petite. European gowns."

I stepped out of the dress, one leg then the other. My heel caught the edge of the zipper. "I'm here with my mother. She's uh . . . getting married, I guess."

I headed toward the back of the room just as the curtain opened. Mother appeared, wearing a sleeveless white satin gown.

"Well?" She ran her hand along the outer seam of the dress. "Fits perfect. I'm set." She flipped the tag over and let out a sigh. "We'll see."

We stepped into the small dressing room. The walls of the room started to close in on me. My breath quickened. An uneasy feeling settled in my gut.

I hugged her, wrapped my arms around the slippery material. I caught a whiff of the air, stale and damp, like a moldy basement.

Mother appeared so excited she wobbled, nearly tripping on the folds of the gown. "I know it's a lot to take in."

"Aren't you nervous?"

"Of what?"

"I don't know. The whole marriage thing. What if Cal's not the right one?"

"You worry too much. Have you forgotten we're not from

this world? My prayers have been answered." Her hands reached behind her back. "Help me."

I sniffed, swiped my hand along my pants, then pulled the zipper down, slowly, as it opened into a deep V down her back.

She reached for the blouse on the floor. "Cal said you were excited. He said he showed you the ring. What's the matter?"

I straightened. What a liar. Dare I say something? Who would she believe anyway? Not me. "Nothing," I mumbled. "It's cool." I leaned against the wall. To the side of me hung a corkboard with a magazine clipping of a bride and groom standing in front of a three-tiered cake. They were both smiling, their hands laced together, holding a knife, ready to cut the cake. I stared at the picture. "Do you love him?"

"Of course." Mother grabbed a tube of lipstick from her purse, leaned close to the mirror and colored her lips a bright red. "The sun and moon are aligned. You know what I mean?" The dim light accentuated the fine lines at the corners of her mouth.

"Sounds like true love to me." I poked my toe through the canvas of my sneaker. "Doesn't anything else matter to you anymore?"

"You matter."

"Then why are you doing this?"

"Doing what? We're going to be a family. That's what we've always wanted."

"Says who?"

"Jasmine, what is wrong with you? You're not making any sense."

"What about us? We don't need anyone."

"He loves me. This is a great opportunity."

"It's not a job, Ma."

"Sometimes life offers us a gift and we need to hold on to it, or it may just slip away." She straightened the collar of her blouse.

My head pulsed. Sparkling lights appeared. I ripped the magazine clipping from the corkboard, crumpled it in the palm of my hand.

There was a loud rap on the door. "How you two doing in there? Want me to bring you anything else?"

Mother finished buttoning her blouse. "We're good." She stared at me. "Please, Jazz. I need you. It's you and me. We're invincible. Phoenix and Dragon. Remember?" She rubbed my shoulder, then flung the curtain open. "Besides, I think the Keeper will leave us alone now."

Just outside the dressing room, the woman waited with a couple gowns hanging from the crook of her arm. She pulled down her glasses. "Ready?"

Mother smiled. "I do want the dress, but could you put it on hold for now?"

The woman nodded. "For twenty-four hours. That's the best I can do."

CHAPTER 27

THE MORNING OF the wedding, I wrote another letter to
my imaginary father.

Hey Pangu,
Lots going on. Today's the big day. Mother and Cal
are getting married. I guess that means I get a stepdad.
Don't worry. You're still my mythological father. The cre-
ator of all.
Mother's been a freak, racing all over the apartment.
Fixing and re-fixing her hair.
She couldn't afford the pretty wedding gown at the
bridal shop. Bummer. She ended up with a red dress
from The Flamingo. The tag said Made in Taiwan.
There's a big brown stain on it that she can't get rid
of. But she seems happy—I saw her smiling and trac-
ing her finger along the silk embroidery, the tiny plum
blossoms and bamboo.
I found a cute red polka-dotted dress for myself. It's
missing a button in the back, but so what. It's much bet-
ter than the red skirt and wrinkled blouse Mother pulled
from a pile of old jeans.
Cal's somewhere with a buddy of his, getting a
boot polish. Go figure. He and Mother were arguing

*about something this morning. Who knows about
what?*

*Basho's been hyper, dashing all over the apartment.
He pooped in the kitchen.*

Wish me luck.

Love,

J

MOTHER AND I arrived at city hall, an older brick building downtown with marble floors, plain white walls and
fluorescent lights that blinked on and off. The air smelled of
Pine-Sol and fruity air freshener. I walked rapidly through
the long corridor with a vase containing sticks of incense
in one hand and a bouquet of red silk roses in the other.
Mother followed behind in the tight red dress, taking tiny
steps in her spiked heels, which made a clicking sound
down the hallway.

"Wait up, Jazz," she said.

At our designated meeting room, a woman at a desk
waved us forward. "Come in. Have a seat," she said.

"We're a little early," Mother replied.

The office had a desk and four chairs, its walls bare except
for a large round clock. The second hand made a grim, steady
ticking sound. Like an aswang. *Tiktik.*

"I have a few things for you to sign," the woman said. She
licked her index finger and shuffled through a pile of papers.
"One o'clock, correct?"

"Yes. One." Mother squeezed my hand. "This is it, Jasmine. He better show up."

"Why wouldn't he?"

Mother hesitated. "We had a talk this morning."

"About what? Sounded more like a fight to me."

Mother shook her head. "It's nothing. You wouldn't understand."

She grabbed the bouquet of flowers. A few of the leaves were bent, and in the center, a missing rosebud. I set the vase on the chair next to me. A musky herbal scent wafted past as I wiped my sweating palm on the side of my dress.

The clock on the wall ticked.

Fifteen minutes passed. I left the room and walked the hallway.

"Where are you? Loser," I whispered.

I returned to the room. Mother sat at the edge of her seat, chewing on her brightly colored pinkie nail.

Another ten minutes passed.

"Is your partner here yet? The Judge has been waiting."

Mother glanced at the clock. "Yes, he should be here soon." She stood and called Cal, but by the look on her face, he must have not answered.

My head throbbed. Scintillating lights blinked in the periphery.

Another five minutes passed. The woman behind the desk straightened her glasses, made a phone call. She shook her head. "I'm sorry Ma'am."

"He should be here, soon," Mother said.

"Ma'am, you're going to have to reschedule."

"You must be joking." She dropped the flowers. The clock ticked louder. "Are you sure?"

"Ma'am. I'm sorry. I'm going to have to ask you to leave."

Mother shook her head, whipped past the woman and out the door into the hallway.

I grabbed the bouquet from the floor, the vase, and

followed. She strutted down the corridor then paused for a minute and glanced out the window. She looked so innocent, stunned like a deer.

I bit into my lower lip till it bled.

IN THE CAR, Mother gripped the steering wheel with both hands. Her knuckles turned a yellowish-white, her gaze fixed straight ahead. The world passed by in slow motion, bits of gray swirling past.

"There must be some mistake," I finally said as we reached the apartment.

She turned off the ignition. "Don't ever open your heart, ever. How could I be so stupid?"

"I tried to tell you. Maybe it's better this way. Maybe he's not the one."

"Shut up, Jasmine. Just shut up." She grabbed the bouquet of roses and threw it at me. Then she started to sob. "You don't know anything. You're just a child." Streaks of black mascara spilled down her cheeks. "You'll never understand."

I was stunned and looked at her in disbelief. It was the first time she had ever thrown anything at me. I gripped the handle of the door. We sat there until the sky turned gloomy with clouds, the wind whipping whorls of dust all around us.

CHAPTER 28

THE DAYS AFTER the courthouse felt like months. Mother became more and more withdrawn. Dishes piled in the sink and the bread turned moldy, the milk sour. She called in sick from work and disappeared in the bedroom for days, hidden beneath the covers.

I brought her tea, bowls of rice, blankets, turned on and off the lights, opened the shades. Sometimes, I'd just sit with Basho and watch TV all day and night as she slept. I'd wait for her to wake up, but when she did, she was unrecognizable, her cheeks bony and sunken.

Her bedroom smelled of sleep. Half-empty glasses of water and a paper plate with dried toast rested on the nightstand. On the dresser was a jar of Tiger Balm and the jade Buddha sitting lotus position, arms resting on his knees, his smile sinking into the shadows of the room.

One day, I was filling her water and saw her bottle of pills on the nightstand.

"You're a saint, you know that?" Mother said. She moaned, a constricting sound escaping. "My sweet angel."

Her eyes looked sallow, sunken. Her hair was tangled and knotted, just barely covering the spaghetti straps of the nightgown she wore. She turned to the side and I curled next to her, rested my cheek on her back, against the sheer softness of her.

In the evenings, I planted myself on the front steps of the apartment, counting the stars and smoking cigarettes, Basho at my side. Rani sometimes stayed overnight and we'd play cards like Blackjack.

"I know this sucks," Rani said. "Don't worry, she'll come around." She curled her upper lip as if she barely believed the words herself.

The school called one morning. They said I was suspended for ten days because I had too many unexcused absences. Apparently they had tried to get a hold of Mother first, but nobody answered.

Suspended. I shouldn't be surprised. At least it was almost the end of the school year.

I remembered what Rani had said. *Who knows who else is after you.*

I envisioned sirens flashing, screaming in the distance, the sound growing louder and louder. Closer and closer.

CHAPTER 29

EARLY ONE SUNDAY, I woke up in the middle of the night. My chest throbbed and my palms were sweaty. A swarm of aswangs circled above my head. I'd been dreaming about the Keeper all night. Officials coming to arrest Mother.

I shot upright. Searched the room as if the dream was real. I got up and headed to the kitchen for a drink of water.

I was shocked to see Mother on the floor, sitting cross-legged. The air smelled of her cooking, garlic and sesame oil. A votive candle burned on the table next to her, its tiny flame quivering in the air. Next to it, a pile of letters, an ashtray with cigarette butts, a purple silk orchid, its stem curved toward the earth. An empty wine glass.

"What are you doing, Ma?" I asked.

Her lids appeared swollen as she held a crumpled piece of paper. She stood, and as if in a trance, leaned toward the candle and held the letter in the wiggling flame until the edges blazed a bright red and bits of ashes began to tumble onto the table.

"Remember, nothing lasts forever. One must detach from all things." Her voice was a high-pitched slur. "Come, give me a hug, sweetie."

I went to her and she wrapped her arms around me and

squeezed. "I can't breathe," I said. She held on tighter, like I was all she had in this world. I told myself it wasn't her fault and I let her hold me until I couldn't take it any longer. Her breath smelled acidic, like bitter herbs.

Basho started barking and howling. I wriggled free, my attention turning to the stove.

The frying pan lit up, engulfed in flames.

"Were you cooking something?"

I ran to the stove and attempted to slide the pan off the burner, but the flames continued. I screamed and grabbed a towel to suffocate them. The fire calmed, but only briefly. Then the oil-soaked towel ignited.

I grabbed the corner of the towel and flung it to the side. The fire on the stove continued to burn. "Oh my god. Help, Ma. You gotta mo—"

When I turned toward Mother, the burning towel had landed on the corner of the table, lighting the tablecloth on fire. The flames spread, bright orange and red, and the orchid melted.

The heat pressed against me, and it felt as if my cheeks and body were on fire, too. Basho dashed toward the living room. Gray smoke rose and filled the air. The fire alarm shrieked.

"Ma! Basho!" I grabbed the Maxwell canister on the floor, raced to the sink and filled it with water, threw it on the stove fire, but that only made things worse. I jumped back as bits of burning oil splattered. Then, it was as if someone had lit a match, and the pan busted into a wildfire of towering flames.

I grabbed the fire extinguisher from the hallway closet and ran back to the kitchen. The smoke appeared denser.

I pulled the silver pin, aimed the extinguisher at the stove, and squeezed the trigger. I moved to the table fire and did the same. Bursts of white spray shot out of the extinguisher. The air burned in my lungs and I covered my mouth. My vision grew watery. I coughed and felt my throat constrict, making it difficult to breathe.

Mother sat in the middle of the kitchen as if glued to the floor, hands at her knees, body swaying back and forth.

"Ma," I hollered. "Get up."

I tried to lift her, but her body sank back down.

"There's a fire. Move. Now."

She shoved me away. "Leave me alone. Let me burn."

"No. Get up."

"Just let me be."

Her forehead was wet with perspiration. I reached under her armpits, crouching down as low to the ground as I could and dragged her out of the kitchen. Basho followed as I pulled Mother out of the apartment, down the narrow hallway and out the door.

In the distance, a loud rush of sirens drew closer.

TIME BLURRED. SIRENS screamed. A fire truck arrived. A couple ambulances. Firefighters at the scene. People in uniform yelling orders.

Apartment residents gathered outside the building—the snoopy neighbor lady in pink curlers, a man in striped pajamas. People wide-eyed and disoriented. Kids in their pajamas crying. A few people yelling and cursing.

I coughed. Flashes of the fire appeared and disappeared in my mind. I thought of Mother sitting on the floor, not moving. Me screaming. The smoke. I couldn't breathe.

Paramedics hovered around Mother. They placed an oxygen mask over her nose and mouth.

I stood, numb and paralyzed. It felt like I was in a movie or waking from a nightmare. I clung tight to Basho.

"Hey, young lady. Are you okay?"

I turned. A tall, brown-skinned man in a navy-blue uniform with large lettering that said CLARKS COUNTY EMS stood next to me. He had a comforting smile and a calm presence. All the noise around me suddenly stopped. He was like a superhero breaking through the chaotic storm.

Suddenly, I found myself spewing out words, coughing. "She was cooking. I think she forgot. I think she forgot. Those stupid meds. It happened so fast. I tried to get her to move but she wouldn't. Cal—" I coughed. "I tried. I tried. I tried."

I couldn't stop shaking. Basho let out a whine and continued to pant.

"It's okay," the EMT guy said. "Let me put this on your finger." He attached a small clip-like device to my index finger. It beeped, gave a reading.

"Do you feel a little tight in the chest?"

I coughed and nodded. "Kinda."

"Let me listen to your lungs, okay?"

He stood behind me and held an instrument to my back. "Give me some deep breaths. That's good." Then with a stethoscope-looking instrument he listened to the front of my chest. "Nice deep breaths. Good job." He checked my throat with a light.

I looked ahead and noticed Mother being whisked away on a stretcher. The doors of the ambulance closed behind her. The emergency lights on the ambulance flashed. Red. White. The siren blaring.

"My mother . . . is she going to be all right?"

"They're going to take care of her. I think we should take you to the hospital. Make sure everything's okay? You all right with that?"

I coughed again. "Is that where they're taking my mother?"

"I think so."

"All right." I thought about my sketchbook. Mother's silk flowers. All our belongings. It was everything we had. "When can we go back to the apartment?"

"They'll need to secure the place and make sure it's safe for you to go back. Might be a little while." He petted Basho on the forehead and gently took him from me. "We'll find someone to take care of your little buddy for now." He handed Basho to another paramedic.

"Wait." I bit my lower lip. "I'll get him back, though?"

"I promise."

"Thank you . . . sir."

The EMT guy nodded and patted my shoulder. He placed an oxygen mask over my nose and mouth as we headed toward the other ambulance. I felt my spirit separate from my body. My body separating from everything I loved.

The sky disappeared as I breathed in and out. In and out.

CHAPTER 30

A SHIVER DARTED through me as I sat in the exam room of the emergency clinic. Strange medicinal smells mixed with body odor floated past.

The nurse asked lots of questions: How did the fire start? Where was Mother? What was she doing? Who are the members of your family? Do you have any relatives close by? She did more tests, checked my lungs again. My body felt heavy. My throat ached. I kept asking her about Mother. *We'll find out*, she said. *They're still evaluating her. She might need to stay for a few more days.*

Eventually, the nurse said, "I'll be back. I have a few calls to make." Then she left the room.

I waited and waited in the room with white walls, wondering if we were in trouble. I was glad I had my phone, even though it was running low on battery. I opened up a message to Rani and started to type. I'm at the hospital. Mother's here, too. I hope she's alright. They took Basho. I'm all alon— Then my phone died.

I grabbed a Post-it and a pen from the desk, to keep my mind off everything. But all I could think of was the fire. I drew flames all over the orange square paper and watched as they lifted and drifted off the page.

Another hour passed. My stomach rumbled. I wanted breakfast. I had lost track of time. It was 11 A.M., yet it seemed like I had been there for a couple days. A flash of light blinked in my periphery. *Pangu? Are you there?*

Tiktik. Tiktik. I smelled danger.

The nurse finally appeared again.

"You have a visitor," she said. "Someone who's going to make sure that you're well taken care of." She opened the door wider.

A woman marched in, her arms swinging by her side. Blood pumped through my veins. No way. No way. I wanted to run.

"Hello, Jasmine," the Keeper said.

I gripped the arms of the chair. I avoided her gaze but she kept moving toward me. *Tiktik. Tiktik. Tiktik.* A hissing sound followed as she drew closer. I looked away as the image of an aswang hovered above her head.

I only caught blips of her words. *Your mom's at the county hospital . . . needs to be there for a while . . . the doctor . . .*

"But she's going to be okay?" I asked, finally turning my head toward her.

The Keeper nodded. "I hope so. They'll figure it out. My job is to make sure that you're safe and taken care of."

"I'm fine," I replied.

The Keeper kept talking.

Then I heard the words, *Emergency foster care.*

My mind went blank.

CHAPTER 31

THE KEEPER LOADED me into her red Chevelle as if I were a criminal. Maybe I was going to jail, like Rani said. Inside, it smelled like citrus shampoo and apple cider vinegar. Something rustled in the back seat. A whimper.

I whipped around.

Basho leaped over the middle console and straight into my arms. His tail whipped back and forth.

I screamed. "Basho!" I turned to the Keeper. "How did you get him?"

She smiled. "Your neighbor took him for a bit. Even brought him to the vet to make sure he was okay after the fire. Good thing she didn't have him longer, she said, or she'd keep him." The Keeper laughed. It's the first time I'd heard the sound of her laugh. It sounded strange, like it was coming from somewhere outside herself.

"I'm so sorry about what happened, Jasmine. Are you doing okay?"

I blinked, waiting for her to shapeshift into a vampire, a snake. I clutched Basho, ran my fingers through his fur. He felt heavier—he weighed at least fifteen pounds now—and I realized that he had grown from a little fur ball into a nearly full sized, curly-haired dog. "I'm good. I want to go home." I felt the wet of Basho's nose as he rested his head on my arm.

"I'm sorry. I can't do that, Jasmine."

"I can stay in the hospital in my mother's room."

"You're a minor, and this is an emergency situation. You need to be somewhere safe." Her hands morphed, claw-like, long fingernails gripping the steering wheel. "You only need to be there a short while. Until your mom's back, okay?" She paused. "You'll have a nice bed to sleep in. Food. It'll be okay."

"I don't have any of my stuff." No clothes. Basho's food. No sketchbook.

"The family will have some clothes for you to wear. Toothbrush. You name it. Don't worry."

"And what about dog food?" Basho licked my arm a couple times. He wagged his tail.

The Keeper glanced at Basho. "The foster family doesn't allow pets—"

"What? Wherever I go, he goes."

"*But* she said she'd make an exception this time. See? Things aren't so bad. Please, Jasmine. In all honesty, I just want what's best for you. I want you safe. You've been through a lot." She reached for my hand and I yanked back. "It won't be forever. I promise. Just until your mother is well."

I dug my hands into my pockets. I didn't like this woman. No one ever kept their promises. I wanted Mother to come and get me. Take me home.

The Keeper kept driving, farther out of town. I touched the rabbit's foot hanging from the rearview mirror. "What's this? Supposed to bring you good luck or something?"

"I don't rely on luck. It's from my mom."

"Wonderful." All I had to cling to at the moment was luck. I sank back into the seat, Basho warm on my lap.

"How far away is this place? And how long do I have to be there?"

"Just a little farther outside of town. The Hempz are a nice family. They have a daughter about your age."

But all I thought of was Mother. I heard her voice. *We're the Phoenix and Dragon, never forget.*

WE DROVE PAST the fairgrounds, then farther north, accelerating onto the highway until we arrived about five miles on the outskirts of town, to a development called Little Bonanza. There were several homes made of brick and stone, a few tucked in the hills, partially hidden by tall pines. We followed a curvy dirt road until we came to the end of the development, stopping at a lone rambler style house made of cedar with a faded wood porch and a string of Christmas lights still dangling along the top railing.

The Keeper parked on the gravel driveway behind a rusted pickup. She swerved to the side, just barely avoiding a tricycle, before coming to a complete stop. As we stepped out of the vehicle, a striped cat darted past.

A tall and husky woman appeared at the front porch, the screen door slamming behind her. She had graying shoulder-length hair, flip flops on her feet, and a white T-shirt with a big pink peace sign plastered on the front. With one arm, she hugged an infant boy to the side of her hip.

"Name's Lida," she said. "Welcome, missy." Her voice sounded scratchy, like she smoked a pack of cigarettes a day. The infant kicked his chubby legs in the air. "This here's one of my daycare kids."

Basho yipped, ears perked forward as he scratched the ground then walked in a circle, finally curling himself on the grass.

Lida glared at Basho. "Keep him away from the kids. Deal? Or no dog."

I already hated it here. I wanted to go home. But I nodded anyway. "Deal."

Lida and the Keeper exchanged glances. "I told Ms. Simpleton I'd make an exception just this time, due to your situation and all."

I reluctantly followed the Keeper and Lida into the house. The aroma of fresh bread mixed with sour milk and sweat filled my nostrils. Knots formed in my stomach. I grew queasy.

Lida pointed in the direction of a door down the hallway. "There's the bathroom. Got you a toothbrush, toothpaste. Everything you need." She looked at me. "You hungry at all? You can get some lunch and join the kiddos."

On the couch in the living room, a teenage girl who looked a little older than me lounged with her long thin legs propped on the coffee table as she watched the television. She took a sip from a can of Mountain Dew. In the middle of the floor, a toddler boy gnawed on a yellow rubber duck, the side of his cheek shiny with saliva. Colored wood blocks lay scattered on the carpet, a couple matchbox cars and a stuffed rabbit with one ear missing. On the far wall hung a large painting of Jesus in a white robe, his hands clasped in prayer. It reminded me of being back at Sacred Sacraments.

"Gena, get up. Show her the room," Lida said.

The girl reached for the remote, turned up the volume.

"Gena. Go," Lida repeated. "That one's mine. Daughter."

Lida and the Keeper disappeared into the kitchen. Gena finally stood, took another sip of the soda. She ran her tongue across her front teeth and let out a heavy sigh.

"You're staying in my room, I guess." She looked at me, her eyes lined with thick black streaks, long sandy blond bangs swooping down half her face. She had on a cropped T-shirt and sweatpants which she wore just below the waist, revealing a small butterfly tattoo on her lower back.

Her bedroom wall was plastered with posters of the Beatles—Ringo, McCartney, Lennon, Harrison. One black and white poster read ALL YOU NEED IS LOVE. The air was infused with sweet floral perfume. The bed was unmade, the floor covered with shirts, a couple pairs of jeans and a pink pair of panties.

"You're over there." She pointed to the rollaway bed on the other side of the room.

Outside, the screen door slammed, followed by the cry of a baby. Lida's voice echoed from the living room. "Gena. Get over here."

"How long you gonna be here?" Gena said.

I shrugged. "Not long." *I hope.*

"Can't believe you don't have to go to school. I ought to get myself suspended. Don't worry, though. My mama will put you to work. You might *want* to go to school." She laughed. "Just don't touch anything. Or I'll kick your sorry little ass." She glanced at Basho before she left the room. "You, either."

I dropped my backpack on the floor and crouched next to the rollaway bed. Basho wagged his tail, his tongue hanging to the side. I rubbed him behind the ears. "This sucks. I don't want to be here. But we better behave or we're in trouble. It's just me and you, buddy."

LATER THAT DAY, I joined the daycare kids for lunch in the kitchen. A little girl with braided pigtails said grace, small hands clasped. "Come, Lord Jesus, be our guest. Let this food to me be blessed."

"To *us*, dearie," Lida corrected. She turned to me. "You like grilled cheese? Tomato soup?"

My stomach twisted and I nodded. I was really hungry.

The bread was crunchy, but not burnt, and the sandwich was gooey on the inside with melted cheese. The toddler next to me in the highchair patted his tray with one hand, kicking his legs in a frantic motion as he sucked on a saltine cracker, bits crumbling between his fingers.

Gena pranced by and tickled the bottom of his feet. He made a razzing sound and spat out bits of wet cracker, which flew in the air and hit my cheek. The little girl with the pigtails giggled.

"Wanna root beer?" Gena asked as she stood by the fridge, one hand on her waist.

I swiped off the cracker from my cheek. "Sure." I never drank soda. We couldn't afford it and Mother said it would rot my teeth. I popped open the can and the soda fizzed. The liquid was icy cold as it traveled down my throat.

The Keeper appeared in the kitchen doorway. "I'm going, Jasmine. Take good care. You've got my number in case you need anything. Don't worry. Everything will be fine. I'll be in touch."

That evening, I hung out in Gena's room, drawing random pictures in my sketchbook while she tried on outfit after outfit, tossing different tops to the floor. I found myself lost in a daydream. I drew strange heroic gods and flying dragons. I checked my phone for any messages from Mother, but nothing. Just random texts from Rani wondering where I was and if I was okay.

She and I both knew—my worst nightmare had come true.

CHAPTER 32

I TRIED TO ignore Gena as she got changed to go out for the night. She wiggled her way into a pair of skintight jeans and stood in front of a full-length mirror, turning to the side, trying to catch a glimpse of her bottom. I thought about the few outfits I had, wondering if they'd survived the fire.

"Quit staring," she said.

"I'm not."

"Hell, you were. I saw you looking at my ass."

I kept drawing and stole another peek at her through the corner of my eye. "Where are you going?"

She flung off her T-shirt. "LA, baby."

"Los Angeles? That's a bit far, don't you think?"

"Not now, you loser." She put on a cropped turquoise top. Her belly button exposed. "I'm going out."

"What are you going to do in LA?"

"Make music. Me and the band."

"You're in a band?"

"Yeah," she said.

I lifted my chin. "I like music."

"You do? What kind?"

"I'm eclectic."

"Yeah? And what the hell's that supposed to mean?"

"A little bit of everything. Pop, hard rock, folk, indie."

Gena opened the window and unlatched the screen. "You coming or what?"

"Me? Are you serious?"

Basho lifted his head and perked his ears.

"You in or what? They're telling us to hurry." She climbed out the window, arching one long, thin leg over the windowsill.

"Who is?"

"The voices."

"What?"

"They're screaming right now. Hustle."

Why not? I thought, even though there were plenty of reasons why not. It sounded like an adventure, and it was better than staying in this house with all the weird smells and sounds, a place where I didn't belong. I hugged Basho. I made sure the bedroom door was closed. "You stay here, little guy. I'll be back."

I slipped on my sneakers and followed Gena out the window. We ran through the back yard, down the dirt road. Fireflies blinked in the tall grass. Crickets chirped.

We finally stopped about a mile or so down the road in front of a small brick house.

"So, what voices are you talking about?" I asked, leaning over, catching my breath.

"They're in my head. Awfully annoying sometimes. Telling me what to do. You don't hear any voices?"

"Not really," I said. "Just my own." And sometimes, Pangu's. The trees and wind. The stars at night.

"Well, you're missing out. Guess I'm the lucky one." She smiled.

We went through the side garage door of the house and

down a flight of wooden steps to the basement. A rhythmic beat vibrated through my body, the music growing louder as we descended the stairs. An electric guitar screeched, then jumped octaves.

"Where the hell you been, girl? You're late." A teenage boy strumming chords stood in the center of the room, the fingers of his left hand moving up and down the neck of his guitar. He had shoulder length jet-black hair and a looped gold earring in one ear. "Who's the chick?"

"Jasmine. She's our foster girl."

"Hey," he said. His eyes were an eerie pale blue. Next to him, a thin boy with blond hair played the drums, head nodding to the beat.

Gena grabbed the microphone and started to sing. Her voice was haunting and raspy and her body moved to the music, each breath audible. To my surprise, she was actually pretty good. She had an indie hipster voice and I admit, I was impressed.

I listened to them practice for an hour, the cement floor of the unfinished basement chilling my bottom as I nodded my head up and down, swayed side to side. The guitar player made eye contact every once in a while, and I debated whether he was smiling at me or if it was just part of the act.

A loud bang against the door startled me and a woman in a fleece robe and fuzzy slippers appeared. "Jimmy. Damnit. How many times do I have to tell you? You're going to wake the whole neighborhood. All of you. Outta here. Or I'll call the cops."

Jimmy—the guitarist—nodded and we scattered out the door like a flock of scared geese. The mosquitoes buzzed, forming thick swarms above our heads as Gena and I made our way back to her house.

I lay awake that night, feeling the rush of adrenaline. I kept hearing the music in my head, over and over. Maybe that's what Gena meant about *the voices*. I heard Pangu, his voice moving over the prairie, along the river, singing with the symphony of crickets at night.

I imagined him awakening, lengthening his gigantic arms and legs, cracking through the black egg of his existence. He'd reach for me and call my name. "Jasmine. I'm here." *Stretch your limbs and save me, Pangu. I will bring you precious stones.*

Mother called the next afternoon, her voice weak and soft. "How's my girl?"

I held on to the cell phone so tightly that my fingers ached. "I miss you."

"Remember, we are never truly apart. I'll be home soon."

What home? I thought.

CHAPTER 33

DURING THE DAY, I helped Lida with chores. I washed dishes, changed diapers, mixed baby formula, scrubbed the floors. She taught me how to make a bed with hospital corners. Gena was right. But it was still better than going to school.

"This here's the proper way," she said. "They teach it in the military. Basic training." Together, she and I made her king-size bed.

"Where's your husband?" I asked, looking at a picture on the nightstand of the two of them.

"He's in Wisconsin, selling hoses and spark plugs. Auto parts salesman." She smoothed out the wrinkles on the bed sheet. "Gone a lot. Nice to have the extra help around here. Bet you're handy around the house."

"Sometimes," I replied. "If I feel like it."

"Mind if I call you Jay for short? Seems to fit you better."

"Sure. My mother calls me Jazz sometimes, but that's only when she's in a good mood. I mean a great mood, which isn't very often."

"Mamas can't be happy all the time. Tell you what, after this, we'll make chocolate chip cookies since the kids are napping. Work hard. Play hard. That's my motto. I grew up on a farm. Meals at noon sharp and another small one at three-thirty."

While the cookies baked, Lida and I sat at the table. She poured herself a cup of coffee.

"Want a glass of milk?" she asked as she headed for the fridge.

"I'd like that." I breathed in the comforting sweet smell coming from the oven.

"How's your mama? She doing all right?"

I took a sip of the cold milk she had set on the table. "I think so. She didn't say much."

"Hospitals drive me crazy. Can't stand the smell. I remember the day Gena was born. Arthur was out of town. I couldn't wait to get home again." Lida took a sip of the coffee. "Then there was the time when she was in the hospital. About a year ago. Anyway. That's another story."

An infant cried from one of the bedrooms. I snatched a couple more cookies and stuffed them into my pocket when Lida wasn't looking.

"Break time's over, Jay. Back to work."

I texted Rani pictures of the cookies. The daycare kids. One of a dirty diaper.

THE NEXT WEEKEND, I followed Gena out the window again. Instead of stopping at Jimmy's house, we went to an isolated wooded lot. A group of teenagers gathered around a bonfire, talking and drinking. The flames of the fire rose and fell, the wood snapping and crackling, reminding me of the inferno in our kitchen. But for once, I felt like part of a group, like one of the cool girls at school.

A dude with long blond hair down past his shoulders greeted Gena with a hug. He looked much older than her. They kissed, then disappeared behind a grove of trees. I sat on an old log by the fire, hypnotized by the dancing flames. I spotted Jimmy across the fire, staring at me, a bottle in hand. He waved, then walked around the bonfire—toward me. He wore all black, his eyes glassy in the firelight, cheeks skeleton-like.

"Kind of chilly tonight," he said. I recognized the label on the bottle, *Jim Beam*, a bourbon whiskey one of mother's old boyfriends liked to drink.

"Not by the fire," I said, feeling daring. I was used to dealing with men, not young boys like him. I could handle this.

He joined me, sliding close.

"Your music's dope. You make it look so easy," I said.

"Been playing since I was six." He took a swallow of the whiskey. "Do you play?" He swiped the back of his hand across his lips. "You seem like the artsy type." He smiled.

"I played the piano as a kid. Pretty bad. In fact, we don't even have a piano. Just my mother's idea. How long you had the band?"

"About a year now. It's been good for Gena."

"What do you mean?"

"She's been pretty messed up. That girl's got some nasty demons in her head."

"The voices?"

"Yep. She tell you 'bout them?"

He swung his hand around my waist and pulled me toward him. I braced myself.

"Sort of," I said. "Kinda freaked me out."

"Everyone has voices, though, don't you think? It's what you listen to—that's the problem."

Jimmy handed me the bottle of whiskey. I took a drink,

felt the liquid burn down into my chest. An owl hooted from the tree and above, stars sprinkled across the sky, taking the shape of my mythical father. A sense of ease flowed over me.

"Have more," Jimmy said. "Don't be shy. Before you know it, it will go down just like water."

"Like water, huh?" I thought of Mother. I took a sip, then another, and another until the blood raced up my neck and to my cheeks.

A few minutes passed and the night sky swam around me in circles. A couple next to us were making out in the grass. I felt Jimmy's hand move under my shirt, beneath my bra. I let out an uncomfortable giggle.

"You look like someone who has never been kissed before. Am I right?" he said.

"No. Been kissed lots of times," I teased. How the heck would he know the truth? I watched the hazy silhouettes creep along the trees then I let Jimmy kiss me, along my neck, on my lips. I pressed my mouth against his, smelled his breath, sour like vinegar. The whiskey. The wild grass and the woods.

Is this what Mother called love? Blades of grass tickled my ankles. I wanted silk flowers. *They live forever. Never leave you.* Then I started to cry, for no damn reason, but the tears streamed down my cheeks and I couldn't stop.

"What the . . . ? Are you kidding me?" He moved back quickly, like I had some sort of disease. "What's the problem?"

"Nothing." I wiped the wetness from my lips. "I don't feel so good." Then, not knowing what else to do, I took off and ran through the night, away from the party.

"Wait," Jimmy yelled. "Where you going?"

Nauseated, my head pounding, I found myself lost in the woods. I dropped to my knees near a tree and vomited. I rested my body on the cool grass. Frogs croaked and the crickets chattered. A cloak of black. Up above, the stars blinked and darted in every direction.

CHAPTER 34

THE NEXT MORNING I woke to the sun. I slid beneath the pillow and groaned. My head pulsed. I sat up and saw the ray of sunlight streaming in through the window, casting a spotlight on Gena. She was sound asleep, legs and arms sprawled in every direction, smudges of mascara beneath her lids, a dribble of spit on the side of her mouth. I flicked a spider off my thigh.

Lida barged into the room. The infant boy in her arms was screaming, his cheeks red. "Ain't no sleeping in, Jay."

She threw me a diaper and a container of wipes then plopped the infant on my lap. His bottom felt warm. Lida reached down and tickled him under the chin. "You little booger. You smell like crap. Jay's gonna clean you up. Thanks, hun." Then she left the room.

I rocked the infant back and forth, but he screamed louder. Basho whimpered and stretched by my feet. I set the infant on the floor and changed him, holding my breath as I ripped open the dirty diaper, using nearly all the wipes to clean him. Gena continued to sleep, snoring loudly.

At breakfast, Lida handed me a letter. "Looks like it's from your mama."

The return address said BRIARPLACE COUNTY HOSPITAL.

It had to be from Mother. Her language of love—words. Poetry.

I hid in the bathroom, Basho by my side as I tore the envelope open.

Dear Jasmine,
The walls are cold and stark here. No color. No movement.
Where are the silk daffodils? The deep red roses? I feel as
though I have died. They call this a place of healing? The
nurses stop in every couple hours to check my blood pressure
and give me medication. I feel helpless. Trapped. I need to
get out of here. The pills make me sleepy. I'm so tired.
I feel as though I have lost everything. I was wrong
about Cal. Are you well? Are they treating you fairly?
I'll be home soon.

With Love,
Mother

I went to Gena's room, grabbed a pen and paper and immediately wrote a letter back. I couldn't scribble down the words fast enough.

Dear Ma,
I'm fine. Eating hotdishy stuff and cookies. Only after
I do lots of chores. I learned how to change diapers and
make a bed the so-called proper way. I went to a party
and ~~drank way too friggin much~~. *I had my first kiss.*
When can I go home? ~~Do you remember what happened?~~
Do you think it's my fault Cal left? ~~I'm sorry, Ma.~~
I miss you.
Love, J

I crumpled the paper in my hand. Who was I kidding? Words were useless, just like empty broken promises. I tore the letter into bits and imagined them floating into the galaxy, my words spinning among the planets, then sucked into a big black hole. I couldn't breathe. She would never feel my sorrow and she probably didn't care. She was in her own stupid messed up world.

I envisioned the Phoenix rising from the ashes. Her voice a song in the wind. A flash of luminescent yellow, red, green, black and white, blinding me. My body shivered as I swallowed back tears.

LATER IN THE afternoon, Lida's husband showed up. A thin, scrappy looking dude with a brown mustache. He snuck into the house and crept up behind her, then draped his arms around her waist as she washed the dishes.

"You scared me, you son of a gun," Lida said. "How did it go?"

"Decent. The Lord taketh and the Lord giveth. I see you've added a child."

"Arthur, this is Jay."

He looked at me. "Welcome, Miss Jay."

After the daycare kids left, we gathered for supper. Lida made some sort of ground beef hotdish with mushy green beans. It reminded me of school and the cafeteria food.

"What brings you to us?" Arthur asked.

"I'm just here, till my mother gets, uh, back," I said, trying to avoid Arthur's gaze. His beady bird eyes freaked me out.

"I hear she's not feeling well?" he said.

Lida set her fork down. "She caught a bad bug. Be back to normal in no time. Right, Jay?"

"I thought you said something about an overdose?" Gena interrupted. "You said her mother lost it and went cuckoo."

The word "overdose" caught me by surprise. My gut wrenched with shame. "That's not true and she's better now," I lied. She wasn't better and I knew she had slipped into that dark ugly world of hers. "I just got a letter."

"Gena, any happenings with the band?" Arthur asked.

She let out a sigh. "Still working on the gig downtown."

"That old coffee shop's not going to bring in a soul," Arthur said.

"What do you know? It's a happening place," said Gena.

"Well, if you got your act together, you'd go back to school, finish your degree," said Arthur.

"You suck." Gena dropped her fork and left the table. Seconds later, a door slammed.

Lida's brows furrowed. "Quit your preachin', Arthur. Ain't doin' no good for nobody."

I stood, ready to follow Gena.

"You leave her alone, now, Jay," Lida said. "She'll be fine."

A few minutes passed. Basho barked and pawed at my leg, so I excused myself and walked through the garage to let him out.

Arthur's car was parked in one stall. I peered through the dirty windshield. A pile of calendars with photos of women in bikinis leaning against shiny automobiles lay scattered in the passenger seat.

"For my clients," Arthur said.

His voice startled me. I gasped and whirled around.

"You're a pretty one."

He approached me and touched my hair. I pulled away. "I need to let my dog out."

"Sorry about your mama. We're sinners. All of us. But the Lord forgives," he said.

"My mother doesn't need any forgiveness."

Turning from him, I beelined toward the garage door and headed outside with Basho, afraid to look back. The skin on my back prickled and itched. He had the wrong sinner. *I'm* the one who needed forgiveness. *I* had started the fire.

THE NEXT DAY, after Gena got back from school, we rode bikes down the road to a gas station. She bought a pack of cigarettes from the convenience store and I searched the aisles, looking for a gift for Mother. Buying a gift gave me hope of seeing her again.

I spotted a dainty crystal, tear-drop shaped, hanging by a thin plastic thread near the window. I spun it around and it seized the light, shades of purple, red and amber. I fingered my pocket for cash, but I only had ten dollars I had taken from our Mason jar.

I looked around.

Gena stood by the magazine rack, snapping her gum, flipping through a magazine. A customer was paying for something at the cash register. I shoved the crystal in my pocket. It didn't feel right, but I had good intentions. It was for my sick mother. She needed it. Now more than ever. I scanned the store for any witnesses. "Ready, Gena?"

She glanced up from her magazine, bangs swooping along the bridge of her nose. "Yup. Let's go."

I pedaled as fast as I could, right behind her, the sky clear and blue as we stopped at an elementary school playground.

We swung high on the swings, pumping our legs. Then we stopped and lit our cigarettes.

I pulled the crystal from my pocket.

"That's dope. Where'd you get it?" Gena asked.

"The store," I said. "I stole it."

"You're kidding. Shut up." She let out a low belly laugh.

"I did." I tilted my head back and waited for a cloud, a bird, to strike me.

"You're naughty." Gena exhaled a swirl of smoke.

"I'm a sinner."

"We're all sinners, Jay." She covered one ear. "The voices. They won't stop."

"Hear them all the time?"

"Kind of."

"Maybe you need to ignore them. Like my migraines," I said.

"That's different."

"How so? You hear things. I see things."

"Like what?" she asked. "Frick'n zombies?"

"Bright lights and crap."

Gena hesitated, then replied, "You should come to LA with me. That's where it's happening."

"Is that what you dream of?"

"Yeah. A place where the noise is so damn loud it drowns out all the voices in my head. How 'bout you?"

I took a drag on the cigarette and exhaled. "An endless sky. Clouds I can grasp in the palm of my hand."

Gena leaned down and plucked a blade of grass. "I hate Arthur."

"At least you have a father." I failed to mention my imaginary one. Maybe there was power in something not seen.

"Well, aren't you miss know it all."

"I'm just saying. Maybe you *should* go to LA." I straightened my back.

"You're right. I should. Seriously. What am I waiting for?"

"You seem happier when you talk about it. I mean, why not?"

"And what about you? It's not impossible, you know? Nothing is. It's only our minds that hold us back."

Images of mythological creatures appeared. The sky lit up a bright purple then faded. She was right. I thought of my mother. I thought of my biological father and my imaginary one. What was I waiting for? I desperately longed for the truth.

LIDA WOKE ME at 6 A.M. the next morning. She had a mop in one hand and a pail in the other. "Time to rise and shine, Jay. Bathrooms and kitchen today. Windows. When you've finished, mow the lawn. And your phone's taken away. Sorry, hun."

I sat up. "You can't take my phone."

"Oh, yes I can, missy. This is my home." Lida dropped the pail and mop. "Arthur wants you to have this." She handed me a wooden crucifix. Before leaving the room, she said, "I paid for the crystal you stole. The owner was livid. Arthur said you were trouble, but I didn't want to believe him."

"It's for my mother," I said, cheeks burning hot.

"Doesn't make it right, hun. Stealin' is against the law. I oughta make you do military push-ups. You need a good boot camp. Didn't your mama teach you?"

I slid the crucifix beneath the pillow. "It's not her fault. It was all my idea."

"I don't understand you, Jay. Different world you come from, girl."

Lida left and I looked over at Gena, a lump beneath the covers. Basho trotted over to her. "Hey, wake up over there. I need your help." I couldn't believe that Lida took my phone away.

I flung away the covers, shocked to find a couple pillows and a bunched-up blanket. No Gena. The curtain flapped against the opened window. She was gone. She had escaped. Free. I wanted to escape, too.

When Lida found out, she stormed to Arthur. "It's your damn fault she took off. For good this time."

"She'll come back. Damn girl won't survive a day on her own."

"She say anything to you, Jay?" Lida asked.

I shook my head. "Nope. Not a thing."

"She have a fight with the boyfriend? What happened?"

"I don't know." I went to the bedroom and opened Gena's top dresser. Nothing but a pair of socks. Cosmetic bag gone. No note. Nothing. She had probably left for LA—took the bus out of town.

Lida notified the police. We hung up posters of her frowning and I took off on a bike to Jimmy's, and then to the bus station, searching for her, but she was nowhere to be found.

At the house, Arthur cornered me, twisting the ends of his mustache while he spoke. "Look, young lady, since you've been here, things have changed. The stealin'. Gena being gone. You're the devil in disguise, tempting all of us. You're a bad seed. You need to leave."

Where was I supposed to go? Back to the burned apartment? I needed Mother.

Lida was in the kitchen, rolling out dough to make a pie. She avoided eye contact. "If you know where she's at, tell me. I can't stand the thought of losing her again."

"I need to go home," I said.

Lida dropped the rolling pin. She had flour on her palms, in her hair. She walked real close, nearly stepping on my toes. She planted her hands on my shoulders and shook me. Her breath smelled of coffee. "Home? You need to help us find Gena. You know, don't you? Little liar. Arthur's right about you. Tell me where she went."

"She just wants to play her music."

"Where?"

"I don't know."

"She must have said something to you. Little weasel. Just think if your poor little mama took off somewhere with one of her boyfriends. You'd want to know. Wouldn't you?"

"My mother would never do that. You're just pissed 'cause Gena took off. Maybe she's happier now."

"The heck she is. C'mon now, Jay. Tell me where she went. I won't tell her. Gospel truth."

"She probably went somewhere warm. Big city. That's my best guess."

I imagined her on the bus. Far away. She had guts. Courage.

"You're no help at all. I need you out of my home." Lida reached for her cell phone and disappeared into another room.

I packed my bag and sketchbook, just in case, even though I knew I couldn't leave yet.

The next day, Lida scurried about the kitchen—preparing macaroni and cheese, strapping a child into the highchair, wiping the kids' noses before the meal. In the living room, an infant boy was crying in the swing chair.

Her cell phone rang. The police had found Gena. She had hitchhiked and ended up somewhere in the middle of Wyoming. She ran out of cash and contacted Jimmy. A truck driver found her at a gas station, screaming and covering her ears. Arthur headed to the garage and took off in his car.

I felt all alone. I had no phone. And I had nowhere to be and nowhere to go.

CHAPTER 35

THE KEEPER ARRIVED later that afternoon and put my backpack into her car. I had been at this place way too long. I lost track of time. It seemed like forever.

A cloud of dust billowed in the air as we drove down the road. Basho lay on my lap as I watched the cedar rambler fade in the distance, nothing but the sound of the wheels turning over gravel. I concentrated on the road, how it abruptly switched to pavement, the car now gliding over the gentle swells of the highway.

"I have a few other places in mind that'll take you," the Keeper said.

I kept looking out the window, my vision growing blurry. "I want to go home."

"I know you do. But home isn't safe right now."

And that place was? Even Gena ran away. Their own daughter. And Lida took my phone.

"I do have good news, though."

I swept away a tear. "What's that?"

"You can see your mom today."

"Really?" I couldn't believe it. Time had washed over all the memories. Nothing seemed real anymore.

"At the hospital."

"She's still there?"

"Yep. And just so you know. Other places aren't going to deal with you stealing and being disruptive."

"I didn't do anything." I ran my fingers along the panel of the door. The thought of flinging it open and letting my body fly out was tempting. Did Mother know I was coming to see her? Was she better now?

"I know a nice family on the other side of town and they're willing—"

"Do we have to talk right now?" I said. "I mean . . . it's been a crappy day. Can I stop by my apartment? I want to grab something."

The Keeper shook her head. "I don't know if that's a good idea."

Lights flashed in my periphery. "I need to get my meds."

"Meds? For what?"

"I get migraines. They're debilitating. Like I can't see."

"Oh?" She frowned. "I didn't know that."

"Good thing I didn't have an episode there. Would have been an ER trip. So, if you don't mind. It'll only take a few minutes to grab it."

"All right. I guess the apartment complex said you'd be allowed to check over your things, now. I'll drop you off and fill gas. I'll be back soon to pick you up."

TO MY SURPRISE, the apartment door was unlocked. I opened the door and held my breath, afraid of what I'd be walking into. It smelled of soot and smoke and flames, but everything was left the way I remembered except for the awful remains of the fire. The damp, cold air burrowed through me. Basho sniffed the carpet and let out a short whimper. He wandered toward the kitchen and I followed.

An eerie silence filled the apartment. Lida's voice rang in my head. Gena's singing. A toddler crying.

I opened the refrigerator and a putrid smell wafted past, rotting chicken and molded broccoli. I found a jar of peanut butter in the cupboard and a box of saltine crackers. Then I heard a sound—a voice—and I whipped around.

"Who's there?" I took another bite of the cracker and walked with soft footsteps toward Mother's bedroom. "Hello?"

The bedroom door slammed shut and I jolted back. Maybe someone from the apartment office was cleaning up? Or maybe it was a burglar.

I grabbed a knife from the kitchen, just in case. Then I headed toward Mother's bedroom. I swung open the bedroom door and a gust of wind blew past, the sheer curtain flapping. Mother's clothes lay scattered everywhere. The dresser drawers were open as though someone had shuffled through them. A suitcase rested on the floor. Had someone been going through her things? I gripped the knife. Her pearl necklace was on the dresser next to the jewelry box.

I heard a muffled voice again. Like humming. This time I could tell that it was coming from the living room.

Something moved among the silk plants. The daisies and roses were still vibrant and untouched. A long slender hand reached out and I gasped.

"Ma?"

I dropped the knife.

She smiled. "Where have you been? I've been waiting for you." She wore a pair of baggy sweatpants and an oversized sweatshirt that I had never seen before.

Was I seeing things? I blinked. My legs grew weak and

I lunged toward her, my body collapsing in her arms. "I thought you were at the hospital?" She smelled medicinal and sterile. My mind raced. An overwhelming wave engulfed me. I wanted to tell her about the foster family, Lida, Gena. The kids. And Jimmy. I had kissed a boy. Things had changed. I wasn't the same person I used to be. I was even a thief. I stole a crystal from the convenience store, for her.

"You've grown up. I can tell." She looked frail, bruised, with needle marks in the crook of her elbow. What had they done to her? She still had the plastic identification bracelet on her wrist.

"I didn't know you were coming home. I was just going to visit you," I said.

"Good thing you didn't, because I left." She glanced at her wrist. "Now get this stupid thing off. I feel like an animal."

"Wait a minute. You mean you just left? You can't do that. They're going to come looking for you."

"They said I was good to go. Just check in—in a day or so."

"I'm not sure I believe you."

"There were no chains binding me. Now, take this silly thing off so I can feel like myself again."

I grabbed a pair of scissors and gently cut the plastic bracelet from her wrist. "The Keeper's coming back. She was going to drop me off at the hospital. She had to fill gas. Did you hear what I just said? She's coming back."

"Let's just give our worries to Pangu, shall we?"

"You didn't even ask about the foster home. Don't you want to know what I've been doing this whole time?"

"I had a feeling that you were fine."

"Well, I wasn't."

"What about me? Locked up like some animal in a colorless place. But I'm healed now. Being away gave me time to think."

I knew better than to believe her, especially when she reached in the wallet of her purse and pulled out three coins. *I Ching. The Book of Changes.* She tossed the coins on the table five times, scribbled down numbers on a piece of paper. She paged through the *I Ching.*

"It's Hexagram 49: Radical Change," she said. "It advises us to move. *Put away the past. Grasp renewal.*"

"What are you talking about?"

I recalled the last time she had consulted *I Ching.* She woke me in the middle of the night to count the stars. On that frosty snowy evening, we created angels, lying on our backs in a blanket of snow, swishing our arms and legs back and forth like windshield wipers, sending a flurry of snowflake fairies in the moonlight. This time, though, was something more real. More frightening.

She gathered the coins. "We're leaving right now. It's called transformation."

"We're in trouble, aren't we?"

"Don't say that. I've got it all figured out."

"That's what I'm afraid of. What do you mean we're leaving?"

"I've been doing a lot of thinking. Self-reflection, you might say. It's time for a change. We're going out west, to Oregon."

The *I Ching* had led us out to the desert one summer. All I remember was the cacti along the highway, getting caught in a dust storm, blinded by a channel of thick, blowing sand. We stopped at a restaurant and ate prickly pear fries and watched the sunset from the hood of our car before heading back home again.

"What's in Oregon?" I said.

"A new life. I know someone we can stay with. A relative, sort of."

"I didn't know we had relatives. Always thought it was just us."

"Don't be silly," she said.

Were we fugitives? Did she escape from the hospital? I would be running again from the Keeper. Our faces would be on posters. WANTED: DEAD OR ALIVE. And yet, the thought of leaving sounded thrilling, too. I could hear Gena's voice. *What am I waiting for? And what about you? It's only our minds that hold us back.* There was nothing holding me back from the truth, now. Nothing.

I went to my room, packed my belongings, again, which wasn't much—my favorite pen, colored pencils, another sketchpad. Clothing. It all smelled of smoke.

I wanted so badly to text Rani. But I couldn't.

Cross-legged on the bed in my room, one last time, I took in the bare beige walls, the water-stained ceiling, the smell of moth balls. Basho curled next to me.

In the mirror, my image dissipated in a ring of smoke, mystic, like a nymph in the forest.

PART II

CHAPTER 36

"WE'RE JUST GOING to keep driving," Mother said. "Till we hit the Pacific."

We drove westward, toward Oregon, in a beat-up Volkswagen Rabbit, a headlight out, which she refused to fix. We took a few boxes with some of our belongings—dishes, blankets, some clothes.

The "sort of" relative was named Auntie Chong. It's the first time I had ever heard Mother mention her name. "You know, the one who lives by the coast. She delivered you, for god's sake. Clipped the cord. And by the way, she rents out apartments. I talked to her and she's saved one for us, fully furnished."

I swelled with bits of hope mixed with buckets of fear.

We traveled beneath a bright new sky, Basho on my lap, cars and semitrucks flying past us at full speed while we crawled along, ten miles under the speed limit—to save gas. I reached in my pocket, forgetting I no longer had my phone. But now it didn't matter. Nothing mattered. We were letting go of the past. Grasping renewal. This is what I told myself, even though all I really wanted now was to feel safe.

What was renewal anyway? Another intangible feeling of euphoria? Like touching a cloud. Like living in a fantasy world? Princes and mythical gods.

I needed answers. Real answers.

From the rearview mirror Mother had hung a Chinese Dragon she bought at the Asian market. It was made of red and gold rice paper and swayed like a pendulum when she took a sharp turn, its long tail and sharp claws hypnotizing me into a trance. To my mother, it was hope hanging by a thread. To me, it was a reminder that *I* was the Dragon. A relentless being in search of the truth.

"Chinese Dragons are powerful creatures," she said as she kissed the tips of her fingers. "You're lucky. Don't forget."

It took us a day to reach Montana, where the sky opened to snow-capped mountains, hills blanketed with tall pines, intercepted by deep valleys, rivers and creeks, a backdrop of aquamarine sky. I pretended I had my cell phone and took snapshots along the way. The road stretched for miles and miles, with log homes tucked and sprinkled in the valley, partially hidden beneath the hills.

We were in the middle of Montana when a car suddenly stopped in front of us. Bumper to bumper. Mother swerved into the opposite lane and a vehicle behind us honked.

"Geez. That was close," I said.

She blinked a couple times, hands gripping the steering wheel. "We're fine. You worry too much."

Her recklessness made me question whether she should be driving. I fixated on the road ahead. "Yeah, but you almost hit that car. Two of them, in fact."

"No, I didn't."

"Yes, you did."

My palms turned sweaty as she switched lanes again at full speed and pulled in front of a semitruck. A horn blasted, and I saw the monstrous grill of a semitruck towering high above our car, ready to plow us over.

"Ma. What the hell?" I screamed, but she didn't answer. We approached another car. Closer and closer. "Oh my god. Slow down. You're going to get us killed."

I petted Basho and glanced behind as we swerved into the left lane then back to the right. I slumped in the seat as another car passed and the woman driver threw up her middle finger.

Mother didn't flinch. "Everything's going to be fine. Don't you see? It's all in the cards. *Fire over mountain. Stay true to your path and the universe will provide.*"

I peered between my fingers. "We're going to die."

"Quit it. You're making me nervous," she said.

"*I'm* making you nervous? Slow down."

She pumped the brakes. "I can't. Something's wrong."

"What do you mean?"

"They don't work. See?" She pressed the brake with her foot but we kept moving forward. I gripped the side door as we weaved in and out of traffic. The car accelerated.

"Let off the gas." I jammed my heels into curve of the mat as if that would slow us down.

"You're overreacting."

"No, I'm not."

"Yes, you are."

"You just told me that the brakes don't work and we're on a friggin' mountain passage." My voice escalated. "Are you out of your mind?"

I saw a gas sign up ahead, grabbed the wheel and veered off the interstate. I pulled the emergency brake and we lucked out as the road turned slightly uphill. We took a sharp turn, which sent our bodies jolting forward then back. Mother's forehead hit the steering wheel and the seat belt pulled tight against my shoulder until the car finally came to a dead halt in front of a gas station.

I unbuckled, flung the door open and stomped away from the car with Basho, rivulets of sweat trickling down my back and along my temples.

I spotted a motorcyclist straddled on a Harley by the side of the road. He was clad in leather and wore tear-drop sunglasses, a gray and white bandana wrapped around his head.

"What are you looking at?" I narrowed my brows. A few feet in front of me lay a dead groundhog.

"Watched the whole damn thing from here. Unbelievable." He squeezed a toothpick on the side of his mouth. A bushy gray beard covered his chin. "Haven't seen a stunt like that in a long time." He let out a long, low whistle.

"Leave me alone." I tasted a bit of gravel on my tongue and spat.

"I don't know where you two were heading, but it looked like the road to hell and back."

"Yeah. What was your first clue?" I said.

"Looks to me like you saved the day."

"The hell I did."

"Might be here for some time."

"Says who?"

"Says me." He smiled. "Just a hunch."

I pretended I didn't hear, and Basho and I followed Mother as she strutted toward the gas station, her purse swinging side to side. I thought of Carnie—Mother's car on the side of the road. Was there a connection?

She rubbed her forehead with the palm of her hand. The motorcycle dude was probably right. We were going to be stuck here for a while. I was still shaking, the adrenaline pumping through my veins. *Fire over mountain.*

Basho whined and yelped. Circled the ground with his tail half-lifted. "I think he's gotta go. Be right back, Ma."

From outside, I watched Mother's hands fling in the air, her mouth opening and closing. The man at the counter kept shaking his head. It didn't look good.

Basho took his time sniffing the grass, chewing on a piece of bark. He finally lifted his leg near a dumpster. Then pooped. Stretched and yawned. Wagged his tail. The Harley man stood close by, leaning against a tree, a pack of Winston Lights in his hand.

"Can I have one?" I asked. He passed me a cigarette and I held it between my fingers. "That your bike?"

"Damn right. Been riding since I was ten years old. Now I sell them." He lit my Winston. "Where you from?"

"Small town. Midwest."

"Drove a long way? Vacation?"

"My mother says more like transformation."

I thought he might ask a follow up question, but he just nodded like he understood. "Could be worse things."

"You're right," I said. "What are you doing here?"

"Resting. Got me a nice shady spot. Put on a lot of miles." He turned his head toward the gas station. "So, what's up with your car?"

The words spilled out faster than I could think. "Not sure. Something with the brakes. Surprised it got us this far. I don't know which is more unreliable, the car or my mother." I pulled Basho's leash. "You're a stranger. So, I can say that."

"For sure." The man clamped down on the cigarette with his teeth and reached in his pocket. "I think you're safe.

Here, hold out your palm," he said. Then he handed me a rolled-up wad of cash. "You seem like a nice kid. My family never had much when I was growing up." His lower lip jutted forward as he blew out a puff of gray smoke.

"Why?" I asked. "I don't even know you."

"Because I feel like it."

Speechless, I looked at him in disbelief. Was this some sort of joke?

"Better move along. Help your mama in there." He pulled the cigarette from my mouth. Crushed it on the ground with the heel of his boot.

I didn't know what to think, except that there was good in this world. You just had to open yourself up to it. Maybe Mother was right. I just needed to trust. Let go. *Grasp renewal.*

I RETURNED TO the station and approached the counter, where Mother was in the middle of a heated argument.

"Look, lady. I don't carry that part. Auto store's not open till Monday morning."

"I can't afford this," Mother said.

"Listen, that's all I can do for you."

Mother's voice softened with defeat. "I'll have to dig into my savings, I guess."

I fingered the cash in my pocket. I thought about Cal. All that had happened. What was next? For us? For me? The air pulsed a faint red. My fingers let go.

I slid my hand out of my pocket and didn't say a word.

WE WERE STUCK at the gas station, so we propped ourselves on the hood of the car, watching the sun dip behind the clouds, the sky bursting a fire-red and orange. Tired and sticky, we pressed our backs to the bug-covered windshield, shoulders touching as we waited for the night to approach.

"Too bad, it's a perfect night for lovers," Mother said. "The moon goddess is out. They say it shines brightest when she's there. An ancient Chinese tale."

I tried to imagine the goddess in the night sky, her skin white as talcum powder, smooth as chrysanthemums, the curve of her body in the shades of the moon, but all I saw was Mother's silhouette beneath a drape of light.

She slept in the front seat of the car and I crawled in the back with Basho. I reached in my pocket and unrolled the wad of cash. I counted the fives, tens, and twenties. I couldn't believe it. Seventy-five dollars total.

Two days later, after the brakes were fixed, Mother let out a yelp of excitement as she started the engine. We peeled out, tires burning against the pavement. She turned up the radio to an oldies station. "See, Jazz?" she said. "The universe does provide. We're on the right path."

Things were different this time.

I reached into my pocket and made a fist around the wad of cash.

I hope so, I thought to myself. *I really hope so.*

CHAPTER 37

OUR THREE-DAY TRIP turned into a week. We passed miles of open land, expansive stretches of fields, and timbered mountains, as our car hugged a curvy narrow road.

Mother promised things would be different this time. She reached for my hand and squeezed. Jazzy piano tunes drifted from the radio and the wind sang through her hair.

Did she really know where we were going? Was Auntie Chong real? Or was Mother just having one of her adventurous episodes again? Feeling invincible?

"Are we lost, Ma?"

"Of course not. We're entering a new world, that's all."

"And do you know where this *sort of* relative lives in the new world?" I stared out the window and allowed myself to disappear into the blue sky, the billowy clouds, the mountains in the distance.

Mother bit into her bottom lip. "Of course. Relax. You're going to love it there." She turned to me and smiled. "You hungry?"

I nodded. Basho lifted his head and yawned then curled into a tighter ball on my lap.

We pulled off at the next exit and stopped at a drive-thru for a burger and fries. Mother handed me the burger but she stole a couple of fries from the bag and sipped hot tea from a thermos as we got back onto the interstate.

Minutes passed and she didn't say much, stared straight ahead. I pulled out a sweet ginger candy I'd found in my backpack. The plastic wrapping smelled of smoke from the apartment fire but I unwrapped it anyway. It stuck to my teeth.

Out of boredom, I grabbed a magazine from the floor of the car, a glamour one I had stolen from Gena's room. I flipped through the pages, which were filled with ads of beautiful women in shimmering gowns and makeup, their images fading in and out. I thought of Gena and her voices telling her to run away. Now, it was my turn.

The road seemed endless. Finally, we passed a large green sign. It said WELCOME TO OREGON. I rolled down the window, let the air race through my fingers. We drove for a couple more hours along a narrow winding highway. Tall pine trees surrounded us and the air felt cool, infused with a damp, earthy smell.

I took in my new surroundings. I felt a strange kind of emptiness, leaving everything I knew, without a word, without a trace. We were fugitives on the run. We were WANTED.

I was tired of running away—from school, the bullies, the Keeper. Tired of being scared. Tired of not knowing what was real. Who was after us this time? I shuddered. Was there a warrant out for our arrest?

"We're almost there." Mother forced a half-smile, an expression that told me she was just as scared and uncertain as I was.

I observed the Chinese dragon that hung from the rearview mirror. I thought of the Keeper and the rabbit foot. I thought of my life with Mother and how at times, it seemed like everything depended on luck. The universe. A mythical god as a father.

"Closer to where?" I asked. To the truth? Discoveries of who I was? Where I came from? I was about to meet a *sort of real* relative, like the pictures on the wall at Rani's home. Auntie Chong. Family. My *real* father, maybe?

"It's Newbay," she answered. "You'll like it."

"How do you know?" I said.

"You were born there."

"I was? Cool."

I tried to sound casual. I believed her. There it was, the truth of where I was born.

"We left when you were just a child."

"And who is Auntie Chong?" I asked. "Is she really my aunt? You've never talked about her before." Or my real father, I thought. Like what about him? Is he still alive?

"She's sort of your aunt. Not technically. She's a very, very close friend. Close enough to call her *Auntie.*"

I felt a wave of disappointment come over me. So, she's not real either? *Close enough to call her Auntie.* What did that mean? Perhaps she didn't really exist. I decided to believe *that* when I actually saw her in the flesh.

Mother pointed out the window. "Look, you can see the ocean."

We drove on Highway 101, along the Pacific coast. It started to rain, a light drizzle, but then the rain came down heavier and pounded the windshield, the wipers moving in a frantic motion back and forth.

"Can you see?" I asked as I leaned forward, struggling to clear my vision as the radio hissed in the background. An angry bolt of light brightened the sky, followed by a clap of thunder. Basho growled, then rested his head back on my lap. "Maybe we should stop."

"It's fine. Only thirty miles."

"But you can't see," I said.

Mother reached down, fingering for her purse. "I need a Kleenex. A damn Kleenex."

"What's wrong?" I tossed her a tissue.

"Nothing."

I looked out the window, pretending not to see her cry.

She rubbed my knee. "I'm sorry."

"About what?"

"It's all so sudden. The move. But it's for the best. Don't be upset."

I rolled down the window. "I'm not." Raindrops swept in sideways.

"C'mon, Jasmine. Look at me."

"Quit it," I said. "Just leave me alone."

"Everything's going to be okay," she whispered. "I promise." She sniffled.

I wanted to believe her. I wanted to believe that our lives were about to change for the better. I wanted to believe that there would be no more secrets. No more lies. "Ma. I think I'm old enough. To like, know more about things. About our lives."

"Of course."

"Like, who is my father? I mean, is he still alive? Did he even know me?"

She turned silent. The rain tapped against the windshield.

"Ma?" Maybe this wasn't the right time. She was driving. It was raining. But I couldn't help it.

"So many questions," she muttered.

"You're driving. I get it. Later?"

She nodded.

The car accelerated and we drove on through the evening. I looked out the window at the large body of water shimmering infinitely in the distance. I'd never seen the ocean before. An overwhelming sensation burned in my lungs. This was real. We were not from the moon. The rain started to let up, a slow drizzle.

Mother glanced in the rearview window. "I think we have company."

Behind us, a white sport utility vehicle flashed its red lights and the sirens whined as Mother pulled over to the side of the road.

I held my breath. They found us. A flash of the apartment fire. A flash of Mother being carried away by the ambulance. A flash of the emergency room. Mother leaving the hospital. The Keeper.

A police officer approached.

He shined his flashlight into our car, swinging the beam of light to the backseat, then to the front. Mother squinted from the bright light. Outside, the rain had stopped and the moon broke through the clouds.

"Good evening," the police officer said as he raised his wire-rimmed glasses. Specs of rain glittered on the lenses. "Can I see your license, ma'am?"

"It's a full moon. You know what they say." Mother sighed and rummaged through her purse. She pulled out her license and handed it to him.

"You were going over eighty," he said.

"I was?" Mother raised both brows as I dug my fingernails into the seat of the car.

"Yes, ma'am." The officer pulled out his ticket book.

"That's impossible. We were flowing with traffic. You must be mistaken." She stared at him, innocent-like. "May I ask what you're doing, officer?"

"Writing you a ticket." The officer continued to scribble in his book. "Lucky you didn't hit that tree," he said. Then he focused the light on her license. "Long way from home." He handed the license back and took another quick scan of the car with his flashlight. "Where's your destination?"

"Newbay," she said.

"Vacation? Business?"

"Home." She handed him a business card.

"Chong's Apartment Complex? That's where you're heading?"

"Yes. Do you know where that is? I seem to be a little lost."

I gritted my teeth. She actually *didn't* know exactly where we were going.

"About seventy miles from here. Follow the interstate till you reach a fork in the road. Stay to your right and it's about a mile from there." The officer eyed Basho. "Allows pets, I hope?" He paused. "You look familiar. Have we met before?"

Mother tipped her head back and laughed. "We're celebrities. Don't tell anyone, all right?"

I exchanged a glance with Mother, the look of *we're in trouble*.

The officer scratched his chin.

"Look, officer," Mother pleaded, "just give me the ticket and we'll be on our way."

"Briarplace, huh? That's awful far away."

I looked past the police officer, to the water, the

shimmering waves. There was a raw excitement in the air. I could feel it in my bones. My deep sense of knowing told me that things were definitely shifting.

"We're kind of in a hurry. My aunt is expecting us," I said, trying to move things along.

"I see. And *that's* part of the problem." The officer finished writing, ripped out a sheet and handed it to her. His attention turned toward the rearview mirror. "Cool paper dragon."

Mother snatched the ticket from the officer. "Yes, its purpose is to bring good luck."

"Absolutely," he said. He glanced at me, then back at Mother, as if trying to figure out the answer to a riddle.

"Ma, I think I'm getting one of those nasty migraines."

"Oh, dear. Officer, we really ought to get going. We've been driving all night. Lack of sleep triggers her poor headaches. And you see that dragon? We really could use a bit of good luck right now."

I grimaced as if in pain and flashed him the most pathetic smile I could come up with.

"All right. All right. Put it this way. I could, no let me correct myself—should—give you a ticket with a much higher fine." He winked. "Consider yourself lucky. Why don't you follow me out?" He headed back to his vehicle.

"Unbelievable," Mother said.

I dug one foot deep into my sneaker, my big toe peeking from a small hole in the canvas.

"Well, you *were* speeding," I said.

"I call it driving with traffic." Mother gave my knee a quick tap. "We're lucky, aren't we?"

She fanned herself with the ticket, leaned forward and

kissed the paper dragon. She started the ignition and I turned up the music on the radio, letting it cut through us.

We followed the police officer out of the ditch, tires screeching as we hit the pavement. A few miles out, Mother grabbed the ticket and ripped it with her teeth. She held her hand out the window and let the pieces of paper catch the wind.

CHAPTER 38

WE ARRIVED AROUND midnight, dripping wet from the rain, standing in front of the apartment complex like two abandoned dogs. A stout woman with a broad nose and dark blunt bangs greeted us just outside the door, a ring of keys in her hand. She wore Batman flannel pajamas and matching blue slippers. She smelled of garlic.

"Auntie Chong," Mother said.

"I can't believe it. It's so late. I waited and waited. I thought something happened. I was ready to call the police." Auntie Chong hugged Mother. "It's been too long."

"Yes, too long," Mother said.

Auntie Chong pinched Mother's cheek. "You are finally here." Her attention shifted to me, her inquisitive stare, peering beneath the lenses of her silver frame. "This Jasmine? Wow. Hun sui."

I glanced at Mother and shrugged.

Mother smiled. "She says you're very pretty. Sui means pretty."

Pretty? Me? A flood of warmth raced to my neck and into my cheeks.

Auntie Chong winked.

I stared at this strange woman and desperately wanted to touch her, pinch her flesh, too. I wanted to make sure she was real. She shined like a bright orb, a treasure chest of memories. All at once, my sense told me that she was the key to my past.

Auntie Chong clicked her tongue. "You are all grown up. And skinny. You don't eat? I remember when you were a baby. You cried all the time. I think you were hungry."

Mother laughed. "She's still hungry all the time."

"Tomorrow we'll have tea." Auntie Chong leaned down and gave Basho a couple quick taps on the top of his head. He backed up, tail between his legs. "Cute."

"Wherever I go, he goes," I said.

"Oh, sure. As long as there's no pee-pee on the carpet." She chuckled.

"He's a good boy," I said.

She exhaled. Her nostrils flared. "You both look tired." She pulled a key off her ring and handed it to Mother. "Number 201."

"Thank you. I can't believe we are actually here," Mother said.

"A young couple moved out. They even left some furniture. You are most fortunate."

THE SUN FLOODED through the crooked blinds the next morning as I unpacked my belongings. The two-bedroom apartment complex was quaint, with two levels, a wood shingle exterior with white trim. It was furnished with two beds, a table in the kitchen with a couple of chairs, and a couch in the living room. The carpet was dotted with brown stains and cigarette burns.

I slid my sketchpad beneath the bed, mesmerized by the dust motes dancing in a ray of light. I took out the crystal I had stolen for Mother and hung it by the window. I thought of Gena and Rani and how far away I was from them.

I found Mother in the kitchen. "Come give me a hand," she said.

We unpacked dishes from a box. She traced her fingers along the rim of a plate as if it spurred a memory. "What do you think of our new place? Not bad, huh?"

"Yeah. It's cool." What I really wanted to say was that the truth was within reach, but I didn't.

I stood and peeked out the window, where a row of black-eyed Susan's beamed a bright yellow and a few pansies hung their heads from last night's rain. There was no ocean view. I wondered if the water shimmered all the time.

"I better go job hunting, or we'll end up on the streets, begging for food," Mother said.

"Not funny. I thought you said the universe would provide?"

She squeezed my arm. "You're right."

The fluorescent lights in the kitchen buzzed. I thought about the Keeper, the ambulance. Cal disappearing. We couldn't go back. I blinked several times, but everything turned wavy and distorted, tiny lights flashing in the periphery, my vision narrowing as if looking through a telescope. Acid rose from my stomach and into my lungs.

I ran to the toilet, knelt down and vomited. The migraine followed and I felt the pressure in my head build, ready to explode. I crouched down on the bathroom floor and buried my face in my lap.

Mother knocked on the door. "You okay in there?"

I squeezed my lids, said a Hail Mary. Mother pounded harder, louder. "Open the door."

Before I knew it, she was by my side, rubbing my back, my scalp. She smelled of Vicks VapoRub. "Look at me," she whispered.

I fought to open my eyelids as Mother dipped her index finger into the jar of Tiger Balm. She smeared the ointment along my temples and across my forehead.

"It's just you and me right now. Okay?"

"Are we done running? Nobody's going to find us here, right?"

"Nobody. We're free. Just you and me. The Phoenix and Dragon."

"Phoenix and Dragon," I repeated as I went to the bedroom and collapsed on the bed, head pulsating. I thought of the quote Mother had scribbled on the bathroom mirror. *The Tao is like a well: used but never used up. It is like the eternal void: filled with infinite possibilities.*

I woke to the powerful scent of burning incense, curls of musky spirits rising in the air. Mother at the kitchen table, a fan of five tarot cards in her hand. "It's the path to beauty and inward truth." She set the cards on the table.

I studied the card with the green dragon dipping its claw into a golden pond with floating lily pads.

Basho yelped and scratched the linoleum floor. He seemed a bit out of sorts with the new environment, barking at every sound. I filled his dish with water and Mother added a couple drops of Bach Flower Essence. Most people moved to pursue new jobs, or careers. But not us. We just followed the stars.

And my sense told me that the answers to the mystery of my life were here, waiting to be discovered.

CHAPTER 39

LATER IN THE afternoon, Mother sent me to the grocery store for soup bones. She wanted to make bone broth. Everything at Newbay, according to Mother, was walking distance. Along the way, I spotted a sign that read CALLOWAY BEACH and followed the arrow to a wooden boardwalk, which led to a sandy beach.

I stood in awe, taking in the vast ocean, the orange-gray horizon. The taste of salty air. A flock of seagulls waded along the shore, flapping their wings amidst the rolling waves. They squawked as if annoyed by my presence.

I kicked off my sneakers and buried my feet in the damp sand. White foam settled along the shore, a rush of waves pushing forward then receding, revealing pink and white seashells and blobs of jellyfish entangled in mossy seaweed. I tossed a pebble into the water, then watched as the waves swallowed it whole.

I spotted some dude maneuvering a prism-shaped kite in the air, his head cocked to the side. He was probably around seventeen, maybe eighteen years old. He had wavy brown hair and no shoes. He wore jeans and a white T-shirt that billowed in the wind. He peered through a pair of retro-black framed glasses, tendrils of hair sprouting in all directions like the tall prairie grass and wildflowers back home.

The kite soared in the sky, a cascade of loops, flips and turns, acrobatic moves against a gray-blue sea. I watched as he tugged and released the strings, jaw cutting a sharp line toward the sky, the kite a puppet, a marionette, as it pirouetted in the air.

The wind shifted directions and the kite suddenly turned toward me, like a war plane. It darted and swooped down. I ducked and dropped to the sand as it skimmed my head. The kite soared higher then dived to the ground again.

The dude dropped the strings and rushed toward me, his body staggered, bare feet digging into the sand.

My throat squeezed as he drew closer. I gripped a clump of sand, feeling like an idiot.

"Dang. I don't know what the hell happened." He stopped right in front of me.

I stood and brushed off the sand. "Your kite attacked me," I mumbled under my breath.

He shoved his glasses up. "What did you say?"

"Never mind." I noticed tiny whiskers along his upper lip.

"Strong wind. Enough to blow anyone over. Sorry. Didn't even see you. I was trying out a flat spin."

"Flat spin?" I asked, unimpressed.

"Kite stunt. Haven't quite mastered it. It's all in the timing. Helps if the wind cooperates." The kite had landed on its side, a bright orange wing pointing toward the sky. He winked—either that, or his eyelid twitched. I wasn't sure.

My embarrassment turned to snark. "You ought to look where you're going," I said.

"Hey. I did apologize."

"If you're already flying stunts, seems to me you have no excuse for hitting an innocent bystander."

"*Nearly* hitting."

"Whatever. You interrupted a moment." An awakening, I wanted to add. A *Zen moment*. It's the first time this Midwest girl had seen the ocean. The first time this girl had touched her feet on wet sand.

"I apologize. Didn't know you *owned* the beach."

"I never said that."

"You sure act like it."

"Look, just go back to whatever you were doing." I rolled my eyes. "Flat spinning."

"C'mon. Let's start over. Name's Blaine."

"Jasmine."

"As in the flower?" He grinned.

"No. As in green tea, my mother says."

"Names are intriguing. Sometimes, they tell a story."

He had an odd gaze. His right lid half-closed in a dreamy squint and his eyes were emerald green. He had a small, beak-shaped nose, like a bird, and brown bushy brows that nearly met at a perfect *V* in the middle of his forehead.

He let out a soft whistle through his teeth, then took off his glasses and examined the lenses against the sunlight.

I suddenly remembered the soup bones. Mother. "I gotta go."

"Wait." He turned his head in the direction of the kite. "I could use a hand."

He took off, waving me forward before I had a chance to respond.

I followed, my feet pressing into the sand. The clouds shivered in the sky.

He picked the kite up by the tip, slowly, as if it were a wounded animal. "Hold right here. The base and center strut, okay?" He handed me the kite then backed rapidly away. I felt the line grow taut as the kite lifted off the ground. "Now let go."

I relaxed my grip and watched the kite soar into the air. "How'd you do that?" I asked. He made flying in the sky look so easy. The wind slapped against me as I ran toward him.

"I'll teach you sometime. Deal?"

"Deal."

I suddenly felt on a high. I wanted to grab the kite string and let it pull me up into the sky. I longed to feel my feet lift off the sand, my body light as a feather. Was this how Mother felt that night on the Ferris wheel, one leg pointing straight in the air? Free.

Back at the apartment, I set the bag of soup bones on the counter, headed to my room and opened my haiku book. The pages were marked and wrinkled.

Dew Evaporates
And all our world is dew . . . so dear
So fresh, so fleeting.
—Kobayashi

CHAPTER 40

YOU'D THINK I'D have some memory of this distant relative of mine, this woman referred to as "Auntie." But it was as though she popped into our lives out of nowhere. I believed it was destiny.

I knew she had the answers to the questions I'd been searching for—but I was still afraid to ask.

Long silk scrolls of rivers and mountains covered the walls of Auntie Chong's apartment.

She sat on the floor in the living room, cross-legged in front of the television. Dressed in a pair of green shorts and an Oregon Ducks T-shirt, a bottle of Tsingtao beer and a bag of dried watermelon seeds at her side. She gripped a control in one hand and maneuvered the joystick while a Pac-Man figure trotted across the screen and through a maze. It made a beeping sound as it ate tiny dots along its path, avoiding the multicolored ghosts.

"That game's so retro," I mumbled as I looked through the glass of her small aquarium. Inside, green ferns waved back and forth and three goldfish swam about, unbothered and barely noticeable in the mossy water. I tapped at the glass. The fish darted back and forth.

Mother always wanted an aquarium in our apartment for good fortune. She came home once, all excited with a fishbowl and one goldfish. It died a week later, after I changed the water. Mother freaked out, calling it a bad curse, so I flushed it down the toilet.

What did Auntie Chong know about my mother? Me? Her past? Were there clues right in front of me? I searched the room for pictures. Anything. In the other corner of the room a cockatiel fluttered about its gold cage, pecking at seeds, scattering shells onto the floor. Birds offered harmony, good feng shui, according to Mother.

"Suck you, Blinky." Auntie Chong smashed her fist on her thigh. "He just ate my Pac-Man." She spat a seed onto the carpet, took a sip of Tsingtao and let out a low belch. She dropped the control to the floor. "Here, you play. I give up." She hobbled to the corner of the room, toward the cockatiel, hand to her rear as she gave her shorts a quick tug.

"Say hello to our guest," she said as she opened the cage. The cockatiel flew out, wings spread wide then gradually folding inward as it perched on my shoulder. I went still, felt a tickle against my cheek.

"What's he doing?" I asked.

"Eating your hair."

"Does he have a name?"

"Ming. I bought him for fifty percent off." She clicked her tongue. "Nobody wanted him. He bites."

"That sucks," I said.

"But he never bite me once."

"Maybe he doesn't like his cage."

Auntie Chong shook her head. "Impossible. This is his home."

Ming flew back to the cage.

Auntie Chong turned to me. "You hungry?"

"Always," I said.

I followed her to the kitchen. She started to chop Chinese cabbage, then onions and garlic, with a large cleaver.

"You live here all alone?" I asked.

"Husband died one night. Many moons ago. He was *very* smart. Told lots of jokes. Always smiling. Then a bad spirit took him away. One day, poof. He was gone."

"I feel like my father must have left the same way. I mean, I don't know if he's still alive. I don't know a thing about him." I laughed and studied her expression for any clues that she knew the truth. What about Pangu? Did she know about him? Maybe it was a way I could connect with her. I decided to test it out.

"Maybe he's like some mythical god or something. Who knows?"

To my disappointment, Auntie Chong didn't reply. She scraped the pile of chopped garlic and onion into the wok. The oil sizzled.

Questions flooded my mind: When was my mother here? Why did she leave? Did you know her when she was my age? What was she like? You saw me when I was a baby? Did you know my father? I held my breath, trying to keep them at bay, then exhaled. "So, you've known my mother for a long time now?"

"Yep. She's a funny lady." Auntie Chong added the cabbage and a handful of dried shrimp to the wok.

"How so?" I leaned in, eager for any little morsel of truth.

"She's a dreamer. A poetic mind. Lives in her own world." With chopsticks, Auntie Chong stir-fried the vegetables.

"You got that right." I thought of Rilke, the haiku book. Her notes. Her silk flowers. *I Ching.* "What else? What was she like when she was younger? How long was she here? Why did she move?"

"Whoa. Slow down, lady." Auntie Chong smirked and unplugged the wok. "I remember she didn't know how to drive. I taught her. Stick shift. She's so bad. We tried to climb up a small hill. The car rolled backward. Almost killed both of us."

I tried not to laugh. I knew I shouldn't, but the thought of Mother learning to drive brought on the giggles.

"I think you were in her tummy. She was excited to have you. And scared, too."

"Why?"

"Different country. Different customs. No family here. Just me."

"What about, you know—boyfriends?"

Auntie Chong sucked in her cheeks. I couldn't tell if she was holding back a smile or something else. "Many. Too many to count. Wow—so many questions. Oh, when you were in her tummy, she said you move too much. You had lots of hiccups." Auntie Chong sighed. "Anyway, sometimes I talk too much."

"No. Please don't stop. I want to know." I *have* to know. I felt trapped in a fantasy world. The aswangs were going to swallow me whole. I was born of something real. I belonged to this world and I'd prove it.

My father, he was—is—real.

"Maybe you go to the beach. It's a nice day."

"You'll tell me more, though. Right?"

"Right. Some time, I'll do that."

It was like she was filling my balloon of curiosity, my search for answers, and I could feel myself slowly rising in the air.

It's time, Pangu. Time to know the truth.

CHAPTER 41

BLAINE FLEW HIS kite along the beach. The sky was overcast and gray.

"Looks complicated," I said.

"Kind of like riding a bike, only without pedals." He tugged at one line, giving slack to the other. He gave a short, sharp tug and the kite flopped upside down and rotated around in a full circle before gracefully curving to the right and left. "Ever hear of Kite Chi?"

"You mean Tai Chi?" About a year ago, Mother and I took a free Tai Chi class offered at the Briarplace Community Center. She moved like a swan on a river, her body smooth and fluid. The Phoenix spreading its wings. And me, well, I was the ugly duckling. Lanky and awkward, hands and legs moving in opposing directions.

"Something like that," Blaine said as he raised his arms over his head, turning his back to the kite, twisting his body back and forth. The kite continued to perform a loop in the sky. "It's a technique I read about. Feel the wind. See what's around you." Blaine faced the kite. "Wanna try?"

"Are you serious? What if I crash it?"

"What if the sky really isn't blue? What if the world ends tomorrow?" He grinned. "Is that a yes or no?"

"I think so."

"Shit. You're hard to read."

"We just met."

"So?"

"How old are you?" I asked.

"Seventeen. You want to try or what?"

"Yes," I said. "But I've never flown a kite before. Especially one with two strings."

He moved the handles in front of me. "Here. It's a stunt kite." I took hold and he stepped behind me, moved his hands over mine. "You've got this."

I turned my attention to the kite, felt his hands pressing on mine. He pulled one string back, letting loose on the other at same time. The kite made a figure eight with big, lazy loops across the sky.

"Just pretend these are handlebars. Pull back on the right, Frankie turns right. Pull back on the left, Frankie turns left."

"Frankie?"

"Named the kite after my dad. It's the best memory I have of him. Him and me flying a kite. A diamond shaped one. It was real foggy that day, but we were out here, on the beach, flying a damn kite. Could barely see the darn thing. It was just speckles of color. But he kept saying, 'Look how the kite rises with the wind. It's all about having that wind. Support.'" Blaine let go of my hands. "Okay. Your turn. Easy now."

I jerked the line back. At least he had a memory of his father. The kite flipped over and crashed to the ground. "I'm sorry."

"About what?"

"Your father."

"I'm over it. Don't really remember much."

"And your kite. I've injured Frankie."

"We're even now. He almost took your head off."

"But I've ruined it."

Blaine smiled. "Nah, Frankie's tougher than that." He ran toward the water. "Come on."

I followed. When I reached the shoreline, I buried my toes in the sand, feeling the sudden warmth of the sun, which had come out from behind the clouds. "Can't believe my mother lived here before."

"She did? I live with my grandfather. Your dad from here, too?" he asked.

"Nope. That's a mystery."

"I like mysteries."

"Awesome. You can help me figure this one out, then."

Maybe Blaine and I were the same. Two lost souls trying to figure out their place in the world.

"Cheers, to mysteries." Blaine made a fist. "Long-lost fathers." He darted toward the water. "Cold water plunge. C'mon."

"Wait," I said, but Blaine was too far ahead, running against the waves. I dipped one foot in the water, felt a wave splash against my ankles, a cold rush. I stepped in farther, up to my knees, a billow of clouds mixed with sun swirling above.

The water was exhilarating. Refreshing and icy cold. I felt alive. *Grasp renewal*. I thought of Tao. *Like a well: used but never used up . . . the eternal void: filled with infinite possibilities*. I splashed in the water, let the waves push me toward shore. The sunlight filtered through a rainbow of colors. Purple, pink, green and blue. I felt like a kid.

A large wave suddenly knocked me down and I became

submerged in the water, head tilted back as I fought for air. Another wave pushed me forward and I went under, panicked. I swallowed gulps of salty water as I thrashed my arms. I heard the faint call of Blaine's voice, but then I went under again, my vision blurred.

Something lifted me up and out of the water. My feet met the sand. The waves roared. I coughed and gasped for air. A cold shiver raced through me and my teeth chattered.

Blaine was standing next to me. Leaning over and catching his breath. "You okay?"

"Yeah."

But truthfully, I felt stupid. Ignorant in that vast ocean. Nobody rescued me. *I* was the rescuer. *I* was the survivor. Hugging myself, I started to walk up the beach, away from Blaine, cold and wet, my clothes sticking to my body. I sat in the sand, pulled my knees to my chest and stared out at the water.

"You sure you're okay?" Blaine sat next to me.

"Leave me alone. We just moved here."

"I didn't know."

The ocean water dripped from my hair. I looked down. "I'm good." I had nearly drowned.

"I don't have a towel or anything. I wish . . ."

"It's fine."

Just don't leave, I wanted to say.

Inside, I screamed, *This is what it feels like to be alive. This is what it feels like to be real.*

CHAPTER 42

I FOLLOWED BLAINE to his grandfather's home, a small cottage along the beach. The door opened to a stone fireplace with amber flames. The air was infused with a strong smoky, cedar smell. His grandfather sat at the side of the hearth in a rocking chair, smoking a pipe. He wore baggy jeans and a red plaid shirt.

I stood in the entryway.

The grandfather leaned forward. "Good gracious, Blaine. What have you brought in?" He chuckled. "Who's your friend?"

Blaine kicked off his sandals. "Gramps, this is Jasmine. She just moved here."

"Pleasure to meet you, young lady." He tapped his wood pipe into an ashtray. "Why don't you get your friend some dry clothes, something toasty to drink." He turned to the empty chair next to him. "You going to say hello or what, Jeanine?"

"She'll talk to Grandma later," Blaine said as he winked at me. In the hallway, he whispered, "Gramps thinks she's still around. Sees her sitting in that chair where she used to knit for hours. She died about a year ago. He still talks to her." Blaine pushed up his glasses. "I know it sounds weird, but I swear she's still here. She's the one who lights the candle in the bathroom."

"Really? I believe you."

In a way, I did. I had a father named after a great god. I crossed my arms, suddenly aware of my clinging wet T-shirt and shorts. I yanked at the bottom edge of my shirt, loosened it from my body. Blaine disappeared into a room then reappeared with a large T-shirt and sweatpants.

"Here you go." He gestured toward the bathroom.

I pulled off my wet clothes and combed through my wet hair with my fingers. A glass bowl filled with seashells sat on the wicker shelf, a lit votive candle next to it, filling the space with the scent of vanilla. The flame flickered and I wanted to believe there was more to this world. Angels and spirits guiding and protecting us. Just like Pangu, a hero of the earth and sky.

I threw on the T-shirt, which was way too big. It smelled like fresh laundry detergent. The sweatpants dragged a bit on the floor, loose in the waist, but I rolled down the elastic band to hug my hips. I stole a peek in the mirror. I looked pale and half-dead. But I felt alive and invigorated.

I strolled into the living room and Blaine met me with a cup of hot cocoa. "Better?" he said. "Your first plunge in the Pacific. You rock."

"No kidding. The water's cold." I laughed and took a sip of the cocoa.

"Yeah, it is." Blaine smiled and I felt even warmer inside.

"Where you from?" asked the grandfather.

"Briarplace. Small Midwestern town." I glanced at the clock, realizing it was past dinner.

"Gets pretty cold there, huh?" The grandfather smiled, as if he'd been there before.

"Winters can be nasty," I added.

"What brings you out this way?"

"Uh . . . a relative. My aunt." *A new life. The truth. Finding out about my father. Finding out about who I am.* "Look, I gotta go."

"Already?" asked Blaine. "You just got here."

"Yeah. My mother's going to kill me." At the doorway, I waved. "Thanks, Gramps."

"Any time, darlin'," he said, smiling. "You come back again, you hear?"

I JOGGED BACK to the apartment, fighting off the jumble of thoughts in my head. When I finally arrived, I nearly smacked into Auntie Chong on the steps. She was hunched forward as she swept sand off the cement.

She dropped the dustpan. "Hey, lady. Where you been?"

"At the beach."

"You look funny," she said.

I tugged at the T-shirt. "Oh, I was swimming."

"Looks like you are drowning in your clothes." She eyed me up and down. "Water's too cold. Not like home. People don't swim in the ocean here."

"Yeah. Right. Where's my mother? At the apartment?"

Auntie Chong squished a spider with her fingers as it crawled along the crevice of the step. She scooped up a pile of litter into the dustpan. "Your mama asked if I knew where you were. Her forehead wrinkled. Right here." She pointed to the space between her brows. "You better hurry or maybe her worry will turn to anger."

"My mother doesn't worry. I don't know what you're talking about." I pulled at the drawstring of the sweatpants, tightened the waistline. Then I caught Auntie Chong's curious stare, her head tilted to one side, waiting for me to continue. I shifted awkwardly. "I mean, I'm older now."

Auntie Chong nodded like she understood. "When I was young, I fell in love with a woman from Taiwan. My parents did not approve. We broke up. Then I married Billie, a Korean, from New York City. My ticket to America. He liked the water. So here I am. What about you?"

I laughed, realizing how silly I must look right now in Blaine's clothes—what she must be thinking. "I just like the ocean," I said.

She nodded and mumbled something to herself—words I didn't understand, then said, "Don't worry. I can keep a secret. But you better get back to your mama."

AT THE APARTMENT, the pungent smell of Mother's cooking surprised me. It had been a while since she made *real* food. She stood at the kitchen counter, chopping slices of gingerroot and scallions. Curls of steam drifted into the air from the kettle. Piano music, jazz, played softly in the background from an old tape recorder.

"Where you been?" she asked.

"Out by the water. Why?"

She lifted her head. "The beach? By yourself?"

"Yeah." Back in Briarplace, I came and went as I pleased. Why was everyone interrogating me?

"You better be careful. Those waves are strong. They'll suck you right in. You don't know how to swim very well."

"I do now," I lied. The waves *had* sucked me in. I was still terrified—but at the same time, it felt intoxicating to plunge into the cold water.

"Really?" Mother slid the large knife along the cutting

board, pushing the gingerroot and scallions into the kettle. She looked stronger now. More confident. "Ginger. It cleanses our body. Once thought to be a healing gift from God." She let the soup simmer a while longer, then scooped steaming broth into two bowls.

"You know," she said. "I was really worried about you. In fact, I started to get kinda angry. Then I told myself—she'll be back." She stared at me and I barely recognized her for a second. "We're not in Briarplace anymore."

"I'm sorry. I lost track of time. I won't do it again."

"And look at you. What are you wearing?"

"I got wet. Found these on the beach." Talking with Auntie Chong gave me courage to improvise. I wasn't ready to share my newfound friend with Mother quite yet. Saying it out loud might turn it into a dream instead.

"I see. You like it here?" Mother asked.

"I do." She was right. The universe had provided. Things felt like they were getting better. There was the ocean. And Blaine.

"Well, just don't get too comfortable. Okay? Life is forever changing."

"Why? Did you hear from the Keeper? Or the hospital?"

"No, Jasmine. Quit worrying about that. Everything's fine."

She made things sound so easy. *Quit worrying. The universe will provide.* Why wouldn't my mind shut up? I took a deep breath and redirected my thoughts. Answers. I needed answers.

"So, you said I was born here. Can you tell me more about that time? I mean, I don't remember anything about being here."

"You really want to know?"

"Yes, I do."

"I was young and foolish. You were just a baby. I was far away from home. I didn't know what I was doing. I wanted a better life for us."

I saw the ocean, the wind in her hair, a baby cradled in her arms. Me. "What else? Maybe you can tell me something real . . . about my father. You said you would," I added quickly.

Mother stirred the soup and blew into the bowl. Plumes of steam drifted sideways. "Your father? Pangu? I hear him call out to us as we speak."

"No, Ma. Please."

Her stories were like a castle in the sand. The tide was coming in. A tsunami about to swallow everything.

"He's everywhere and anywhere. Maybe what I tell you is better than the truth."

"That's for me to decide, don't you think? I'm not a baby. No more stories about creatures that don't exist."

"Ah, but I hear the gods. They're angry. Especially the all-powerful one. His blood flows across valleys and mountains."

"Enough, Ma."

Just then, her cell phone rang. She answered, her voice shifting to a soft whisper. She nodded. "Just a second." She turned to me. "Give me a minute, Jasmine. Why don't you go change."

I walked away, Blaine's T-shirt brushing against my back, and I was suddenly aware of the baggy sweatpants. I could be anybody I wanted to be. I wondered what it would be like to be a little girl again, have her tuck silk cherry blossoms in my hair. But I wanted them to be real, so I could smell the sweet perfume. I wanted it all to be real.

CHAPTER 43

THE CLOUDS PARTED the following afternoon and the sun broke through, revealing patches of bright turquoise sky. I brought my charcoal pencils and sketchpad to the beach. I had the sudden urge to paint the ocean and everything else, in case it all went away. It was as if the mere act of painting would lead me to the truth. Or at least capture some essence of it.

I painted to forget, too.

I planted myself as close to the water as I dared. The tide rushed in as a group of seagulls wobbled along the shore. Basho barked and darted toward them. They scattered and flew in the air. I flipped open my sketchpad and began to draw the water, the clouds, white cotton against the azure sky. The ocean roared back, its waves desperate, like fingers, pulling me in.

In the distance, a long-legged bird—curved thin neck, bluish-gray with rusty colored thighs—stood motionless on a rock. Everything flowed from my pencil with ease. The movement of the water. The ebb and flow of the tides.

An hour must have passed when a shadow spread across the page, covering half my drawing. Basho growled and barked, then wagged his tail.

"Not bad."

I dropped my pencil, scooted on my bottom in a semi-circle, and hugged the sketchpad.

"The clouds are good. And I like the way you drew the blue heron."

"It's you," I said.

"Don't sound so excited." Blaine slid his glasses up with his index finger. "Do we have to start all over again? Blaine. Jasmine. Nice to meet you."

"What's up?" I grabbed the drawing and stood.

"Am I supposed to be impressed?"

"About what?"

"You being an artist and all."

Artist? No one had ever called me that before. I pretended I didn't care, that I heard things like that all the time. "I'm just doing this for myself, that's all. Think whatever you want."

"You should draw me."

I laughed. "Why?"

"Intriguing subject matter? Plus, I want to see how an artist like you perceives me."

"You sound serious."

"I am." He took off his glasses and shook his head back and forth, fluffing his hair with his fingers. "I'm working it, can't you tell? I want to redefine myself." He put his glasses back on.

"I don't usually draw people." But then I thought about all the sketches of my imaginary father, a fantasy figure I had conjured in my mind. Did that count?

"C'mon. Just try. Draw me." Blaine sat in the sand, legs crossed as he lowered his gaze. "Okay, I'm ready."

"Whatever. This is silly."

Still, I sat down again and flipped to a blank page in my sketchpad. A light breeze ruffled the edges of the paper as I outlined Blaine's face, his forehead, his chin, his cheekbones. "Now look at me."

Blaine's lids flung open and the intensity of the moment surprised me. I grew suddenly aware of my fingers grasping the pencil, the edge of the notepad touching my arm. My breath quickened. With my charcoal pencil, I drew each pupil, switching to saturated blues and greens.

"Let's take a look." Blaine leaned close. "Hey, not bad. Not bad at all. I mean it's a start, anyhow."

I covered half the page with my arm. "I'm not finished. Sit."

I filled in another section of his cheekbones and took my eraser, rubbing out the shadows, playing with the light. The drawing blossomed to life.

"Almost done. Still need to add some final touches." I studied the sketch, admiring my work. The sun faded beneath the clouds. "Time's up." I closed the sketchpad.

"Hey, I want to see what you've done."

"Not yet. When I'm finished, I'll show you." I gathered my pencils, brushed off the grains of sand from my legs. When I looked up, he was gone. Nothing remained but his footprints in the sand.

"Blaine?" Where did he go?

How odd. How rude. It made everything feel like a dream.

I walked along the beach, the tide splashing against my ankles. Up ahead, a couple of young boys skipped along the shoreline, chasing a bright kite shaped like a fish. It darted back and forth in the air in spastic motions, making a kaleidoscope of color. I turned my attention to the blue heron, wings spread across the sky, neck tucked in, moving in slow, deliberate wing beats.

When I returned home, I found a note stuck to the door. *Be back in a few hours. Mother.*

There was an opened box in the middle of the living room, surrounded by a few pots and pans, scattered utensils. She must have been unpacking. I started to put the pans in the cupboard but decided to go to her room instead. I dug in a box of clothes and discovered Mother's favorite porcelain lamp shattered at the bottom. Next to the lamp was a photo album wrapped in a towel. I pulled it out and opened the book.

The pages were warped, worn on the edges, and gave off a musty odor. I held my breath as I looked at the pictures— a handsome but stern-looking Asian couple, a photo of a garden with palm trees and blooming orchids. But the sepia photo of a little girl with long pigtails caught my eye. She had a solemn expression and wore a white ruffled dress, matching anklet socks and shiny black shoes.

I turned the page and something fell to the floor—a thin blue envelope. I opened it and found a letter, its writing barely legible with no date. I examined it more closely. Chinese characters were mixed with English on the page. All I deciphered was: *It is all for the best. This child will never know.*

CHAPTER 44

I BECAME OBSESSED with my new discovery. On the couch with Basho by my feet, I ate one dried mango after another, paging through the old photo album, looking for more pictures of the little girl, but there was only the one photo. I read and reread the words, trying to make sense of it all. *It is all for the best. This child will never know.*

My lids grew heavy, the shriveled fruit, sweet and tart. Mother was still gone. It was past dinner, and the fridge was mostly empty—a jug of orange juice, an open can of lychee fruit, and a stalk of rotting bok choy. The clock on the wall ticked.

An hour had passed when I heard humming and singing coming from the foyer of the apartment. A jingle of keys. I slid the photo album beneath the couch as Mother pranced in, her hair swept in a bun. She had on a beige dress with a crimson floral print, one I'd never seen before, and on her feet, red stilettos. I breathed in the scent of floral. I couldn't help but notice her makeup, the black eyeliner that made her eyes shrink, the sparkling blue eye shadow.

"I'm starved," she said as she kicked off her stilettos. "Let's go out, get something to eat. I know this cool café downtown."

"I'm not hungry. In fact, it's past dinner. And what's with

all that stuff on your face? Where were you?" It was my turn
to interrogate.

"You won't believe it, Jasmine. I found a job, downtown
at the Jade Buddha. The owner, Mr. Jin, is someone I've
known for a long time." She removed the clip from her hair.
"I can't believe he's still there." She rubbed my shoulder. "I
left such a mess, but I needed to go for a drive. Serendipity
you might say, that I just happened to pass by the restaurant." She pulled me close. Her hair smelled of grease and
Chinese food. I wanted to hug her, but my body stiffened.

The clouds hung heavy downtown, the faint glow from
the streetlights peeking through as we passed several shops.
A boutique with a mannequin in a sun dress, a French
bakery displaying croissants, scones and berry tarts, and a
manicure salon, its window splashed with bright fluorescent
writing that read PRETTY NAILS HEAD TO TOE.

Mother didn't stop talking. She was on a high, waving
her arms in the air, repeating the incident over and over:
how she walked into the restaurant and how surprised she
was to see the owner, an old friend of hers, and even more
surprised when he offered her a job.

We reached a little café with frosted cube windows.
Sam's Diner. The inside held '50s décor with pictures of
Elvis, a black and white checkered floor, vinyl red booths
and a jukebox in the corner belting out rock and roll. On
the back wall hung a chalkboard with a handwritten list
of pies: apple, blueberry, strawberry-rhubarb, coconut, and
lemon cream. I ordered a burger, fries and a chocolate peanut butter milkshake.

"I thought you weren't hungry," Mother said after our
food arrived.

"Changed my mind." I looked around. "Must be almost closing time."

Most of the tables were empty except for one, where an elderly man in a trench coat, hunched over the counter with a mug of coffee. Mother drummed her fingers on the table and sipped on the blueberry shake she ordered, smiling like she had just won a prize.

"So, what do you think of the place?" she asked.

"It's cool." I reached for a french fry. "I like the music."

"Changed a lot since I've been here. Used to be wood paneling and no Elvis."

"Really? I can't picture that." I glanced in the direction of the jukebox. "Just like I can't picture a lot of things lately. Like being born here." Elvis's voice dimmed in the background. "Why'd we leave again?"

She sipped her shake again, then put it down on the table. "I never had a true home. I told you, remember? You were just a baby. And I was young." She twisted the corner of the napkin. "Young and scared."

"About what?"

"For gosh sake, I had *you* for crying out loud. And I was only a child myself."

"Then why'd we leave?"

"I was restless. I wanted to start all over again. Maybe I was searching for something I could never have."

I straightened. Here was another chance. "And what about my father? Tell me. I'm old enough now. You promised you'd tell me."

I knew the real answer was there, hidden in the forest of pine trees, the misty gray clouds in the sky. She crossed her hands, rested her elbows on the table then leaned forward. "I've taken care of you. What more do you want?"

A slow rage brewed inside me. "I want the truth."

"I'm your mother. Isn't that enough?"

"I just want to know what happened to him."

Should I tell her about the picture I found? The words sat on the tip of my tongue. But then I could see that she was feeling threatened. Her entire body shutting down.

"Jasmine. Please." Her voice shifted. Almost pleading.

She wanted me to forget. Forget about the past. And I despised her for it, I realized, for the little secrets she kept. I wanted to shake it out of her. I could hear the ocean waves crashing against the shore. I wished for the truth. I felt robbed. Betrayed. Fire rose in my belly. I held the power of Pangu. "I need to know who I am," I said in a harsh whisper. "Where I came from."

She inhaled sharply. "All right."

"All right?" I repeated.

"It's just . . . I felt trapped. I was far away from home. I was all alone. I didn't know what to do." She paused and part of me wanted her to stop talking. Part of me was afraid of the truth. But I continued.

"And what about my father? Is he still alive?"

"Remember in the beginning of the universe? How heaven and earth were inseparable? I think he draws near."

I gripped the cold glass of my milkshake. I wouldn't play along this time. I felt something inside me snap. A volcanic eruption, spewing out molten rock and magma. The truth. I needed the truth. "I'm too old for that now. The big black egg. The hairy giant who cracks the shell, splitting apart heaven and earth. My father, the immortal man. The god of the universe."

"You must leave the past alone, Jasmine. We have to move on."

"I need to know about my father. You owe me that much."

"Owe you?" Mother's voice cracked. "My gosh. Where is all this coming from? Don't talk to me that way. Did you hear a word I said?"

"You always think you know what's best for me. Maybe you don't." I choked on my words. "Maybe I *don't* feel safe at home. Maybe I'm afraid of fire. Of hospitals." A lump formed in my throat. I could barely breathe. "Maybe I'm afraid . . . of being left alone. You should have gotten rid of me." I pulled out the picture from my pocket as well as the letter and slapped them on the table. "And who is this?"

Mother blinked and stared. "Where did you get that?"

"I found it in the photo album. Who is she?"

"She doesn't exist anymore." Mother started rocking back and forth. "It's me. When I was an innocent little girl." She was looking at a ghost of herself.

"And what does this mean?" I pointed to the letter, the words. *It is all for the best. This child will never know.*

"I'll tell you more another time. I promise."

Exhaustion overtook my body and I slumped back into the diner booth. Images of Pangu, my heroic father, flashed before me. I shoved the dream away, longing for reality to emerge.

ON THE WAY back to the apartment, Mother and I stopped at the beach and stood by the water. The waves slammed against the shore in a white fury.

"It's freezing," I said as I hugged myself.

"I'm trying to do right for us," Mother said.

"I want to go back now."

She took a step toward the water and grabbed my hand. "To our knees?"

I squeezed her hand. I felt small and vulnerable. I felt like a little girl again. I took a couple steps and continued until she and I were both knee deep, the icy cold waves slapping against our legs.

Gray clouds slid across the night sky. The moon was a beacon of light reflecting off the water. My mother and I were swimming in the ocean, not knowing where we were going.

We were just riding the waves, hoping something, someone would find us.

CHAPTER 45

MOTHER WORKED OVERTIME at the restaurant, an attempt to get us back on track financially. Auntie Chong gave us a break on the rent, but still, we struggled. We washed our clothes in the bathtub and ate tuna fish sandwiches and rice porridge for dinner. Auntie Chong visited, unannounced, with plates of noodles and rice.

"You need to eat," she said. She invited me to her apartment to play cards and video games. "Too much solitude. Not good for a young mind." She thought I might get an anxiety disorder, something she saw on an afternoon television show. Little did she know that I was already diagnosed by the counselor. Too late.

The one she should have been worried about was Mother. Ever since our conversation, she'd been acting strange, isolating herself and constantly talking on the phone. She'd shoo me away then continue to talk in soft whispers. I thought maybe it was the electric or telephone company threatening to cut us off. At dinner, she picked at her food, barely talking before quickly leaving the table to clean the dishes.

At first, I blamed it on the argument we had, and then I wondered if she was going into her funk again. But then she started dusting and vacuuming the apartment, washing the windows and rearranging the couple of silk flower arrangements she had in the living room. Basho watched her with concern as she raced about the apartment. I'd catch her looking out the window, as if expecting someone or something.

The Saturday evening after the diner incident, Mother insisted I go to work with her. "There's no food at home and Auntie Chong keeps telling me not to leave you and Basho alone at night." I think it was more out of guilt that she brought me with, especially after our fight.

A large bronze statue of Buddha greeted us in the entryway as we arrived at the Jade Buddha restaurant. Candle flames wiggled in the dim light. Paper lanterns of red and gold glowed as Mother and I walked past customers, laughter and conversation filling the room as I followed her to the back of the restaurant to Mr. Jin's office.

"He said you can stay in here. Be good, now." She kissed me on the forehead and disappeared.

Mr. Jin's office smelled of cigarettes. Magazines and papers were piled high on both sides of the desk. I grabbed a magazine of Asian movie stars and made myself comfortable, flipping through pages, unable to read it yet intrigued. I propped my legs on the top of the desk and pictured myself as one of the actresses, dressed in designer clothes, surrounded by famous men, fancy cars.

My stomach growled; I hadn't eaten since morning. I pulled open the top drawer of the desk and discovered a bag of M&M's tucked in the far back. Before I had a chance to rip open the bag, a lean man with black coarse hair walked in, a cigarette dangling from the corner of his mouth. He snapped his fingers and spoke through clenched teeth.

"Look who's here. Keeping an eye on your mother, eh?

Make sure she keeps busy." He tapped the burning ashes of the cigarette into an ashtray on the desk and ran his fingers through his dark hair, creating tall peaks, like a rooster. His button-down shirt hung loose around his torso, nearly untucked from his trousers. "I'm Jin."

I shut the drawer. "I was just looking for a pen." I glanced at the bag of M&M's.

"She made you come here?"

"Who? My mother?"

"Yeah. Yeah."

"Sort of. I guess I didn't put up much of a fight. Beats being all alone with Basho in the apartment."

"Tonight could get long. She closes. Might as well settle in."

"Great." I grabbed a pen, rapped it on the desk.

"Your mother said you draw. An artist, she says. Me. I have no talent. All business. Always business." His hand shook as he took a slow draw from the cigarette.

I scanned the room. A picture of a temple rested at a slant against the wall. Next to it, a framed photo of when the restaurant probably first opened—a much younger Mr. Jin in a navy blue suit and tie, smiling in front of the building.

"You've been here a long time?" I asked.

"So many years. I've lost count. Your mother came back. Just in time."

"You knew her before?"

Mr. Jin laughed. "Yes. Forever." He knelt and opened the bottom drawer of his desk and reached inside. I smelled the cigarette on his breath, a hint of cologne. "Here. You like sweets?" He tossed a handful of rice candy onto the desk.

I sprang up, realizing I had made myself a little too comfortable in his chair.

"Sit, sit. Want a soda?"

"That would be cool." I unwrapped the rice candy. "Sorry. Kinda hungry."

"Eat. Eat. I send someone in. You relax." Mr. Jin grabbed a can of soda from the mini-fridge and handed it to me. "You are much different than I remember. No longer a baby."

He laughed and left.

The evening dragged and I wished I was back at the apartment. I did a few push-ups on the floor, just to get the blood pumping. Smoked one of Mr. Jin's cigarettes. I thought about Blaine and the picture I drew of him. How he called me an artist. Then I shuffled through the other magazines, and half an hour later found myself rummaging through the drawer of his desk again.

I found a photo of a man and a woman standing in front of the restaurant. The man was definitely Mr. Jin, only younger. I could tell. He had his arm around the woman's shoulder. They were caught in the middle of a laugh. I looked closer and realized it was Mother. I barely recognized her. She looked much younger with bangs and shorter hair.

Just then, one of the servers barged in, carrying a plate of fried rice and sesame chicken. She snapped her gum. "The boss sent me. Famished?" She set the plate on the desk.

"I am." I stood and reached for the fork, inhaling the sweet spicy aroma.

She had on a black apron and beneath it, the same green silk dress Mother wore, only it looked sort of odd against her blond hair and auburn roots. She had Pillsbury white, doughy skin, spotted with acne on her forehead and cheeks.

She must have been in her twenties. She pulled out a handful of dollar bills from the apron.

"Cheap bastard." She counted the cash. "Just got done serving a table of ten. The asshole tipped me three bucks." She stared, wide-eyed, batting her pale lashes. "Geez, girl, you look just like your mama. It's frightening."

"Seriously?" No one had ever compared me to Mother before. At least I had more sense than to coast down the highway without brakes, stand on a Ferris wheel with one leg in the air. Love a man who leaves you stranded and alone on your wedding day. I stabbed a piece of chicken with my fork and reached for the soda.

"Like you both have the same mojo. Know what I'm saying?"

"Heck, no. Are you kidding me?"

"Calm down, girl. Ever thought about it?"

"About being the same as my mother? I mean, she's beautiful and all, but . . ."

"C'mon, girl. Screw our physical selves. We're all floating through life, atoms bouncing off one another, connecting only when we feel the charge, the ionic bond." She paused. "What brings you here?"

"My mother and aunt are afraid too much alone time will have an impact on my mental health. Some call it guilt."

"That's intense."

"For sure."

"What are you drinking, girlfriend?" she asked.

"7UP." I took a sip and swallowed.

"Let's get you a *real* drink."

I followed her out the door and passed Mother, who stood by a table of four. She looked radiant in her snug dress as she held a pot of tea. I was still mad at her for not telling me the truth about my father.

The server took me to a small bar area with a granite countertop and above it, glass shelves stacked with bottles of liquor, bowls with wedges of lemon, lime and maraschino cherries. She poured a couple tablespoons of thick syrup into a glass, adding soda and orange juice.

"How old are you?" she asked.

"Eighteen." I watched as she added a couple shots of vodka to the glass. I decided I had the right to be eighteen for the night if I wanted.

"You look so young. I remember when I was your age. Couldn't wait to leave home." She added a cocktail parasol, hung it along the edge of the glass. "This one's on me." She grabbed another glass and filled it with club soda.

"Cheers," I said as we clinked glasses.

She raised the drink in the air. "To freedom."

"Freedom." I took a moment, admiring the pink color of my cocktail, the fancy parasol. I felt taller. Smarter. I twirled the paper parasol between my teeth and crossed my legs. Time passed as I enjoyed each sip of the sweet liquid. The lights dimmed and glowed in hazy halos. Halfway through, a warm tingly feeling swam through my body.

"Look at you. You're red as a beet." She laughed, exposing her pierced tongue, the silver stud.

I swirled the drink. "Want some?"

"I'd love to." Her doughy cheeks contracted. "But Boss will be mad. He's been more agitated since your mama came. Wants everything perfect."

I glanced at her name tag. Victoria. "So, Vick, what do you know about Mr. Jin?"

"He's my damn boss. My paycheck."

"He knew my mother. Before, I mean. A long time ago."

"God, I think they go way back. I mean *way* back. Shit. They could be brother and sister."

"Or husband and wife? Father and Mother?" I said.

"Who knows? Like I said. We're just atoms, colliding with one another." She tapped her fingernails on the counter. "It's that time. Back to work. Girl, do me a favor and drop your glass to the kitchen. Dishwasher will take care of it."

I finished the last bit of liquid, the instrumental music dulling my senses as I walked toward the kitchen, glass in hand. The lights blinked on and off and everything looked wavy, like the ocean. I heard Mother's voice, the flirty laugh. I nearly bumped into her as she busted through the swinging doors, her fingers balancing an oval tray with several plates of food.

"How you doing? Did you get something to eat?" She whisked past. Honestly, why did she bother asking?

The cook stood at the long grill, frying a cluster of broccoli, carrots and cabbage. He nodded and smiled, forehead damp with sweat. His apron was spotted with large brown greasy stains. On the opposite side, the dishwasher leaned against a sink full of dirty dishes. He turned around.

"Jasmine?"

I knew I recognized that head full of hair. "Blaine? I didn't know you worked here."

He lifted his soapy hand, pushed up his glasses, leaving tiny bubbles at the bridge of the nose. "First job I could find this summer." He swiped his hand across his apron. "You?"

The room started to spin and I swear I saw two of him for

a second. "My mother. She, uh, works here." Was I tripping on my words? I couldn't tell.

"Suchou? She's your mother?"

I nodded, pretending not to be annoyed.

"No kidding? We were just talking about your trip here, the car, and how the brakes went out. What a ride."

I didn't like the way he said, "we," and it left me with a sick feeling in my stomach. My imagination lit on fire. Blaine and my mother standing side by side, Mother flipping her long hair over her shoulders, tilting her head back and laughing.

"She's unbelievable." I laughed. "Vick told me to drop this off." I set the glass by the sink and the room continued to spin.

"See you later?" he asked.

"Maybe. I mean, we'll see." I felt off-balance. I waved and left the kitchen before I embarrassed myself further.

The door to Mr. Jin's office was partially shut and through the narrow opening I caught sight of Mr. Jin and Mother. They stood close, facing each other. He said something and she inched away. She looked strange, with an intensity I'd never seen before.

He handed her a white envelope. Mother took it and headed toward the door.

As the door swung open, I backed away, nearly losing my balance.

Mother looked up, startled. "Jasmine?"

"Who'd you think it was? The bogeyman?" I started to laugh, more like a cackle, and it caught me by surprise.

"Are you okay?" she asked.

"I'm good."

She grabbed my arm and yanked me forward. "It's time to go."

The lights in the restaurant dimmed, and the music in the background—a flute and a depressed guitar—grew faint. Mother marched ahead of me at a rapid pace, strands of hair falling loose from the bun on the back of her head. I kept seeing Mr. Jin, how he looked at Mother. How she looked at him.

A line of rice paper lanterns blushed a faint red and gold. Colored moons beneath an evening sky.

CHAPTER 46

MY HEAD PULSED from the evening's drink. I had fallen into a restless sleep. Nightmares of Mr. Jin licking Mother's nose. Electrons and protons exploding in outer space. In the middle of the night, through the thin wall separating our rooms, I heard Mother pacing back and forth, the floor creaking beneath her feet. She was on the phone, her voice switching back and forth, from high to low octaves.

Silence followed. I listened for any signs of her leaving. Outside, I swear I heard the sound of an ambulance. A red siren flashing. A vision of an empty bed. Me all alone, beneath the artificial light. I reached for Basho, clutched him to my side. He panted and kept licking my chin and cheek.

I woke up the next morning in a cold sweat and went into her bedroom. She was asleep, her hair covering her face like stringy seaweed.

I longed to be close to her again, like the time when she was on a zafu, sitting lotus position, her palms up. She said she needed to clear her monkey mind and I tiptoed past, careful not to interrupt her peaceful place, but she opened one eye, tapped the floor by her side. I joined her, in silence, breathing in the woodsy scent of incense, feeling safe and comforted. Afterward, she tickled my side and we laughed till we couldn't breathe, our bodies warm on a carpet of rectangular light.

I gently shook her arm. "Are you okay?"

She groaned and turned to the other side. "What do you want?" she muttered.

"Nothing."

She sat up. "What do you need?" She sounded irritated, upset.

"Nothing."

"My gosh, Jasmine. What time is it?"

"You look kind of freaky when you sleep," I said.

"I'm resting, my dear."

"I heard you on the phone all night."

"It was important."

"Are we in trouble? Was it the police? Are they looking for you?"

"For god's sake. Everything's fine. Quit worrying."

I didn't believe her. And lately, Mother's phone calls were more frequent and secretive, and I worried that one day the police would come after both of us and throw us in jail.

Mother sat upright. "You liking it here?"

"You already asked me that. Remember? What's not to like?" I stared at her, waiting for another question that didn't make sense. Waiting for the temperature in the room to turn chilly.

"It rains a lot in the winter."

"It's summer right now." I shrugged. "Who cares."

"I've been doing a lot of thinking lately. Maybe it's time for a change. I'm not sure how long we should stay here."

"What are you talking about? We just got here. We're

starting over, remember? *I Ching?* Forget the past. Grasp renewal or whatever it was."

"What would you say if we headed back to Briarplace?" she said.

"Briarplace?" My entire body clenched. For a second I couldn't breathe. "Are you joking?" What was she thinking? We had just arrived and I was liking it. A lot. Being by the ocean made me feel alive. I was painting and drawing more. In the fall, there might be a school that I didn't hate. And of course, there was Blaine.

"It's just a thought." She stared out the window. The curtain rippled from a light breeze. I wanted to smack her, wake her up from whatever crazy thoughts she had floating in her head.

"Maybe you should just meditate on it, see what the universe wants," I said, in a tone I knew she wouldn't appreciate.

"Lovely thought. Life is an ever-changing universe."

Go ahead and live in your fantasy world. Shouldn't her spiritual practices save us? I grew quiet, afraid where the conversation might go and part of me really didn't want to know.

CHAPTER 47

AT THE BEACH, the tide was low. A few seagulls squawked, flapped their milky wings in the air, swooping downward, skimming the surface of the water. Bright tangerine and purple sea stars clung to boulder-sized rocks, surrounded by clams and coral buried in the reef.

I planted myself on a piece of driftwood and opened my sketchpad, listening to the roar of the ocean. Basho sat by my feet, nose lifted, ears perked. I spotted Rani in the sky, flames of fire, the foster home, Gena. A couple days ago, I had found a box. It had pictures of Cal and the three of us together. Wrapped in tissue was the diamond ring and a box of matches from a restaurant where we had eaten. The memory faded in and out amongst the waves.

I concentrated on the clouds, how unruly they appeared, shifting languidly across the sky. I started to draw a smear of concentric circles along a horizon. Long hair. Strong jaw. Hairy chest. Large biceps, arms holding up the sky. Feet planted in the earth. Pangu, my father.

I felt a tap on my shoulder and spun around.

"We need to stop meeting like this," Blaine said from above me. "My picture done?"

"Not quite."

"Why not?"

"I'm still working on it. Do you live at the beach or what?"

"I come out every morning and check on the seagulls. Take Frankie for a spin. Depends on the conditions of course."

I dropped the sketchpad to the sand. "I like it here, too. Reminds me how small I am, how insignificant."

"Small, yes. Insignificant, no."

"But the ocean's so big and vast. Doesn't it make you feel like there's more out there? I mean, I feel in awe, and kind of fearful, too."

"Of what?"

"I don't know."

"Sea monsters? Water creatures?" Blaine folded his arms.

I giggled. "Sounds silly. Maybe I'm afraid to be swallowed by its vastness. Sometimes I wonder what my purpose is in this world. Don't you?"

"That's deep. Maybe you think too much. And you can't be so afraid of everything."

"Like you're real tough, Blaine."

"I'm always aware. Never know when there might be a damsel in distress."

"Oh, please." I rolled my eyes.

"I'm kidding." Blaine turned all serious, like somebody had socked him in the gut. "I bet you're brave. But I'd protect you." He looked past me and I felt bad then for mocking him. "Anyway, you got my eyes wrong."

The sketchbook was sprawled open on the sand.

"They're too close together. And the nose . . . hmmm." Blaine crouched down, staring at the picture. "But, the body, right on."

"Sorry. It's definitely not you." I snatched the book and covered the page.

"Who is it then?"

"No one you know."

"Is it your boyfriend? I'm good at keeping secrets."

"I can't tell you. You're going to laugh."

"I won't," he said.

"Promise?" I didn't know if I trusted him enough to tell the truth.

"I promise."

Blaine sat down next to me. Our fingers touched, pinkies entwined. "Okay," I replied. "It's an imaginary person."

"Cool. I dig the creative process."

"It's my father," I said. "My hero. I've never actually met him. But, this is how I've always known him and imagined he would be. When I was little, my crazy mother fed me all this crap about him being a god and I believed it."

"Sounds kind of cool to me. Your dad's a superhero."

"Whatever."

That's when I told Blaine everything. Don't ask me why, but it all came spewing out—about Cal and Mother, the Keeper, the fire, and how I stayed at a foster home. How she and I were in big trouble from the law. He listened, in a curious and kind manner.

"Your turn," I said.

"Well, for starters," he said, "I hate goodbyes. Don't believe in them."

"That explains things. Why you just disappeared. Like a ghost. I thought you were rude for not saying anything."

"Ever since I can remember, I've had this reoccurring dream about me and my dad flying a kite at the beach. The kite soars into the sky. My dad grabs my hand and I hold on real tight as we float higher and higher. Then his grip loosens, and I start calling him back as he vanishes, past the kite, toward a clearing in the clouds."

"I have a similar dream," I said. "Only it's my mother flying far away into the big blue sky. She scares me sometimes. I'm afraid we're going to be apart again."

"That sucks. Well, my stepfather's always telling me what to do. How to live my life. And he can't even hold a job for more than a month. I don't know if I can take it much longer. I feel like I'm going to lose it sometimes." Blaine's voice sort of cracked. "I'm saving money now. I want to be an architect."

"Sweet," I said.

"How about you?"

"I don't know. Guess I'm still trying to figure it out. Haven't given it much thought."

"Artists. Always searching. Let's go for a walk."

Blaine grabbed my hand and we hiked along the beach, looking for seashells, Basho trailing behind.

"One thing I do know is that I'll meet my father one day," I announced, looking toward the horizon.

"How do you know for sure?" Blaine asked.

"I just do." I really didn't know if I would ever meet my father or if he was even alive, but maybe he was closer than I thought. In my mind, he was still larger than anything I could ever imagine, a hero, his blood turning to rivers and seas.

"We better find him, then."

"*We?*" I asked.

"Don't you think you might need a little help? It can be sort of a mystery. Bonnie and Clyde."

"They were outlaws. Robbers."

"Right. Then Sherlock Holmes and . . ."

I pulled out my best English accent. "You know my methods already, dear Watson." I felt the warmth of the sun against my cheeks. "My mother and I are fugitives, running away from our problems. Maybe if I found my father, we'd just stay in one place. She's already talking about moving again."

"You just got here," Blaine said.

"Right? She's nuts."

"Well, maybe you've found where you belong. For a little while, at least."

"Here, you mean?"

"Yeah. Here. Newbay. What's it like where you come from?"

"Flat prairie, a few hills and rivers, but I've seen mountains and the desert from the seat of my car. Who knows when my mother will decide to pick up and move again."

"I hope you stay this time," Blaine said.

"Me, too."

"You know, you look just like your mom."

"I do?"

"Only prettier."

I felt my face flush. No one had ever told me I was prettier than my mother.

CHAPTER 48

BLAINE AND I came up with a master plan to search Mr. Jin's office for any clues of the past: pictures, notes, letters, receipts.

"So, Mr. Jin is the suspect, huh?" he said.

I nodded. "I think he could be a relative. I don't know. Maybe he's the answer." I held back from telling Blaine what I was truly thinking. Perhaps he was my long-lost father. I just didn't have any proof yet.

Outside the restaurant, we peeked through the windows like a couple of spies, watched Mr. Jin pass by as he greeted customers at the tables. Mother scurried about, taking orders, filling water glasses, removing plates.

Near closing time, we headed to the back of the restaurant, Blaine by my side. We waited in the parking lot, crouched on our knees next to a dumpster.

It was fairly quiet, except for the crickets chattering and the wind rustling through the lone pine tree that stood awkwardly in the center of the lot. A foul odor rose from the dumpster like rotting fish, the wind carrying a sweet and sour greasy smell from the restaurant. Only a few vehicles remained in the back parking lot.

I shivered in the damp cold. I stood, stretched, then crouched back down. The night sky dazzled with a thousand pinpoints of lights. The bright moon reflected off the damp pavement.

"I don't get it, Jasmine. Maybe there's a better plan. Do you really think Mr. Jin has the answers?" Blaine said.

"It might be him," I said.

"Wait a minute. Like your *father*?"

"Yeah."

"You said he was maybe a relative. You didn't mention anything about him being your father."

I felt the weight of Blaine's words.

"Think I'm nuts?"

"No. Not at all. It just doesn't make sense. Why would your mom come back here after all these years? Does he even know?"

"Nothing in my life makes sense, Blaine. And to tell you the truth, I don't know. It's just a hunch."

"So, we're here on a hunch."

I glared at him. "You're the one who was all excited. Bonnie and Clyde. Sherlock Holmes. If you want out, then leave." I paused and waited for him to tell me how crazy I was, but when I glanced over, he was scraping his shoe against the pavement. "What are you doing?"

"Damn it, there's gum on the bottom of my shoe."

"Leave it alone. You're going to give us away. Keep it DL."

"DL? What's that?"

"Down low. Inconspicuous."

"I get it." He pulled out a pair of sunglasses from the front pocket of his shirt and put them on. "How about this? I feel like a spy. A real-life CIA agent."

I shook my head. "What the hell are those for?"

Blaine grinned, like he was proud of himself. "I can see

clearer now. Way better with my sunglasses at night. X-ray vision. What do you think, Sherlock?"

"Real cool. Honestly, you're ridiculous."

He shrugged. "Just trying to lighten things up." He pulled off the sunglasses.

I flinched when I thought I heard something. "Quiet, okay? This is serious."

After a half hour passed, my lids grew heavy and I tried to separate the real world from my imagined world. Blaine stood, stretched one leg then the other. He paced back and forth behind the dumpster, hands in pockets.

"Sit down. Someone's going to see you," I whispered.

"There's no one around. It's closing time." Blaine scratched the side of his head, glanced up toward the sky.

I searched my brain for encouragement. I wasn't ready to give up. "What happened to the whole spy thing. The CIA?"

"We've been squatting by a stinky dumpster for the last hour. Just saying."

I felt my irritation bubble up, ready to explode. "Sit . . . please." I pointed to the ground as I scanned the area for any movement.

Blaine continued to pace back and forth. "Maybe we should go." He squatted. "It's getting late. And to be honest, I don't know how much longer I can stay here."

"Shhh," I snapped. "A few more minutes. He should be coming out any second."

"And then what?"

"Not sure, but I'll figure it out. Trust me."

Another half hour passed with no sign of Mr. Jin. I was just about to surrender when a figure appeared near the exit.

"Here he comes," Blaine said.

I could barely recognize him, but I knew it was Mr. Jin by the way he moved his hips with a sort of strut, like a model walking down the runway.

Blaine's jaw dropped. "Well? What are you waiting for?"

I watched Mr. Jin head toward a brown Camry, a cigarette clutched between two fingers. He flicked a few ashes to the ground.

I made a fist. "He looks like he's in a hurry."

Blaine laughed. "You better catch him, then."

"Shhhh. He's going to hear you."

"That's the point? Right?"

"No, you idiot," I muttered.

"I thought you wanted to meet with him? Ask him a few questions?" Blaine paused. "Did you just call me an idiot?"

"Like I'm going to walk up to this man and say, *Hey, by the way, do you know who my father is?* Or— *Are you my father by any chance? That's* nuts. I don't know why I brought you along in the first place."

"Wow. Okay."

"Sorry. It's just—I need to figure this out. You have the keys, right?"

"Keys?"

"I thought you had access to the restaurant."

"I'm the dishwasher."

"Never mind. He's going back inside," I said.

We watched Mr. Jin saunter back in.

A few minutes later, Blaine gestured toward the restaurant. Mr. Jin reappeared with Mother. I stiffened and listened.

"I'm so glad you're back, Suchou."

"Me, too."

"You told her yet?"

"I will, Jin."

"She's going to find out one way or another. You know that."

And before we knew it, they hopped into the Camry and drove away.

"Did you hear that, Blaine?" I said.

"Uh. Yeah. Shit."

I was dizzy. "They were talking about me. I know it."

Blaine waved a pair of keys in the air. "Guess I do have them."

"What are we waiting for? Let's go."

We walked through the back entry of the restaurant to Mr. Jin's office. I searched the drawers of his desk while Blaine rifled through a file cabinet.

"What are we looking for?" Blaine asked.

"Not sure," I said.

"So, I'll know it when I see it?"

"Yeah. Hang on. Look at this."

I discovered more old photos beneath a pile of bills. Mr. Jin with a younger Auntie Chong. I recognized the bangs, a razor straight line across her forehead. Next to her was Mother with a protruding stomach. In another drawer I found a picture of a baby in a stroller.

"Is that you?" Blaine asked, leaning over my shoulder.

"I don't know. I think I'm going to puke." I sank to the floor with the picture in my hand. "Let's go."

"You sure? Did you find what you were looking for, Sherlock?"

"Maybe. I don't know." I felt sick inside, like I had discovered something that wasn't meant for me to see. Maybe

I didn't want to know the truth. Maybe I didn't really want to know who my real father was.

My insides swirled in a tornado of emotions.

I shoved the baby photo into my pocket, and Blaine and I left the restaurant.

CHAPTER 49

I STUDIED THE baby photo all night, as if it contained some hidden cryptic message. The chubby cheeks. The wavy brown hair. Could this be me? Why was I getting so emotional? Would the picture lead to answers about my childhood?

A wave of sadness swept over me. An urgency. I wanted to protect this innocent baby and shield her from harm. Just like Pangu protected me. I wanted to wrap my arms around her and tell her everything was going to be all right.

I placed the photo in my pocket, careful not to bend the edges, and headed to Auntie Chong's.

I was getting closer to figuring out the mystery of my father.

Once a week, she and her lady friends gathered at her apartment for tea, rice cakes and several rounds of mahjong. When I arrived, five- and ten-dollar bills were already piled in the center of the card table in the living room where four ladies sat, a row of colorful tiles in front of each of them. The air was filled with the sweet scent of talcum powder, floral perfume, and Bengay rub. From the corner of the room, Ming whistled and hopped about the cage, tail feathers wagging.

"Pung!" a woman with short brown hair squealed as she revealed two matching bamboo tiles.

"Pung," Ming squawked. "Pung."

Shiny jade jewelry adorned the woman's wrist and neck. She smelled of gardenias, her cheeks red and shiny, her hands slightly deformed and arthritic looking.

She waved me forward. "Jasmine, come here. You call me Auntie Pearl, okay?" She pinched my cheek. "So pretty. I'll take you shopping some time. Yes? I have a seamstress. I'll have her sew you a nice dress."

Auntie Chong reached for a tile, placed it on the wooden rack that sat in front of her, alongside the other tiles.

"What's up?" she asked.

"Not much," I replied. "Been hanging out with Blaine. And I found something kind of interesting."

"Oh? Haven't seen you for a long time." Auntie Chong sounded a bit annoyed. "I think you forget about me already. Boyfriends take a lot of time."

"I'm sorry." I frowned and rubbed her back. "He's not my boyfriend, though. And it's only been a couple days."

Another woman with her hair in a bun laughed. "You mustn't tease this poor girl so much. It's okay, Jasmine."

"Yes," Auntie Pearl said. "She's just giving you a hard time. Your auntie loves you."

A slender woman with hair down to her waist, just like Mother's except for the silver color, sat next to Auntie Pearl. She pulled me close and whispered, "Shall I tell her to leave you alone?"

Auntie Chong chuckled. "Don't worry. This girl is tough. She can handle anything. She swims in the ocean."

I adored Auntie Chong, especially at this moment. My mind latched on to the word *tough*. Yes. *See Pangu. I'm just like you. Tough. Strong. Powerful.* I elongated my back. Made a fist. A surge of energy ran through me. I suddenly had the courage to inquire about the photo. I pulled it from my pocket and slapped it on the table in front of Auntie Chong. "Quiz time. Do you know who this is?"

She flinched, then made a clicking sound with her tongue. "Where did you get this?"

The ladies leaned forward.

"So cute," Auntie Pearl said.

"It's me. Isn't it?" I said.

"You think so?" Auntie Chong picked up the photo. "You don't recognize yourself?"

"I just want to make sure."

She pointed. "See the red cap? Your mama made you wear it all the time."

"Interesting," I said, staring at the red beanie. "Red for good luck. Right?"

"She always wants to protect you. Don't forget." Auntie Chong turned to the ladies. "Anyway. This game reminds me of the time Billie and me went to Vegas." Her voice grew louder. "You've heard of Las Vegas? Gambling? Billie and me made lots of money. Blackjack." She took a bite of the rice cake and they continued to play, voices escalating, laughing, making bets, tossing crumpled dollar bills on the table.

Auntie Pearl waved her hand at me. "Hey. I think you are good luck. You must stay. I insist."

The four of them continued playing mahjong while I stood by Auntie Pearl's side. For good luck.

After another round, I tucked the picture in my pocket and left. I felt a sense of satisfaction, validation. The picture *was* me. I had lived here before. No wonder it felt like home.

• • •

BACK AT THE apartment, an eerie quietness hung in the air. The sweet scent of jasmine rice.

A soft giggling came from Mother's bedroom. Was she on the phone? No. I noticed a jean jacket hanging on the back of a chair in the kitchen. A pair of cowboy boots. I paced back and forth on the linoleum floor, sand scratching the bottom of my feet. I spotted a yellow rose, a real one, on the counter. It was still partially wrapped in tissue paper.

I pressed my ear against her bedroom door. Mother giggled again. Then I heard the low, soft voice of a man. Then the door flung open and she jumped back at the sight of me. She clutched the edge of her robe and slid it across her chest.

"Oh, god, Jasmine. You frightened me." She shoved her hair to the side.

"Who's here?" I asked. I held my breath. The air grew heavy.

Mother pulled the door shut behind her. She leaned close, the sourness of her breath overwhelming me.

"You won't believe who came to visit," she said.

I shifted my weight from one leg to the other, dug my toes into the carpet. Before she spoke, I turned. I didn't want to hear his name. Didn't want to think of him here.

Mother reached for my shoulder and swung me around. "Don't be like this."

"It's him, isn't it?"

"Please understand. It's complicated, okay?"

"You're just messed up. What's so complicated? Things are different now. Can't you see? We escaped. You're free, Ma." I stared at the door. Reptilian claws. Amber eyes. The aswang was back for blood. "How did he find us?"

"He called."

"And you actually answered? Why?"

"We had to discuss something very important."

"Like what? We just got here and you're going to take him back. Just like that. After all he's done?"

"He's just visiting," she said.

"In your bedroom."

"Don't do this."

I threw her a mean-spirited look. "Don't be the sane one? Is that what you're saying?"

"You don't understand. You never will."

The door swung open and Cal appeared, barefoot, wearing jeans and a striped shirt, partially untucked. "What's the trouble?" He reached for Mother, but she wriggled free from his grasp and stormed into the kitchen.

Cal combed his hair back with his fingers. His eyes flashed amber and back again to a greenish-blue. He took a step toward me. "Just let your mother be. She'll calm down." He took another step. A hissing sound like a snake followed. "You okay?" Red squiggly vessels ran along the whites of his eyes.

"You don't fool me," I muttered.

A rush of adrenaline took hold as I edged myself along the wall. I was tough. Powerful like Pangu. Basho stuck by my side. He tilted his head and wagged his tail.

"He remembers me." Cal leaned down and exhaled, his breath a lethal vapor. He petted Basho, then took another step, drew me close before I could move. I tried to pull away, but he only held on tighter. I could feel his claws clutching onto my arms.

"Let me go," I said. I could smell Mother's perfume.

He released me and I stumbled backward.

"Look, I know I hurt you both, but I had a lot to think about. Truce?" Cal stuck out his hand.

There was a time when I thought he might be the one, but he was no different than all the rest. My mind went blank. All I saw was one big claw. Pointed sharp talons. *Where are you Pangu? Help me.*

I froze. The silence was deafening.

Basho barked and barked at me.

Leave, I heard a voice say. *Leave now.*

CHAPTER 50

OUTSIDE, GRAY CLOUDS shifted across the sky like angry spirits. A heavy mist hung in the air. I ran out the door of the apartment, past the parking lot, past Cal's pickup. I raced by a few more houses and a motel. I kept seeing an image of Cal. I wasn't about to let him manipulate us again.

The sky split open into a sheet of bright light and gray shadow. Clouds shifted and fanned open like black wings in my midst. A giant aswang. I felt myself being pulled toward the earth. A deep chasm. Falling. Falling. Falling.

I had no choice. Run. Just run. Run till you reach the end of the earth.

I slowed down when I thought I spotted Blaine. I blinked and blinked, my vision clearing.

He was almost unidentifiable in a black leather jacket, but I recognized the wild curly hair and black retro frames. The way he stood with his weight on one leg. He leaned against a motorcycle. Probably the Honda he had talked about, the one he'd bought last year with half his savings. He held a black helmet to his hip, conversing with an elderly man.

I stopped, my throat raw, my head ready to explode. Blaine caught my eyes. My mind exploded. Why did Cal have to come back? He was going to ruin everything again. He was playing with us. How could Mother be so stupid?

Why was this happening? Why? I couldn't breathe. My nose felt stuffy and runny.

Blaine waved me over and parted ways with the man.

My mind spun and I darted to him, charging forward and straight into his arms.

His body stiffened. "Whoa. What's going on?"

With the back of my hand, I wiped my nose and took a couple steps back. Left a smear of wetness on his jacket. I leaned forward and caught my breath. "Is that your bike? I need a ride."

"Where are we going?" His forehead wrinkled. He lifted his chin, his tone gentle. "What's wrong, Jasmine?"

"Nothing." I held his gaze, unable to speak. My vision blurred again, into a smear of watercolors. Purple. Pink. Blue. I had to escape. Away from the aswang. Away from my thoughts. Away from Mother. "Can I have a ride or not?"

"Yeah, but . . ."

"Now. Please. I need to get out of here."

"All right." He tossed me his helmet. "Here, put this on."

I hopped on the back of the seat and the engine revved. I held on tight as we drove along the street and onto the highway. Part of me wanted to let go, let my body catch the wind.

"Where are we headed?" Blaine asked, turning his head.

"Vegas, Los Angeles, New York. I don't care," I bellowed. "Just keep going, okay?" I squeezed my arms tight around his waist. I moved my foot and the heat from the muffler scorched my ankle.

We rode for a few miles along Highway 101. I lost track of time. Scintillating lights reflected off the water. "Faster," I hollered.

Blaine accelerated, weaving between cars and trucks. He

took a sharp turn, veering east onto another road. A thick grove of tall pine trees rose on both sides of us, as if we were cutting through a heavy forest. Images of Mother and Cal appeared. I thought of Mother, how far we had driven. All the way to Oregon. Away from him.

Blaine didn't say a word. Minutes passed and he finally said, "You with me?" The sun began to drop in the sky. "We should head back."

The air felt cooler and I nudged his side. "No, keep going."

"I'm running out of gas."

"No way."

"Yes, Jasmine. I'm not kidding." He sounded agitated and he pulled onto the side of the road and stopped. Cars whizzed past from both directions.

"Please don't make me go back there," I said. "I can't."

"We have to."

"Just leave me here, then."

"I don't know what's going on, but we have to go back or we'll end up hitchhiking."

"All right."

So much for my escape plan. I needed to retrieve Basho also. I had left him back at the apartment in my rage. *But whatever happens, I'm not going back to Mother and Cal*, I thought.

Blaine gave the bike gas and made a sharp U-turn. We stopped at a gas station, then headed back on the road again. I clung to Blaine, the momentum of the bike pulling me back, the cold wind barreling through me. The smell of pine.

We returned to Newbay. He stopped and parked along the side of the road, across from Calloway Beach. I pulled off the helmet in a fury, swung my leg around and jumped off the motorcycle. I didn't want to be here. I wanted to be far, far away.

"You're welcome," Blaine mumbled.

"Excuse me?"

"I said, you're welcome. For the ride."

"I don't want to be here. You don't understand."

"What did you want me to do? Keep driving till we ran out of gas?"

"I don't know. I just wanted to keep moving." I touched the inside of my ankle and it stung.

Blaine pushed up his glasses, his gaze drifting downward. "Look. I know you wanted to ride—like really far away. But I'm confused. Can you tell me what's going on?"

"Not really."

Blaine wouldn't understand. He lived with his grandfather. Where would I start? Too much had happened. My life was too complicated. "Just go home." I marched toward the beach. "Oh, and don't worry. I'm not going to say *goodbye*. So feel free to just disappear."

"Hey, you can't just take off like that."

"Watch me."

I picked up my pace and kept running, acting as if I knew what I was doing.

Along the shore, the tide was high, cutting through the gray skies, the pounding of the surf not far, waves curling and unfurling, spreading thin across the wet sand. Towering sea cliffs rose above the water.

Blaine caught up and I stopped, our bodies next to each other, facing the ocean. "I'm not going anywhere until you tell me what the hell's going on. Did something happen with your mom?"

I thought for a moment about my life, its lack of clarity, my longing to grasp onto something real, and it occurred to me that maybe *I* was the crazy one. Something had changed. My mythical world had turned into a complete nightmare. I felt lost. Alone. I peered out at the ocean. The endless horizon.

Blaine reached for my hand. "You're cold." He took off his leather jacket, threw it across my shoulders. "Listen. You don't have to say anything. I'm sorry." His voice was barely audible against the sound of the water, the wind.

I took a deep breath, tried to clear my head. I struggled to formulate words. I felt like if I talked, everything inside me would rush out like a tsunami—and swallow me whole. I sank to the sand, crossed my legs.

Blaine sat down next to me, his shoulder brushing against mine. "You okay?"

"I don't know." I paused and thought of Cal, his coming and going. "You think a person can change?"

"Like how?"

"Like commit. Keep a promise and not run away all the time?"

"Hmmm . . . I'm not sure. Depends on the commitment. The person, too. Don't you think?"

I shrugged. "Sometimes I want to believe. But I'm always getting disappointed."

"Can't lose hope, though." He turned and looked at me. "Right? Every moment counts, I think. Like right now."

The sun dropped beneath the horizon and a heavy mist hung in the air as we watched the encroaching tide. Blaine slid off his glasses, wiped the lenses with the edge of his shirt.

"It might be better to leave those off. You probably don't want to really see me right now. I'm a mess. Let me be blurry, okay?" I said.

He set the glasses down.

"All I need is right in front of me." He moved closer, kissed me lightly on the forehead, then on my lips. I smelled the ocean, the forest, on his skin, his clothes. We stretched out on the sand, he on his side, facing me. I inched closer and our bodies became entangled. At first I felt awkward. Suddenly aware of his body. Aware of my body. Could he hear my heart pounding? But the look in his eyes washed away my fears. My chest exploded. The roar of the ocean echoed, a hunger, a longing, and I didn't want this moment to end. Ever.

CHAPTER 51

I RETURNED HOME just before sunrise, shocked to see a couple of police cars parked out front. One of the police officers was talking to Auntie Chong in front of her apartment. She kept shaking her head back and forth and shrugging her shoulders. Maybe they were looking for me and Mother. Or just me, I realized, for being out all night with Blaine.

I crept past and raced upstairs. Inside, our apartment was drowned in darkness except for a vanilla candle burning in the kitchen. Its tiny flame quivered as I removed my sneakers and wiggled my toes, sending speckles of sand to the floor. I reached for the light switch, but then stopped at the sight of Mother at the kitchen table. Her bare legs were propped on a chair, silk robe wrapped around her, a glass of red wine in her hand.

"You scared me," I said. "Did you see the cop cars out front? One of them is talking to Auntie Chong."

"Oh?" She looked up. "Maybe there's trouble in one of the units on the other side. Come here, give me a hug."

"They're probably looking for us. We're wanted, you know." I gave her a weak squeeze, felt her arm lightly touch mine.

"It's fine, honey. You worry too much."

"Maybe we should be hiding right now." I looked out the

window and pulled the curtains tight. "You're up early." I
stared at the wine glass.

"I'm waiting for the sun." She traced her finger along the
rim of the glass. "Restless night. And you? Where have *you*
been all night?"

"Nowhere." I dug my nails into my palm, preparing for
her reply.

"Nowhere with who? That boy again?"

"You mean Blaine? You work with him."

"You two have been spending a lot of time together.
What is he, your boyfriend?"

"I don't know." I still felt his kisses on my lips. Smelled
the salty ocean on my skin. The sensations of Blaine's fingers
touching my face, my body. The awkwardness mixed with
longing still there. The heat of the moment etched in my
memory. I hesitated, afraid talking about it might smear it
all away.

"He's too old for you." Mother licked her upper lip. "A
cutie, though. Hiding behind those glasses. I know that type."

"I didn't know there were types." I reached in the cupboard for a glass then poured the last swallow of orange
juice from a carton in the fridge.

"Boys at that age. Only one thing on their minds."

I wondered if she could sense where I'd been and what I'd
been doing. I felt myself blush and rubbed my toes together,
felt the little kernels of sand again. I knew what it was like
now to be in love.

Mother set the wine glass down and pulled out a folded
sheet of paper from the pocket of her robe. "I wrote a haiku."
She grasped the corners of the paper. "For Issa, the Japanese
Poet." She recited the poem.

Don't weep, blooming flower—
Lovers, clouds, like night and day
Must part

She waved the paper in the air. A dizzy array of red ink flashed before me. "Think he'd like it?"

"Who?"

"Issa. Of course, silly."

"I thought he was dead."

"Ah. But poets live forever." She tossed the paper in the air and it swirled, landed on the floor, a splotch of red ink bleeding onto the other side. "So? What do you think? Am I worthy of his fondness? His admiration?"

"What?"

"Have you not been listening? Issa. How does one love? How does one trust again?"

"Is this about Cal?" My skin prickled even though I was grateful her attention was no longer on me.

"He can't stand it when I cry." She took a sip of the wine.

"Who *do you* trust, Ma? Mr. Jin? Is he any better?"

"Mr. Jin is a good friend of mine. He saved me. A long time ago. If it wasn't for him . . . Anyway, he's helping me. Us, now."

On the table, a crystal vase with the single yellow rose caught my eye, a reminder of Cal's return. I held it up against the light and wondered how long this one would last. I paused. Thinking about love. Thinking about feeling beautiful. Feeling wanted. I touched a petal, felt the silky softness between my fingers. "So, where's he now? He coming back?"

"Why do you ask?"

"Because I want to know." I went to the window, peeked outside. The police cars were still there in the parking lot.

"Don't worry," she said. "He'll be back."

"Were you fighting again?"

"No. We had something to discuss. Something we should have talked about a long time ago."

"Like what? I mean, why is he even back? I don't get it. Thought we were rid of him."

A momentary pang of guilt struck me. Here and gone. "It's like a stupid game. He's manipulating you, just like you use other men to feel good about yourself."

She looked alarmed, the hurt and rage forming lines on her forehead. "What's happening to us? We're the Phoenix and Dragon. Remember?"

"Why is he back? Why?"

"To see us again. He missed us."

"Bullshit."

The room spun, the wine glass glinting in the dim light.

"Cal wants us to go back to Briarplace."

Her words pierced me like a poisonous dart.

"That's why you said we might be moving again."

"He's come to take us back," she said.

"He can't do that. *He* left us."

"Yes, but he said he made a mistake."

"And what does that mean?" I asked.

"It won't happen again."

"And you believe him?"

"I want to."

"Why?" I asked. "Do you still love him?"

"I think I do." She let out a soft whimper. "Damn it. I still love him."

• • •

I COULDN'T TAKE it anymore, so I left the kitchen. On the way out, I picked the poem off the floor and went to my room. I smoothed out the crumpled paper and read the words out loud.

Don't weep, blooming flower—
Lovers, clouds, like night and day
Must part

A sudden rage brewed inside me. *I'm not going back to Briarplace*, I thought. I searched the drawers for a pair of scissors, but I found a box of matches instead. I lit a match and touched the flame to the edge of the paper, watched as it disintegrated into feather light ashes, tumbling to the floor.

CHAPTER 52

I SLEPT WITH the light on that evening, anticipating a knock on our apartment door. The cops busting through and cuffing us both. But they didn't.

Mother fell into a funk and for the next couple days I took care of her. Since I didn't have a phone, I met Blaine briefly at the beach and told him that I'd be *busy* for a bit. I didn't mention Mother, that seemed too weird.

I tried not to think of Cal or moving back to Briarplace. Instead, I occupied myself by sitting on the living room floor by the window, drawing pictures of faraway places and alternate universes. Mystical worlds to call home.

When Cal showed up late one afternoon with a brown paper bag tucked beneath his arm, hair slicked back, I just shook my head and continued to draw.

"Back again?" I asked.

He flung off his boots, tossed the brown sack in front of me. "Asiago cheese bread. Got it at the bakery down the street."

I looked up and shot him a look of disgust, but didn't say a word.

"You always so cheerful? Thought my absence might make you appreciate me a bit more."

"For what? And why?"

"Never mind." Cal cracked his knuckles. "What are you drawing?"

"An alternate universe. A home. Something you wouldn't know about." I closed the sketchpad, felt the weight of his presence.

"Home." He nodded. "That's what I'm going for. It's why I'm back." He glanced around the corner, toward the kitchen. "Where's your mom?"

"Resting."

"It's almost supper time."

"She wants to be left alone."

"C'mon." He swung his hand in front of me, palm outward. "High five? Fist bump?"

"Cut the crap, Cal. Just tell me why you're really here." I held his gaze, trying to find a speck of truth. In the light, his eyes fluctuated from amber to green to a deceptive blue.

"You know the reason. I missed you both."

"I hear you want us to go back. You can't do that. She likes it here."

"Who? Your mom?" He stroked the side of his face, like a man with a full beard.

"She's better here. Know what I mean?" I thought about Mother's words: *Put away the past. Grasp renewal.*

"And what about you?"

"This is where I belong."

Cal smiled. "That's good. We all need to find that place."

"Look, I don't know what to say. You're messing things up."

"C'mon, Jasmine. You can't mean that."

"What was last time? A practice run? Did you just *pretend* you were going to marry my mother? Go back."

"I can't."

"We weren't the ones who left. You did. Remember?"

Cal looked at me. "We're family now. You understand?"

I dug my toes into the carpet. How dare he come back and act like nothing happened. Like nothing changed.

"I should have chased you away the first time."

"You sure tried."

"Not hard enough. I should have made you go away."

"Still got those lovely freckles. I had a ton of freckles when I was a kid. Looks better on you, though." He sat down next to me. "I swear I didn't know."

"Didn't know what?"

"When she told me, I kinda freaked out. I need to be here for you guys."

"What are you talking about?"

But his words hit me hard, like a slap in the face.

I swear I didn't know.

When she told me, I kinda freaked out . . .

"Things are going to be different from now on." Cal looked down. "I didn't know if I could do it."

"Do what? I'm confused."

I held my breath.

My fingers turned cold.

"Remember when you asked me about the scar on my side? Well, my ma and pops were in a big fight. I thought he was going to hurt her. I charged after him. He shoved me through the glass sliding door. I got up and lunged forward and I—I—punched him and . . . he fell. It almost killed him."

"Why are you telling me this?"

"Because, from that day on, I swore I would never want a family of my own."

"And?" I felt my brow furrow. "What's that got to do with anything?"

Cal just shook his head. There was more he wanted to say. I could feel it. But he had already said enough.

CHAPTER 53

Watch birth and death: the lotus has already
Opened its flower.
—Natsume Sōseki

THAT EVENING, I read my haiku book. Through the bedroom wall, I heard Cal and Mother, at first arguing, followed by the soft murmur of their voices, the giggles, the rustle of their bodies.

I swear I didn't know. My head spun with Cal's words. Over and over. What didn't he know? The hairs on my arm prickled. Bolts of light flashed in my periphery.

Cal.

No. It wasn't true. It couldn't be true.

I went to the kitchen and pulled out a box of Lucky Charms. Dumped half of it on the counter and picked out all the marshmallow bits: hearts, horseshoes, clovers, blue moons, unicorns, red balloons, and rainbows. I read the back of the box.

Heart—gives life to objects
Star—power of flight
Horseshoe—power of speed
Clover—luck

Blue Moon—power of invisibility
Unicorn—brings color to the world
Rainbow—power to teleport
Red Balloon—power to float.

I plucked out all the Blue Moons and ate each one. The power of invisibility—that's what I needed right now. Then I continued to eat the rest of the marshmallow bits. One by one until they were all gone.

CHAPTER 54

MORNING LIGHT PRESSED harsh against the curtains. Cal had left to run a few errands, and Mother and I sat on the edge of her bed, a flurry of dust fairies in the air. The room smelled stale of sweat.

"I don't feel so good," I said. Maybe it was all the marshmallow bits expanding in my stomach. Maybe it was the thought of moving back to Briarplace. The thought of Cal—

"What's wrong?" Mother held the back of her hand against my forehead.

"My head hurts and I feel weak," I said as I shoved her hand away.

"Are you worried?" she asked. "Things are going to change. You'll see."

"They already have. For the worse."

"We're going to be a family. Cal's going to offer us a better life."

I grasped the edge of the blanket with a tight fist and started to panic. "You think so?"

"Things are different now." Mother looked down. "He knows."

"Knows *what*?" I surprised myself with the harshness of my own voice. Basho leaped onto my lap and licked my chin. "Say it."

I needed her to say it out loud. Only then would it become real. Only then.

Mother hesitated, then spoke. "He knows that he can't just walk away. He wants us to be a family. I know that's what you've always wanted. A real home."

"I gave up on that a long time ago."

I needed the truth.

"Surely, you can't mean that? I know you like Blaine. There will be others. You might have to use those predator skills of yours and chase him away. You're good at that."

I thought about what she just said—if we did move back to Briarplace, she was right. For once, she had told the truth. I'd have to get rid of Blaine, just like I chased away Mother's boyfriends. Now it was my turn to feel the pain.

AFTER MOTHER LEFT for work, I heard every creak and movement in the apartment, the water running through the pipes. I needed to tell Blaine that we might move. What was going to happen to us? Was there even an *us*?

Basho barked each time he heard footsteps, voices outside the apartment. I grew more and more restless, so I went knocking on Auntie Chong's door. Maybe she had the answers to my mixed-up life.

The door swung open and Auntie Chong waved me in. "Lai. Come." She gnawed on a toothpick as if it were a piece of gum. "It's my favorite lady."

I kicked off my sneakers by the doorway and followed her as she waddled into the apartment, her hair matted on the back of her head like she had just woken up. In the corner of the living room, Ming ruffled his feathers and chirped.

I breathed in a sweet salty aroma of garlic, ginger and soy sauce. A pot of rice gurgled in the corner of the counter.

"What are you making?"

"Zongzi. Sticky rice. Going to the waterfront to throw in the river." Auntie Chong folded a couple of banana leaves over a scoop of sticky rice. She tied it with twine into a triangular pyramid, clutching part of the string between her teeth.

"You're making all this to throw into the river?"

"Dragon Boat Festival. In memory of Qu Yuan."

"Who's that?"

"A poet during Zhou Dynasty. Accused of treason. He killed himself by drowning in the river. We throw food in the river so the fish eat rice, not Qu Yuan's body. Here, you take a bite." She dropped a heaping of rice onto a new set of banana leaves. "If you like, I'll teach you how to make."

"I'd like that."

We sat in silence as I fumbled to find the right words to ask her what to do about Blaine. What she thought about us moving. Cal. All the questions started to make me delirious.

"Everything okay?" Auntie Chong finally asked.

"I don't know. Lots going on, I guess. Why?" I had no idea where to start.

"You are here, unexpected." She pointed to my forehead. "And you have that wrinkle right there like your mama, when she's worried about something."

"Honestly, I don't feel like being alone right now."

"You have love troubles?"

I laughed. "Blaine and I are just hanging out. I mean. I'm not really sure what we are." I sighed. "Why does everything have to be labeled? Marriage. Family. Boyfriend. Girlfriend. Why can't we just be? You know?"

Auntie Chong shrugged. "You got me. Confusing world. In my language we say s*iao*. Crazy."

"*Siao* is right." I took another pinch of rice and ate it. "Auntie Chong. Can I ask you something?"

"Sure. Anything."

"You knew me when I was just a baby, right?"

"Uh, huh." She nodded as if to reassure me. Then she started to move to the living room.

I followed her. "Hey, what are you doing?"

"It's Blinky time." She plopped herself in front of the television, legs crossed, a remote control in one hand.

I stood toward the front of the television, blocking half of it from her view. "I know I'm asking a lot of questions, but I'm just curious about my life. Like I just need some questions answered. Stuff like that."

Auntie Chong craned her neck to see the screen, then slid to the side for a better view. "Have you talked to your mama?"

"Yes, of course I have. But she's the queen of secrets." For so long, I tried not to think about things. I escaped into my fantasy world. But now that world was crumbling. "Are you listening to me?"

Auntie Chong nodded, still staring at the television.

"She keeps telling me my father is a mythical god. The great Pangu. I'm fifteen. *Fifteen*. It's time to quit believing in mythological gods." I felt the warmth of my blood crawling up my neck.

Auntie Chong shrugged. "Myths are a way of explaining things we don't understand. The mysteries of the world."

"You sound like my mother. Things we don't *understand*? I'm talking about my father, Auntie Chong. My father.

What's the mystery? It's all bullcrap, and you know it. Now that I'm here in Newbay, I have to know. The past keeps haunting me."

Auntie Chong set down the controller and turned off the screen. "Hey, now. Lai. Come sit. Of course you need to know. You deserve to know."

I slid next to her and she patted the top of my hand.

I tried to calm myself. "You know what, you're the only person besides my mother who can tell me about my father." I sniffed. "And I don't even know why we're here."

"You're here because this is home. You've been running too long. The police came to the apartment, looking for both of you."

"What? I knew it." They *were* looking for us. My palms started to sweat.

"Your mama's speeding ticket was not paid."

"What did you tell them?"

"I told them you weren't here. I took care of everything. Okay?"

"There's the Keeper. And Mother left the hospital. And . . ."

"Yes. I know. You're too young to worry about these things." She patted my shoulder. "I take care of it all. Don't say anything to your mama. Otherwise *paiseh*. That means embarrassing. Your mama might not like that. Too proud, maybe."

I forced a smile, even though I was on the verge of losing it. On the verge of a big ugly cry. "*Paiseh*," I whispered back.

I hugged Auntie Chong, holding back a wave of tears. "Thank you," I whispered. "You don't know how much this means. I've been so scared. I have nightmares that some-one's going to take us away and put us in jail."

"Of course you are scared. I am, too." She rubbed the top of my hand. "Everything will be okay."

I felt lighter, like she had lifted a huge worry off my back. But there was still Cal. Moving. And Blaine—I probably should tell him.

What did I know about love?

CHAPTER 55

"WHAT DO YOU think?" Mother asked as she held up one of my drawings the next day. The colored pencil sketch of the ocean. It appeared harsh now, the water faded against a colorless sky blurred with streaks of clouds. She had it framed, matted with an awful yellow border that offset everything, an odd combination of color and light. "Surprise," she said.

My shoulders tightened. "Where'd you get that?"

"I found it when I was packing. Thought it might be a nice touch at our new apartment."

"Packing? You were literally just un-packing not that long ago."

"There's an apartment on the north side of Briarplace, all set up for us."

I barely recognized her—skin ashen, bluish half-moons beneath her lids. The living room was claustrophobic with boxes half-full of clothes, dishes and her silk flowers.

"I don't want to go back," I stammered. Ever since I had found the baby photo and letter, I carried them in the front pocket of my jeans, like a guide, a talisman. I fingered the edge of the photo and took a deep breath.

"I know you're infatuated with Blaine, but there are plenty of birds in the sky. Trust me." She set the drawing down. In the dim room, the pewter frame reflected a metallic sheen.

She lifted a mangled bouquet of flowers and tossed them into a box. "I don't think you really have a choice. We—as in you, me, and Cal—are moving."

"Did you *I Ching*? Just to make sure? And what about Cal? What does he say? More false promises?" My voice sounded desperate and I hated it.

"He wants us to be together. We're moving. And that's final."

"Can't we stay a little longer?"

She reached for a plate to pack, wrapped it in a dish-towel. "Please, Jasmine. I just want us to be happy."

"We were. Until Cal came back."

She set the wrapped plate on the floor. "You sound angry. Is something wrong?"

"Nothing's wrong with me. It's you. You're delusional. And blind."

"Don't worry. We're still the Phoenix and Dragon. But now it's you, me and Cal. A family."

The sound of his name ripped through my chest. Cal didn't make us a family. Where was the transcendent path? Harmony and beauty? The truth? "I'm not going anywhere with you this time, even if he's—he's my—"

"What?" She turned pale, like she had seen a ghost.

My voice escalated and cracked. "Say it, Ma. *Say it.* I need to hear it from you." I took the drawing and tossed it to the floor. "Now. Tell me the truth."

A voice came from the hallway.

"She's right, Suchou." Auntie Chong stepped into the living room. "It's time for the truth. No good for both of you. You feed your daughter too many tales."

"You stay out of this," Mother said.

"I think she's ready."

"The truth might destroy us all," Mother said.

"You tell her the truth or I will," said Auntie Chong.

I glanced at my drawing—lifeless and upside down on the floor.

Pangu, please help me.

Anything was better than this moment, of wanting and not wanting the truth.

"You're right ... Your father ... is Cal," said Auntie Chong. Mother turned paler. "I didn't know what to do. I was scared. I was young. I didn't know how he'd react, so I never told him."

I knew it. The words were finally real. But now the truth was tainted with an overwhelming sense of despair. A wave so heavy and deep. *Your father is Cal.* It felt like my spirit had left my body, a feeling of emptiness like never before. I could barely speak. "You kept me a secret from him. All these years? Why?"

Mother took a step back. Then the world of fantasy vanished in the reality of her voice as she told me everything. How she and her father first moved to this country. How at a young age she tried to hide the life within her. How, when her father found out, he shook his finger and said, *I have to look at you every day. We came to this country to live a better life. Now you have ruined everything. Our family name. You are a disgrace. I never want to see you again.* He told her to leave. That she was no longer his daughter. *Paiseh.* Embarrassment. Shame. How she had no choice but to bury secrets and leave.

I stood there, listening. Everything I believed about my father, my hero, dissolved before me, until it was just a wash of endless gray.

"You never told my real father I existed," I whispered. "Is that what you're saying?"

"I did what I thought was best for all of us. I protected you. Even though I didn't have the means to take care of you."

Mother lifted the picture from the floor, flipped it right side up.

I studied the drawing, the waves no longer like water, but claws, sharp and pointy, fingers grasping for air. "Maybe *you're* not even my mother."

"We're the Phoenix and Dragon," Mother stepped toward me and reached for my shoulder.

I shoved her hand away. Turned and leaned against the wall. "All these years, I was just a secret. And you made me believe my father was a hero." I spun around. "Did you hear me? He was the sun and the moon. I worshipped my fantasy father, like a god. It was all in my screwed-up head."

Mother looked past me, as if she didn't hear a word. "Mythology is the music of the universe."

"But they're *lies*. All of them. I hate you. You allowed me to believe anything I wanted to. How could you?"

No, Pangu. It isn't true.

"What difference does it make?"

I held Mother's gaze. "It matters. All of it. Who I am. Where I came from."

Mother frowned. "I was young. I didn't know what to do. Where to go. Who to trust. Jasmine—"

"Why? All this time."

"I only wanted to protect you. I didn't know how to tell you or him the truth. I was afraid. Now look at us. Fighting over the past. Over things we can't change."

Auntie Chong walked to my side and squeezed my hand. "You come with me."

CHAPTER 56

AT AUNTIE CHONG'S apartment, I fidgeted with the hem of my sleeve, pulled at a loose thread, the two of us side by side on the couch, my leg shaking up and down. I felt numb. I tried to stuff everything down, down, down inside. I wanted to bury it all for now.

Ming opened his beak and whistled. Puffed his feathers.

"She wants to move," I finally said.

"I know. Back to Briarplace."

"She told you?"

Auntie Chong nodded. "Yes."

"What else did she say?" I asked.

"Not much." Auntie Chong got off the couch and threw a handful of bird food into Ming's cage. He dove and pecked at the seeds.

"I don't know what to do." I stood and paced back and forth. "I can't go back there. Especially not now." I tapped at the glass of the aquarium. The fish scattered. "Do you think I'm like her?"

"You both want the same things. You both want to be loved. That's all. Love is complicated. People do crazy things to protect those they love. Remember? Siao. Crazy."

"Why is it so difficult?" I pulled the baby photo and letter from my pocket. "What about this? What does it mean?"

It is all for the best. This child will never know.

"That's from me," Auntie Chong said. "After her papa find out. She had nowhere to go. Your mama didn't think she could take care of you. But I told her we would make it work. I would help. It was our secret. I took care of her. And you. Mr. Jin, my friend, also helped."

"But she let me believe I had a father who cared about me. Stories that aren't true. Heroic creatures that don't exist. Fathers that aren't real."

"She told stories to protect you."

I dropped the letter to the floor. I couldn't breathe. I imagined Pangu, his presence encompassing the entire sky, his arms like limbs wrapping around me in a tight embrace. Protecting me. Then the image vanished into feathers of smoke. The black egg cracked wide-open. With nothing left inside.

I swallowed the swell of emotion rising within me, determined not to let Auntie Chong see me cry.

CHAPTER 57

BLAINE AND I met at the beach. Me, trying to figure out what to say to him in my head. Trying to figure out how to tell him I might be moving. Trying to figure out if we were even *a thing*. Maybe it was all in my imagination. Just like my father, Pangu.

It rained, a slow drizzle as we hiked along the shore, the cool wet sand between my toes.

Blaine hunched forward, wavy hair flat against his forehead. "How you doing?" His voice was faint through the beats of rain.

I knew he was referring to the other night. Me being all messed up. And now me *totally* messed up after talking to Mother and Auntie Chong. "I'm okay." I didn't know what to say.

I was a swirling cyclone of thoughts. It all seemed so complex. I was still processing everything about Cal. The reality of my world was struggling to settle in my brain. I wasn't ready to talk. It all felt way too raw. But I needed to at least tell Blaine the truth—that we'd be moving. Far away from here. And what about *us*? That night on the beach?

"You've got that look. What's up?" Blaine blinked through the rain drops.

"Can I ask you something?" A thick froth gathered along the shore, the tide rising.

"Okay? Sure."

"About the other night . . ."

"Yeah. I meant to talk to you."

"I mean, it doesn't really matter."

"Well, what happened *does* matter to me. I care about you, Jasmine. A lot."

Shit. He said he cared about me. This was real. Not some fantasy I had imagined in my head. I dug my toes into the sand. "I care about you, too." Should I tell him about Cal? Should I say something about moving? Maybe it wasn't necessary. Maybe Mother would change her mind.

"We shouldn't be out here much longer." He pointed to the sky. "See those clouds moving in?" The wind picked up, the sky became suddenly stippled with streaks of gray. Intermittent claps of thunder.

I dropped my head back, let the droplets pelt against my neck. It started to pour, a blistering shower of rain.

Blaine reached for my hand and pulled me forward. "Let's get out of here. Head home to Gramps."

I thought about what it meant to have a home. Briarplace? The foster home? And now Newbay? "You're lucky you have a place to call home."

"You're right. Gramps is my refuge."

AT THE COTTAGE, I felt the immediate warmth of the fire. Gramps was reading a book as he rocked back and forth in the chair.

"We're back," Blaine said.

"I see you brought your friend." Gramps lifted his head and grinned.

"Sure did." Blaine gave Gramps a hug. "Hope you don't mind."

"Good heavens. Not at all." Gramps turned to the empty chair. "Right, Jeanine? We like company. Make yourself at home. Awfully stormy today."

"It is," I said. My teeth chattered and I watched the flames of the fire flicker and crackle. I smiled at a picture of Gramps and Jeanine on the mantel. She was a petite silver-haired woman with a kind face.

Blaine and I nestled by the fire and played a game of dominoes, sipped hot cocoa while Gramps snored in the rocking chair, the opened book resting on his lap. I shoved away the image of Cal. I tried not to think about Mother or Auntie Chong. The letter. All the secrets.

We moved to the study and sat on the couch. I spotted a stack of books along the wall—*The Art of Kite Flying*, *Zen and Stunt Kites*, *Architectural Designs*, and *The Sound and the Fury*.

I reached for *Architectural Designs*, paged through the chapter on Frank Lloyd Wright, waiting for the right moment to talk to Blaine.

Blaine pushed up his glasses. "Do you believe in spirits?"

"I used to. Why?"

"Just curious."

"If you lived with my mother, you'd believe in tarot cards and mythical fathers. Flying phoenixes and dragons."

"Gramps says the best part of his day is when Grams visits. Used to make me sad, but now it doesn't. I feel her presence, too, sometimes." He turned and stared at me and

I suddenly felt naked. Like he could see right through me. "I'm glad to have met you, Miss Jasmine."

"I'm glad to have met you, too. Mr. Blaine." He slid close and stole a kiss. I tasted sweet cocoa on my lips as I inched away. I had to tell him the truth. I felt the familiar tug of awkwardness and longing coming over me, just like the night at the beach. "I need to tell you something," I whispered.

"Okay. Go for it."

I closed the book and set it down. "I mean. What are we exactly? Not that we have to be anything. Or something."

"I told you. I like you, Jasmine. A lot."

I slid back. I didn't want to be like my mother. Love wasn't a game. It was hard to believe in something. Then watch it slip away. Maybe it was easier not to love.

Streaks of red and orange light pulsed in my periphery.

"What's wrong?" he asked.

"Nothing." I couldn't bring myself to look at him. "Everything's screwed up." I swiped away a tear that escaped down my cheek. Our bodies were still slick and damp from the rain.

"Did I do something wrong? Is it about the other night? I would never . . ."

"No. Not at all. It's not you. It's just . . . there are so many things I don't know right now."

"What are you talking about?"

"Well, for one, I'm not sure how much longer we're going to be here."

"What do you mean? I thought you and your mom liked it here?" His expression turned serious in the dim light.

"I do. But we might have to leave." I started to feel dizzy, my body and mind separating into an endless void. "I can't keep seeing you—knowing it's all going to end."

Blaine shook his head. "I don't get it. That's not a good enough reason."

"I know. It's not you. It's me." I shivered from the dampness of my clothes. "I don't want to be like my mother. She keeps secrets." I wanted to tell him everything. But the words were locked deep inside. It would hurt too much to tell the truth.

Outside the room, the fire crackled and snapped, all the ugly secrets burning a hole right through me.

CHAPTER 58

Dreaming—
Mother and I are the Phoenix and Dragon.
Our wings take flight as we fly among the clouds.
Our shadows dancing across the sky
a fan of iridescent reds, yellows, greens.
Across mountain tops and above the sea,
our silhouette against the pink and orange horizon.
"C'mon Jazz. Higher. Higher," the Phoenix calls.
I follow—chasing the moon in dips and turns, pirouettes.
My tail thrashing, the wind carrying me beyond the sky.
I blink and blink.
Then lose sight of her—
watch as the Phoenix's wings fade.
Smoke fills the air.
Flames of color erupt in the sky.
Blinding ashes.
Feathers fall to the earth like rain.

CHAPTER 59

I SLEPT WITH the lamp light on, tossed and turned with Basho at the foot of my bed. I got up, pulled out the crumpled picture of me as a baby, in the stroller. The red beanie on my head. I pulled out the sepia photo of Mother as a child and placed the two pictures side by side.

I could see it now, the resemblance, the longing, the loneliness, the wanting to be loved, carved in our expressions. I felt a sudden loss for something I never knew existed. I tucked the photos beneath my pillow and lay my head down.

THE NEXT MORNING at breakfast, Cal was at the table when I left my room. His expression was long and sullen, his eyes dull in the faint tissue of light. "Got a minute?"

"I guess." Did I have a choice?

"I'm sorry, Jasmine. About everything. Had I known, things would have been different."

I repeated the sentence in my head. *Had I known, things would have been different.* But how could he not have known about me? "You're full of shit," I said.

Cal stared at me with a weird desperation on his face. He continued talking as if he didn't hear a word I just said. "You know what I mean? The truth is . . . I can't forgive your mom. Not just yet. She kept me away from you all these years."

I froze. My pulse quickened. *Stop. Stop talking*, I wanted to say.

The air turned wavy. "I care about you. You know that."

I wanted to scream. "I'm not moving back to Briarplace."

"I should have known better. She should have told me I was your father," he whispered.

I looked at him in disbelief, sizing him up in my mind—this man I tried to get rid of. This man who came and went as he pleased.

Cal shook his head and I could tell his mind was spinning—spinning out of control. "She told me the morning of our wedding day. It felt like a trap. I was in shock. I thought I was ready for a family. But I'm not. I told her a long time ago I never wanted a child of my own. I was always afraid to become . . . like . . . heck. Never mind." He sighed. "Maybe that's why she never told me the truth."

Basho barked and ran out of the kitchen. Mother appeared, cast in shadow. "What's going on?" She looked frail, the straps of her nightgown loose along her upper arms.

Cal stood. "Just saying goodbye to Jasmine."

"Goodbye?" Then it was as if something in her snapped. "I should have never told you."

He didn't budge. "Don't worry. I'm leaving. Calm down."

"Leave. Stay away from her. From me." She grabbed a plate from the table and flung it against the wall. It shattered into pieces.

"You're insane." He reached for her arm. "I can say goodbye to my daughter if I want."

"I'm not your daughter," I screamed. "I'm not."

Mother sobbed. She waved her index finger in the air.

"You know what? You're just like him. Just like your *own* father."

"Don't, Ma," I cried out. I wanted the fighting to end. I thought of Auntie Chong's words. *This girl is tough. She can handle anything. She swims in the ocean.* I was a Dragon. I was strong and powerful. Just like Pangu. Just like the waves of the ocean.

Cal grabbed her shoulders and I thought for a minute he might hurt her, but he let go.

"I'm not like him," he said. "And you'll never know because you never gave me a chance. And that's okay."

Mother hugged herself with a look of desperation. Her hair was wild and tousled and she looked like a stranger to me. "I did it to protect her. You would have only brought disappointment."

"You lied, Suchou," he said, his voice low and piercing. He shifted his attention to me. "I'm sorry, Jasmine. She should have never kept you a secret from me."

Mother crouched in the corner of the room like a little girl, her body tight as she swung side to side. "Leave," she repeated over and over. She was not my mother. Her voice even sounded different, off pitch and small.

I imagined myself transforming into a mythical dragon. Hands turning into talons. My body stretching toward the ceiling, toward the sky. Tail thrashing. "I'm not afraid of you," I said to Cal.

"I don't want you to be." His body slumped. "We're the same. You're . . . you're my child for crying out loud. I never want to hurt you, Jazz, or your mother. Had I known. I could have been there. You have to believe me."

I wanted to run, but I felt numb at the same time, a rage

welling up inside. "I'm nothing like you. You make promises you can't keep." I thought of Pangu, the heroic creature I believed was my father. All knowing. All loving. Protector of all. But the man standing in front of me was the complete opposite. He was a coward. Someone I could never trust. He was not my father. He could never be my father.

"It's better this way." Cal shook his head. "And honestly, I don't know if I have it in me, to be the father you deserve."

"Go," I said. "And never come back."

Then Cal left. The room shrank into a veil of haze, geometric lines of achromatic light.

CHAPTER 60

I TRIED DESPERATELY to erase the thoughts, the memory, of Cal—as if he never existed, as if the other night never happened. My head throbbed, asymmetric lines of light surrounding me. I couldn't shake the heavy sensation of hopelessness. My body felt caught in quicksand.

In the kitchen, I filled a glass with water and gulped it down. My throat felt scratchy and sore, my voice hoarse. A damp coolness chilled the air despite a ray of purple squeezing through a crevice in the blinds.

I called for Basho to feed him, but he was nowhere to be found. I searched my room again, the bathroom, the living room, but he had disappeared.

Mother was taking a nap. Her room smelled stale with a hint of perfume.

"Ma? I can't find Basho. He's gone." My voice cut through the air, a dry, raspy croak. Afraid to touch her, I tugged gently on the blanket. "Wake up. Do you know where Basho is?"

She rolled onto her side, let out a groan and shooed me away with a flick of her hand. A half-filled glass of water along with her bottle of meds sat on the nightstand.

"Ma, I need to find Basho. Help me." His name exploded in my head as I surveyed her room. A pair of jeans on the floor. The faint smell of Cal still lingering.

I paced back and forth, stepping over flowers, orchids, tiger lilies. Then I spotted the picture of the ocean she had framed for me. It was leaning against the wall. The waves moved and twirled, clouds lifting off the canvas, hanging in midair.

I recalled the time when I was a little girl, standing at the edge of a pool, peering down into the clear blue water, toes gripping concrete. I called out to her. It was a game we played. Catch me if you can. I had no fear as I jumped into her outstretched arms, my body dipping into the cool water. I longed for that moment, to feel safe again, the unwavering trust of her not letting me fall.

With Cal gone, I saw the lonesome river of her soul. The Phoenix had lost her wings. Color vanished from the walls.

My father appeared, a vision, just like I've always known him, Pangu the Creator, hairy and muscular, stretching the heavens and earth. He smiled, a toothless grin, the moon in his eye. He touched my forehead and like magic, my hair grew longer and longer, shiny, down past my knees, spiraling around me and my mother like a silk cocoon.

"Help me find Basho," I pleaded.

I noticed the apartment door cracked open, so I raced outside, up and down the block. I whistled and shouted his name. *Basho. Basho. Come here. Where are you?* I searched the sidewalk for any signs of him.

Cars whipped past and my mind filled with dread. Where could he be? Had someone taken him?

I circled the area another couple times. After an hour of searching, I dropped to the curb, my body slouching as I sat. I heard a bark and looked up, devastated when I spotted a little pug crossing the street with its owner.

I caught my breath then continued to search.

It felt like I was in a dream, trudging through a heavy swamp. Moving through thick, muddy water. Lucky Charms marshmallow bits suddenly appearing, suspended in the air. Little stars giving me the power of flight. Red balloons allowing me to float. I swallowed and swallowed. The sweet bits dissolving to acid on my tongue.

I started to cross the road to the other side, my mind exploding with thoughts of Cal, Pangu, my mother, the thought of losing Basho.

A sudden flash of lights blinded me, followed by the screeching sound of a car coming to a shrieking halt.

Then pitch blackness.

Silence.

CHAPTER 61

FERAL PUPILS AND a bright light dazzled, oscillating back and forth. I clamped my lids shut and a clown appeared with balloons. His nose bled, a red trickle dripping down and onto the ground while Mother lay in a field of bright dandelions, hair entangled in the tall grass.

Was I dreaming? I moaned, tore through a web of hair and moss. A couple of aswangs fed off flesh from the crook of my arm.

I screamed, but nothing came out.

It was the carnival all over again. Shattered mirrors. Cockroaches with spiked antennae. The inside of my throat slashed and raw. The Ferris wheel spun faster and faster, so I had to jump. I watched Cal flying past, masked in a black shroud. Gena down below with a microphone, waving me forward. Rani spinning in a ribbon of smoke, nodding. Laughing.

I transformed into a fearless dragon, with a horse-shaped head, snake's tail, claws of an eagle. I was benevolent and wise. Empowered with the mystical ability to fly. I took a step into the sky and flew, my wings fanning open.

"It's the medication," a voice said.

I woke to a sterile room, the faint hum of the television. I had died and entered either heaven or hell. I searched the room for angels, white feathery wings, an aura of lights, the saints. I swallowed and my throat lit on fire. *I must be in hell*, I thought. I started to panic when I heard the sound of a chair scraping against the floor.

"Look who's awake." I felt a tight squeeze on my arm and turned to a bewildered-looking Auntie Chong, locks of hair sticking up on one side of her head. "You are making all kinds of funny noises. Bad dream?"

I blinked a couple times, my vision fading in and out of focus. The room rotated sideways, the floor to the ceiling. I swallowed again and a sharp pain followed, like bits of broken glass lodged in my throat.

"Where am I?"

"You want some water?" Auntie Chong asked. She stood and reached for a Styrofoam cup.

I took a slow sip, grimacing with pain. I searched the room for another bed, another body. The field of dandelions wilted. "My mother. Where is she? And Basho?"

Before Auntie Chong had a chance to answer, a nurse entered. She took my temperature and blood pressure.

"How you feeling, sweetie?" she asked. She placed her fingers on the inside of my wrist and took my pulse. "Hungry at all?"

I shook my head. "My throat. It hurts."

"I know, honey. You need to drink lots of fluids. I'll bring you a popsicle. Maybe some Jell-O?"

I nodded in agreement.

When the nurse left, Auntie Chong tossed what looked like my sketchpad onto the bed. A box of colored pencils. "Blaine told me to bring you this. In case you get bored."

"Blaine?"

"He's the one who found you on the street after a car almost hit you. It didn't stop. You fell and hit your head. He called the ambulance. Saved your life."

"That can't be."

"He was looking for you."

"Why? What day is it?"

"Saturday. You've been here all night—you sleep then wake. Sleep then wake. Oh, and he found Basho."

I sat up. "He did?"

"By the road, wandering around."

I started to hyperventilate. "Is he okay?"

Auntie Chong nodded then looked down, interlaced her hands. "And your mama . . ."

"What? Where is she?" Scenarios raced through my mind. I pictured her with Cal, the two of them driving away, back to Briarplace. I had blocked out everything. "She's gone. Isn't she?" Thoughts swarmed in my head like a drone of mosquitoes. "She left with Cal." I made a fist and squeezed.

"She's not with Cal. He's gone. She's at home, but worried about you. She's having a hard time and will see you soon."

"She's a liar." I flipped to the other side, tugged at the IV as I hugged the pillow to my chest. "Maybe you should just go."

"Just give her some time. And I'm not going anywhere. I stay right here with you."

"Whatever."

I was glad Auntie Chong stayed by my side, day and night, while I remained at the hospital, under observation. She brought her Pac-Man game and hooked it up to the television. The yellow figure marched across the screen in linear patterns, eating dots along with pink and blue ghosts. "Suck you, Blinky," she said as she focused on the screen.

"You're *siao siao*," I said. Crazy crazy. "You know that?" I laughed, even though it made my throat hurt.

"Of course. Me siao siao and proud of it."

I tried my best not to look at the screen. The doctor told me that I had to rest my brain. Not to think about anything. I embraced the whole idea of not thinking about anything. The beeping sounds from the television made me laugh as I tried to ignore the tweets and stir of the medical monitors, the nurses in their blue scrubs coming and going. Poking and prodding at me.

A nurse brought in a tray with dinner and I played with the mashed potatoes and gravy, picked at the meatloaf with the fork.

"When can I go home?" I asked Auntie Chong, even though I knew she was only half-listening.

"Home?" she asked. "The doctor must check you first."

"For what?"

"See if you're okay to go home, I suppose." Auntie Chong moved the joystick up and down.

"I feel fine," I said.

"The doctor said you had concussion. You need to rest. Tough to do, I know. But it helps your brain heal. Better listen, okay?"

"Okay." All the sadness, anger and confusion churned within me. "I'm glad you're here. It would suck being all alone."

She turned and smiled. "We are family. Never, never forget."

LATER THAT AFTERNOON, Auntie Chong surprised me. She snuck Basho into the hospital for a quick visit. He was wrapped in a blanket like a baby, his tail sticking out and whipping back and forth to the sound of my voice. She set him on my lap and I scratched him behind the ears as he licked my cheeks and pawed at me with excitement. He whined with yelps of joy.

Beeps and clicking sounds filled the gaps of silence, the smell of disinfectant, whiffs of urine, Auntie Chong's chamomile tea and kimchi punctuating the sterile air. I thought of Blaine and opened my sketchpad even though I was supposed to rest my brain. Auntie Chong snored in the chair next to me, her head tilted back, mouth wide-open.

I really wanted to see Blaine. I wanted to thank him for finding Basho. For saving me.

I attempted to finish his portrait, shading in lines and curves, but the sweep of my pencil turned into scribbles, circles, and pretty soon, slashes across the entire page.

CHAPTER 62

THE NEXT FEW days at the hospital were murky. It felt like the world had come to a halt. I longed for the marshmallow unicorns to bring color to my world. Rainbows to teleport me out of here. Frosted Lucky Charms to make my world *magically delicious*.

I just wanted to go home.

I couldn't believe that Mother never came to visit. I was pissed, but more crushed than anything. The thought spread like a river—rising, rising, until I overflowed with emotion. It felt like I was drowning. I gasped for air.

But Auntie Chong had come. I thought of the ocean. Looking out at the endless water. I wasn't alone, I told myself. I wasn't alone.

I was finally able to leave with Auntie Chong after the doctor gave her approval.

THE SMELL AND sounds of the hospital stayed with me as I entered Auntie Chong's apartment. Basho was excited to see me and he wagged his tail as he crept toward me in slow bursts. It was like he sensed that something had changed.

Crazy dog. His nose twitched, his ears pasted back as he sniffed my jeans. He yelped and pawed at my shoes as I kicked them off by the doorway. I scooped him up into my arms. "I missed you, Basho."

Auntie Chong smiled. "He was very well behaved. He can come over anytime."

I could tell she was excited that I was staying with her until I was ready to return home to Mother. We pulled out the sofa bed in the living room. Kernels of popcorn and plum candy wrappers lay scattered on the mattress. Ming squawked and cocked his head in curiosity.

THE NEXT DAY I went down to the beach to be alone with my thoughts. The cool salty air greeted me. The sound of the waves, hypnotic and mesmerizing. I felt lost. The world I had imagined was no longer vivid in my mind. Dreams— faded, washed away.

What was I to do? Where was I to go?

A light fog settled in and I thought I saw Blaine.

He was flying a kite, a silhouette of movement in front of me. He caught my eye and the kite stalled, floated backwards. Basho circled and barked, then took off toward a flock of seagulls. The birds dispersed in the air, a flurry of white wings. With his ears perked forward, Basho came charging back to my side.

I hesitated, then ran toward Blaine.

"Hey," I said, out of breath, as I drew closer.

Blaine held his attention toward the sky, toward the kite wavering in the wind. "I see you're back." His voice sounded cold and strange.

"I thought you might want a little help flying Frankie." Stupid reply. What I really needed to do was thank him for saving my life. For finding Basho.

Blaine continued to focus on the kite, his words sharp and short. "We don't need anything."

"Let me explain."

"I don't need an explanation, Jasmine. You said you wanted to end things."

"Please. Just listen to me. I need to . . . thank you. For saving me that night. And you found Basho. I thought I had lost him forever."

Blaine shoved up his glasses and finally looked at me, the kite taking a slow dive to the ground. "I don't remember why I went looking for you. I guess your aunt was worried when she couldn't find you." He pulled on the kite strings. "She called you something. It was in a different language. Said you were a crazy girl who swims in the ocean."

"She kind of told me what happened. Honestly, I don't remember much, either."

"You were out cold. It was pretty awful." He crouched and petted Basho. "And you, little buddy."

"I'm sorry."

"For what?" He looked up. "Almost getting killed?"

"No." I gazed down at the sand. "For cutting you off. I was confused."

"I thought we had something."

"We did. We do. But it's complicated." A sudden wind blew through my hair. The ocean waves crashed against the shore. "I found out who my father is."

"You did?" His brows furrowed. "Mr. Jin?"

"Nope." I looked away. "Part of me wishes I didn't find out."

"Why? You were so determined. You needed to know. It was eating away at you."

"I thought I knew who my father was. But the ugly truth is, I really didn't. He's nothing like the image in my mind." I made a fist, trying to fight back the disappointment ripping through me.

"Who is it?" Blaine asked. He looked concerned.

"It's Cal."

"What? You're kidding. Oh my god."

"My mother never told him about me until the day they were supposed to get married. That's why he never showed up. He was too shocked. He said he came here to make up for lost time. But in reality, he chose to leave again." I let out a bitter laugh. "So, he left. Can you believe it?"

"He left? I thought he wanted you and your mother to move back to Briarplace?"

"I thought so, too." I blinked several times. My vision grew watery. "He said . . ." I swallowed. The pain of his words was stuck deep in my chest. I swallowed again. "He said he . . . he never wanted a child of his own."

"That's horrible, Jasmine."

I swiped away a tear. "I told him to never come back. I don't want to see him again. Ever."

My whole body tensed as Blaine pulled me close. Part of me still clung to the fantasy of Pangu. Part of me wanted to believe I was truly loved. A seagull swooped down in the distant water. I looked at Blaine. "The truth stinks."

He nodded. "You got that right."

"And I'm pissed at my mother for keeping me a secret."

"I don't blame you. I'd feel the same way. Will you have to go back?"

"You mean to Briarplace?"

"Yeah."

"That's not my home anymore." I paused. "It's here."

Blaine stopped. "And what about us? Did you really mean it? Not wanting to see me anymore?"

"I meant it at the time. But things have changed."

Blaine tilted his head to the side. "So, there's hope?"

"I think so." I didn't know what else to say. "I gotta go now. I told my auntie I wouldn't be long."

"Wait. One more thing. Did you finish it?"

"What?"

"The picture of me. I want to see it."

I recalled the mad scribbles, the slashes across the page. "I kinda have to start over. Like everything else in my life."

"Fair enough," Blaine replied. "But I'll hold you to it. And one more thing."

"Yeah?" I turned and looked at him.

"You're not insignificant, Jasmine. No matter what you think."

CHAPTER 63

Dear Pangu,

You may not be my father
yet I feel your presence
among the stars at night
hear your voice, a whisper in the wind
for you are the earth beneath my feet.
You are the salt of the ocean.
You are the smell of rain
giving me strength
giving me wings to fly.

Yours,
J

CHAPTER 64

I FOUND AUNTIE Chong busy in her kitchen, a tray of freshly made crescent moon–shaped dumplings on the counter.

"You making potstickers?"

"Jiaozi. Yes. You come help." Auntie Chong barely lifted her head as she folded a thin layer of wonton skin over a dollop of ground pork. The table was cluttered—a bottle of soy sauce, a bowl of ground pork, the cutting board with remnants of chopped garlic, gingerroot slices, green onions. When she finally glanced up, I noticed that she had bits of green onion caught in her hair, a smear of soy sauce on her cheek. And her lips were pursed in a smirk.

"What are you smiling at?" I grabbed the spoon and scooped up a heaping of ground pork.

"Me? Why do you say that?"

"You're laughing at something. Funny thought? Something I just did?" I shrugged. "I don't know. You tell me."

Auntie Chong rolled her mouth inward. Another smirk.

I pointed and laughed. "See. There it is. The sneaky smile."

"I remember when you were a little girl. How much you like to eat dumplings. You eat and eat until your stomach hurt."

"Ha. Very funny."

"It was."

I reached for a wonton skin and dropped the pork onto the circular wonton. Dipped my finger into the small bowl of egg white and smeared it on the edge like glue. Then pinched the edges together to form a crescent moon shape. "I guess I still remember how to make these."

Auntie Chong reached for my hand and squeezed. "How you doing?"

"Um. Fine."

She raised her brow in disbelief. "You sure?"

I knew she was talking about all the secrets. The new revelation. Everything that had happened. How do you tell someone that your world has turned upside down? "I guess I feel kind of numb. Like I can't breathe sometimes. It all seems surreal. You know?"

"Yes, of course. Not easy. You are tough, though."

"I wish."

"I'm serious. You are brave like Pangu." Auntie Chong got real quiet. "Guá tia di."

"What does that mean?"

"It means I love you. In my language." She smiled. "I'll take care of you, okay? No matter what. We are family."

CHAPTER 65

THE FOLLOWING DAY, I wanted to return home to Mother. Part of me felt ready, but I dragged out each step back to our apartment, taking in the sunshine, Basho at my side. A queasy feeling gnawed at me and I tried to wish it away. I was afraid to see Mother, especially after everything that had happened, and I was still upset that she never came to see me at the hospital. Why didn't she come? I didn't understand.

When I arrived at the apartment, Mother was in the bathroom so I sat at the kitchen table and doodled random things I missed—Mother's purple orchid, Rani's long braided hair, Blaine's kite, Frankie—in my sketchbook. My leg jittered up and down and I bit into my bottom lip.

When she finally came out of the bathroom, I couldn't help but race toward her.

"Jasmine. You're back." She wrapped her arms around me and I took in the sweet and sour scent of her. "Are you okay?" She stepped back. "Let me look at you."

I nodded and forced a smile. "I'm fine."

"You look well. Auntie Chong took good care of you."

"She did." My voice went hoarse. Finally, I said, "Why didn't you come to the hospital?"

After a pause, she said, "I was afraid to lose you. I couldn't take it."

"That's lame. And you're right. You *could have* lost me." The words spewed out in a harsh tone. "You should have been there."

I crossed my arms. And then I realized beneath the anger was a brokenness I didn't quite understand. *I just wanted a real mother,* I thought. I needed her.

"I'm sorry, Jasmine."

She pulled me close again, stroking my hair. I watched the movement of our shadows along the wall. The light above us blinked on and off. I wanted to believe that she loved me, even if it was in the only way she knew how.

"We're alike, you and I. But you are much stronger and so much smarter." She paused. "I'm sorry he had to leave. It's going to be okay. We have each other."

Mother squeezed me tight and we sat in silence. I felt like I had been gripping on to something so tight, like the strings of a kite. And I finally just let go. I cried. I let the tears fall.

Is this what forgiveness feels like? I wondered. *A letting go?*

From the front pocket of my jeans, I pulled out the crystal I had stolen when I was with Gena. "I got this for you. I . . . stole it."

"Stole it?"

"I wanted so badly to get you a gift. I thought if I took it—I would for sure see you again. It's weird. I know."

"Oh, Jasmine. You are the gift."

She kissed my forehead and placed the crystal by the window.

It glimmered, dispersing a rainbow of colors all around us.

CHAPTER 66

I PULLED OUT my sketchpad and redrew Blaine's portrait. His look of concern when I told him about Cal was seared in my memory. I tried to recapture all our times at the beach. Ribbons of watercolors danced across the page. Frankie, the kite, soaring above us.

I started to draw, letting the charcoal pencil take over. My fingers moved lightly at first across the blank canvas. I worked in layers. Shading and softening, adding the angles, the contours, the shape of his lips. Defining his eyes, brows, nose. Spinning and twisting the pencil like a magic wand.

It felt healing. Calming. The portrait coming to life.

Blaine's tender eyes staring back at me.

CHAPTER 67

A WEEK LATER, I hiked up a wandering path through a lush forest of spruce and redwood at a National Park just north of Newbay. It was dawn. The sky was submerged in swirls of pink and orange. Sunlight penetrated through the tree branches. I felt a sudden shift in the air, a pull toward the earth with the same kind of urgency I had when I wanted to draw or paint.

I looked up and searched the sky.

Thank you, Pangu. You saved me.

I closed my eyes and saw a reflection of my own face, the freckles on my cheeks now dappled in morning light.

A dirt trail stretched for miles along the coastline. I stopped at a clearing, a grassy bluff near the edge of a cliff that overlooked the Pacific Ocean. I stood, gazing over the raging water.

In the distance, a ridge of mountains unfurled beneath the sky. The last veil of shadow moved across the mountain-side, chased by the sun, slowly dissolving.

"Sunlight playing over a mountain," I whispered.

At the edge of the cliff, I found a rock and tossed it into the water below.

The waves pushed out to sea, farther and farther away.

The wind moved through my hair and I caught a glimpse of something silver floating on the water.

I paused and felt each breath. I dared not lose sight of the two gems, hovering above the endless ocean. In its mist, the Phoenix and Dragon rose above the ashes, above the waves, soaring higher and higher, slowly vanishing into the deep blue sky.

ACKNOWLEDGMENTS

MY WRITING STARTS alone in a room, but everything I've done in my life that's been important to me has been made possible with the help and support of others.

I'm forever grateful to my fabulous, steadfast agent, Linda Camacho of Gallt and Zacker Literary Agency, for believing in me and Jasmine's story from the very beginning and never letting go. You are my rock on this journey. How incredibly fortunate I am to have someone like you in my life. You are not just a fabulous agent, but an incredible human being. I'm humbled and honored to be a part of the GZLA family, an amazing team of generous and passionate people.

To my brilliant editor, Alexa Wejko. Thank you for taking a chance on this story and for your tireless enthusiasm and dedication to help me bring this novel to life. I'm immensely grateful for your keen eye, your insight and vision. This book is what it is because of you.

Special thanks to artist Xuan Loc Xuan and Janine Agro, Art and Production Director at Soho Press, for the gorgeous cover and design—it's beyond anything I could have imagined.

I'm so very grateful to Rachel Kowal, Managing Editor at Soho Press; Mia Manns, copy editor; and Sarah George, proofreader, for your guidance and editorial expertise. A heartfelt thanks to all at Soho Press, for your enthusiasm and for bringing this book into the world.

It wasn't until much later in life that I took writing seriously and I'm deeply indebted to my mentors and professors in the MFA program at MSUM, who continue to be a source of inspiration and guidance. Lin Enger, I've run out of words to say thank you many moons ago. I'm extremely grateful for your insightful feedback, your generosity and endless words of support and encouragement. Thank you for the meaningful conversations about writing and life. Al Davis, the first day I attended your prose class, I knew I had found a place to study the craft of writing and your encouragement inspired me to dig deep and work hard. I'm so grateful for your support. Mark Vinz, you sparked my love of language with your words and teaching. Kevin Carollo, a deep thanks for the poetry and music and for inviting me to do my first ever public reading. What an honor to read with you and Thom. Shari Scapple, you lit the fire of young adult literature in me and your class had a true impact on my writing journey. Liz Severn, thank you for the all the guidance and support. Thom Tammaro, you and your work are an inspiration. Reading with you and KC was a dream. Many thanks to my peers and friends in the MFA program, especially Linda Lein, MaryAnne Wilimek, and Rob Neuteboom.

My writing journey has not been without disappointment and challenges. Community definitely matters. With love and deep gratitude to my writing musketeers: Linda Lee Sand and Tory Christie—thanks for fueling me with laughter and always lifting me up. To Sarah Beck, my invaluable writing companion and confidante. To Jill Kandel, for your friendship and guidance. To the Fargo SCBWI writers, for your inspiration and support. Many thanks, Taylor Hewstan, for welcoming me into your home and creative world. Love and heartfelt gratitude to Jill Badonsky: You changed my life. Vinita Pappas, my lovely Zoom creative soul and friend. Here's to PUT. To my KMCC Mastermind group, for the encouragement and community and to all my other KMC-Cers, my kindred spirits—thanks for reminding me that it's about trusting the process and finding the joy. Special thanks to Allison Pottern Hoch, for all things marketing.

To my family: You teach me about life and remind me of what's important. Kevin, I'm forever grateful for your patience and love. I couldn't have done this without you. KK, your insight and thoughtful reads made a huge differ-ence and you never stopped believing. Tan, for being there and for sharing your creative skills. Mase, for listening and making me laugh when I needed it most. To my sisters, Sharon and Rach, for their love and support. To Mick—for being at my side from the very beginning and for shining the beacon of hope when I've lost my way. To Ross—I miss you, Cuz. This one's for you. Love to my relatives in the States and the Philippines.

To Mom and Dad: I love you beyond words. Thank you for the sacrifices you've made. Mom, for your courage and resilience, for bringing the four of us girls to the library and instilling the joy and value of reading and books. Dad, for your wisdom, your stories, and your voice. To Shakes and Mandi—my teachers of love and patience. I could never do this work without you by my side.

To you, dear reader, for sharing your precious time with these pages. I'm truly grateful.